GOT A MAN

GOT A MAN

Daaimah S. Poole

KENSINGTON PUBLISHING CORP.
http://www.kensingtonbooks.com

DAFINA BOOKS are published by

Kensington Publishing Corp.
850 Third Avenue
New York, NY 10022

Special book excerpts or customized printings can also be created to fit specific needs. For details, write or phone the office of the Kensington Special Sales Manager: Kensington Publishing Corp., 850 Third Avenue, New York, NY 10022. Attn. Special Sales Department. Phone: 1-800-221-2647.

Dafina Books and the Dafina logo Reg. U.S. Pat. & TM Off.

ISBN: 0-7394-3586-8

Printed in the United States of America

To Robin Dandridge Sampson and Auzzie Pool.
Thank you for all your love and support.

Acknowledgments

Thank you Allah for making this possible.

To my family, I love you all of yall. Thanks for telling your coworkers, friends, and strangers about me and my work. Thanks for supporting me one hundred percent. My son Hamid, I love you. Thank you to my mother, Robin Dandridge Sampson, and my father, Auzzie Poole, for all your love, support and guidance. Alvin Cooke, thanks for always being there for me. My sisters Daaiyah, Nadirah and Najah Goldstein. Grandmothers Delores Dandridge and Mary Ellen Hickson. My aunts Bertha Dandridge, Elaine Dandridge, Edith White, and Cynthia Cargill. My uncles Teddy and Aaron Dandridge, Herbie Kidd Jr., Steven, Julius, Eric and Leon Poole. My counsins Keva, Iesha, Tiffany, Arron Dandridge Leno, Lamar Quattlebaum, Khalif Mears, Jamal Kidd and Al-Baseer Holly. My stepmother Pulcheria Ricks Poole. All the kids, my first and second cousins. The Pooles, Wertzes, Grahams, Saunders, Dandridges, and Goldsteins.

Thanks to Deidra Potter, Sherlaine Freeman, Pulcheria Ricks-Poole, and Shana Higgs for your insight and for reading the early versions of *Got a Man*.

Thanks to Helena Gibson, Maryam Abdus-Shahid, Miana White, Katrina Elliott, Tamika Wilson, Dena Riddick, Gina Delior, Carla Lewis, Tamika Harper and Tamika Floyd, my girls at Ebauche Envouge Hair Salon: Aisha Murphy and Aida Allen, Qolour Shynes Hair Salon, Candance Irvin, Knots And Tangle, Nisa McGough, April Williams, Shawna Grundy, Dinyelle Wertz, Leonna Maddox, Linda Womack, Loraine Ballard Morrill, and Kia Morgan. Everyone at Keystone Mercy, Basic Black Books of Philadelphia, Liguorious Books of Philadelphia, Our Story of Plainfield N.J., The Black Library of Boston, Yasmine Coleman APOOO Books, Howard University bookstore and all the African American impendent bookstores, PMA Literary and Film Management. Thank you to everyone at

ACKNOWLEDGEMENT

Kensington books: Karen Thomas, Jessica McLean, Ebony Alston, and Mary Pomponio.

Thank you to Karen E. Quinones Miller and Camille Miller. Thanks to everyone who has bought, read and spread the word about *Yo Yo Love*. Thanks to all my new and old readers. Thanks so much for all the support and the e-mails; keep them coming. If I forgot you, it was not intentional and thank you.

Thanks for the love,
Daaimah S. Poole

GOT A MAN

Chapter One

Shonda Nicole Robinson

Have you ever woke up in the middle of the night, and regretted something you did the day before? The scene keeps replaying in your head over and over again. You wish you could take back your action, and you keep telling yourself, *I should have done this, or I should have said that.*

You have? Yeah, me too, only it's not the middle of the night, it's 4:30 P.M. and I just made a complete fool of myself by showing up at my boyfriend's wedding. I couldn't help it, though. All I know is that I was running up the church steps past huge arrangements of red and white roses and white and gold bells. I caught my breath and walked into the church. I sat on the last row so I would go unnoticed. Then the rev asked did anyone see why this man or woman should not be joined in holy matrimony, yadda, yadda. So I stood up and said, "Malik, you can't do this, you know this is wrong."

Everyone turned around and stared at me like, *bitch, are you crazy?* Then everyone stared at each other, shook their heads, and started mumbling amongst each other. Kim ran into the pew crying. Malik just stood there with his mouth open. One of Kim's girlfriends or cousins tried to act like they wanted to say something, but I didn't give them a chance. I said what I had come to say and I

1

was out. The wedding was interrupted and I ran to my getaway car that I had left running outside. I called my godsister Tae as soon as I got in the car. I shouldn't have called her at all, since she refused to come with me. She could have been my backup, if things got ugly ya mean. But she said I was wrong and she would not be my accomplice.

I frantically dialed her number on the phone. It began to ring, then she answered and I said, "I did it."

"You did what?" she asked.

"I stopped the wedding."

"No, you didn't, cause if you did I'm not speaking to you anymore. Come on, Shonda, I thought you were joking."

"Well, don't speak to me anymore. I told you I was serious."

"You're serious? Girl, you're crazy!" Tae screamed.

"I'm not crazy!"

"Really! You know how much heart it takes to go and stop a wedding."

"Uh, I don't know, a lot," I said as if I had to think about it.

"No, it takes a sick, crazy individual. CON-GRAT-U-LA-TIONS, it should have been me." Tae finally laughed between trying to sing like Vesta, this singer from back in the day, who sang about going to her ex-boyfriend's wedding. They used to play the video all the time on BET. Now I can't believe I'm acting this shit out.

Well, I could have let it happen, but I didn't. No, not after what I have been through with Malik—let alone men, period. If I told you my story, it would take a book and a half. I wouldn't know where to begin.

It's so cliché to say it all began when this happened. So I'll start my story like this. My name is Shonda Nicole Robinson, I'm twenty-five, and I have a story to tell.

I was in Atlanta for six months trying to get myself together, or so I thought. My plan was to go to Atlanta and come up. A.T.L. was supposed to be the new black Mecca, right? For everybody else maybe, for Shonda, I don't think so. My six months in A.T.L., the only thing I managed to do is meet a stalker.

I stayed with my Aunt Jackie in College Park, right outside of Atlanta. I went down there because me and my daughter's father Brian had broken up after seven years of being together. I didn't feel like being bothered with him or his family. He was so upset that I left, he married somebody else three months later. Atlanta wasn't really for me though, there were too many damn yellow waffle houses; and forget about trying to learn the confusing ass highways, they didn't make any sense. Plus, I didn't have the help with Bree like I had in Philly. I could barely go to the store without having to drag her along, because my aunt rarely baby-sat. She was one of those women in her late forties trying to date young men and go to the club herself. It really was not like home.

I lived in Philly all my life, with my dad and my grandmother, who I call Gram. My mother Angela is a deadbeat mom. Not typical of a mother, but true, but I'll get on her later. Let me finish telling you about my ex.

My stalker's name was Mike. I met Mike at my job at the Holiday Inn Airport hotel. I was a front desk agent. He had stopped in and asked for directions because he was lost. I gave them to him. Then he came back almost an hour later to thank me for the directions I had given him. He then asked me what was I doing when I got off. I told him going home and going to sleep. He asked me if I would like to go to out with him to breakfast when I woke up.

* * *

I took him up on his offer. We got together and it was like we knew everything about one another in a few short days. Mike showed me all around Atlanta. On our first date he took me to Justin's, on Peachtree Street. It was really nice and we really enjoyed ourselves talking, joking, and taking in the scenes. After our first date, we went out almost every night. Dinner, movies, even a Braves' baseball game. I even allowed my daughter, Brianna, to meet him. That was a major no-no. Bree had never been around any men besides her dad and my father. I was really starting to be into Mike until, well, until he became an outright crazed maniac. I mean, I'll agree all men are a little jealous, but there is a line. It shouldn't have taken me months to realize that Mike was crazy as hell. My first signs should have been when he began checking my messages on my cell phone. People would tell me they called and I would be like, no you didn't. But I never got the message because he was erasing the messages. I don't know how long he was doing that. The only reason I found out he was listening to my messages is because he confronted me about a message Brian left about Brianna. I asked how did he know her dad wanted her to come up and he confessed that he had dialed my voice mail by accident. How do you accidentally get my voice mail password? When he wasn't busy checking my messages, he was asking me had I met anybody else. I paid him no attention.

Anyway, Mike showed his true Gemini colors the night a coworker asked me to accompany her to a party after work at Vegas Nights. I called my Aunt Jackie to see if she would watch Bree. She said yes, so then I called Mike and told him I was going out.

"Hey, babe. I'm going to stop past Vegas Nights with Lori from the job, okay?"

"You're going where?"

"Vegas Nights."

He yelled in the phone, "So you going to start going out, huh? What, I'm not enough man for you? You got to take your little hot ass out?" Mike was going ballistic. I totally ignored his comments. I thought he must have been pissed about something else and was taking it out on me.

"Listen, baby, I'm going out. I'll talk to you later," I said and I went out with Lori to the party.

I got to Vegas Nights about 11:30 P.M. Already the club was almost jammed to capacity. Lori and me had to say excuse me every other two seconds, trying to maneuver our way to the dance floor. As soon as we reached the dance floor a guy approached me to dance. He stood about six feet even, with chocolate-colored skin, dark mystic eyes, and seductive lips. "What's up, you want to dance?" the stranger asked.

"Sure," I responded. The stranger grabbed my hand and we danced on the crowded dance floor. The stranger's friend invited Lori to the dance floor. They danced beside us until the next song came on and I saw Mike. How Mike found me in a club full of thousands of people, I will never know. But what I do know is he came up to me looking deranged. His eyes crossed. He asked me could he have a word with me.

"No, leave me alone!" I said, annoyed.

"Let me talk to you, Shonda," he said as he grabbed my arm.

"No," I said as I jerked my arm out of his grip.

"Please."

"Okay. Okay," I said, and I told Lori I would be right back. The guys we were dancing with looked at Mike suspiciously, then they turned their heads—I guess deciding it was better to mind their own business. I walked with him to the front of the club. Mike said he couldn't hear and asked could we go outside. I went outside with Mike and sat in his car and we talked.

"Look, Mike, you tripping, it's only a party. Okay? I'll call you later." I went to exit the vehicle when Mike locked the doors, put the key in the ignition, and started the car.

"What are you doing?" I asked as I tried to get out of the car. Mike pulled off.

"What is wrong with you?" I yelled as the car began moving. I couldn't believe he would just take off like that. Mike said nothing. As soon as the light turned red at the intersection, I unlocked the door and jumped out of the car. I ran in the opposite direction of traffic. I thought Mike would keep going but he didn't. He backed the car all the way up the street making a loud shrieking noise and drove onto the pavement, blocking my path from running.

"Get in the car, Shonda."

"No, leave me alone!"

"Get in the fucking car, Shonda," Mike said as he grabbed me by my belt buckle and started dragging me toward the car saying, "Sometimes life isn't worth living when you give a person everything and they don't give back."

People were passing by but he didn't care. I knew someone would call 911 because it looked like I was getting kidnapped. He opened the driver-side back door and threw me in. Then he slammed the door, crushing my feet against the window. I tried to sit up and gain my balance, but I couldn't because he sped off so quickly. Mike ran red lights and was scaring the shit out of me.

"Where are you taking me?" I asked, as tears streamed down my face.

"Home, where you need to be. All I want to be is happy. But you don't want to be happy. You want to go out and party. I can't take having my woman in the club."

Mike pulled up to my house, dropped me off, and left. By this time I didn't even care about going out. I just wanted to go in the house. I wiped the tears off my face so Bree and Aunt Jackie wouldn't see them. Aunt Jackie was lying on the sofa with her powder blue robe on and curlers in her hair, watching *ER*.

"You're back early," she said.

"Yeah, it was too crowded, so I just came home. Bree 'sleep?"

"I just sent her to bed."

* * *

I went to the bathroom and glanced in the mirror and saw my puffy red eyes. I looked like a bee had stung me, they were so puffy and red. My eyes and face swelled every time I cried. Crying made my golden honey skin look pale. My black hair weave was out of place. I didn't even feel like calling Lori to tell her why I left. I just wrapped my hair around, and put on my scarf and went to bed.

I turned on the television and fell asleep watching Jay Leno. The phone rang.

"Hello."

"Yeah, you ain't even call me to see if I was all right. You know what, Shonda, you ain't shit."

"I'm not shit, you pulled me out of a party and I'm not shit. Please," I said as I banged on Mike.

He called back and said the same thing. "Shonda, you ain't shit. You ain't nothing but a Philly whore."

"What? Mike, cut it out. Look, I'm going to sleep. I'll holla at you tomorrow."

The third time Mike called back I don't even know why I answered the phone.

"Hello," I said with much attitude.

"Shonda, you know it's real fucked up how you treating a nigga, but it's cool. You ain't shit. Nothing, you hear me?"

Okay, by now I was tired of hearing that I wasn't shit. I hung the phone up and turned my ringer off. Minutes later my Aunt Jackie came in the room handing me her phone.

"It's Mike," she said.

"Look, it's over!" I screamed into the phone.

"I'm sorry, I didn't mean it."

"I'm sorry too . . . and tired, so do me a favor and don't call me back tonight." I hung up the phone. I turned off my light and went to sleep.

A strange feeling awakened me. I felt a presence coming toward me. I opened my eyes and saw Mike standing over me. I jumped up and screamed, "What are you doing here?"

"You don't want to call nobody back, huh?"

"Look, Mike, leave." He leaped on top of me like a football player.

"Aunt Jackie! Aunt Jackie! Help, call the police," I screamed. Mike then placed his hands over my mouth and throat. I couldn't breathe. I still tried to scream, but it was muffled. I continued to kick and scream.

"You don't want to answer the phone, huh, Shonda?" Mike demanded as he began to shake and choke me. He took his hands off my mouth, but I was too shaken to do anything. I just lay still as he hovered over me trying to figure out what his next move was going to be.

What was Mike doing in the house? Who let him in? Was he going to hurt Bree, Aunt Jackie, or me? I nearly passed out before he lifted his hands from over my throat. I coughed and gasped for air, as I took long breaths. Mike then let me go. I stared at Mike and tried to figure out what his next move was going to be. He surprised me by saying, "I just want to be happy. I love you, Shonda," he said, crying, as he began to hug me.

"I love you too, Mike," I said as I tried to pacify him. Suddenly my aunt appeared in my doorway; she flicked on my bedroom light.

"Y'all all right?"

"Yeah, we're fine," I said as tried to conceal my face.

"Mike, I didn't know you were here. Shonda, let me talk to you," my aunt said as she glanced at my face and turned toward Mike. "Mike, what's going on?" she asked.

Boom! Boom! I heard someone banging on the door. My aunt went to answer it and I jumped off the bed to find out who the hell was knocking on the door this late. Mike stayed in my bedroom. When I reached the living room, I saw red and blue lights flashing. I opened the door and it was about five cops standing in front of the door. *Who called the cops?* I thought. My aunt walked in front of me and said, "Yes, may I help you?"

"Miss, we had a report that a man was climbing through the window. Is that true?"

"No, that's not true," I blurted out.

"Are you okay?" the other cop asked.

"Yes," I answered without thinking. My aunt must have been as confused as I was, because she just stood there.

"Well, why are you crying and why are your neck and arms red if you're okay?" a white, short, brown-haired cop asked as he flashed his flashlight in my face, almost blinding me.

"Is anyone else here with you?" another cop asked.

"Yes, my daughter and boyfriend."

"Where's your boyfriend?"

"In the back room."

"Can you call him out here?"

"Mike, come out here, the cops want to talk to you."

Mike walked into the living room.

"Is there a problem, son?" one cop asked.

"No, sir."

"Why is your girlfriend crying?"

"I don't know."

"Come with me, son. Let's talk."

As the cop escorted Mike out the house, the lone female cop pulled me to the side. She took off her hat and took out a small note pad. She then asked me what was going on. I told her I didn't know. I really didn't know.

"Did you let him in?"

"No."

"So how did he get in here?" she asked.

"I don't know," I answered.

"You know you don't have to put up with an abuser, we can take him to jail. Just say the word. All you have to do is file for a protection order," she said as she stared me directly in the eye. What the police officer was saying made sense. But I needed to think. I didn't want to get Mike in trouble, but he was acting crazy. I mean, he never acted like this before. He had me really scared.

The lady cop asked me again, "Do you want us to lock him up?"

"Can you just make him leave? I need to think, and he wants to talk."

"You just want us to make him leave?"

"Yes, just make him go home." I didn't really want to see Mike go to jail.

The lady cop went outside. Then she came back and said, "He's gone. Have a good night."

The cops left and I went back into my room. My aunt shut the window that Mike had entered through. We made sure everything was secured. I got back in the bed and wondered what the fuck Mike was thinking about when he climbed through the window. I lay back in the bed ready to fall back to sleep when I heard Mike outside again banging on the door.

"Shonda, I want to talk to you. Shonda, I love you, I need to talk to you now!" I heard Mike scream as he banged on the door. "Shonda, open this damn door."

He woke my daughter up. Bree screamed, "I'm scared, somebody's at the door!" and ran into my room.

My aunt came back into the room and said, "Look, I'm going to call the cops."

"No, I'll talk to him," I said as I went to the window.

"Mike, go home. I'll call you tomorrow. You're disrespecting my aunt and my daughter. I promise I will talk to you tomorrow."

"Okay, what time you want me to call you?" he asked.

"Like twelve. We can go to breakfast, okay?"

Mike said fine and I went back in my room, assured this time he would leave. That would be too much like right. I heard more banging against the door.

"Shonda, I need to talk to you right now. Come out or I'm going to—" and with that I heard my aunt's door get kicked in. I called the cops back. The operator answered.

"Yes. Um, my boyfriend just kicked in my front door, hurry, please!"

"What's your address?"

"121 Hollydale Road."

"We'll send someone right away. Is he in the house?"

"I think he is." I ran into Bree's room and picked her up and ran into my aunt's room. I locked her door, and we sat on the floor near the closet until the cops arrived for the second time. When I saw the blue and red flashing lights I felt safe to open the door. I peeked out the door and saw the police locking Mike up.

"Miss, this is our second visit. We're going to take him in. Did he do this to the door?"

"Yes."

"Well, this all could have been avoided if you would've talked to us the first time. I mean, if you want to let a man beat on you that's your business."

"I didn't get beat," I said.

"Well, again, that's your business."

This time I got Mike arrested. I got a restraining order, but that still didn't stop him from harassing me. He started calling my job, sending me flowers, fruit baskets, and sing-o-grams.

I was so sick of him and distraught that I tore up all the pictures of him and me together. He must have been digging in the trash, because he mailed them back to me taped up with a note asking me why did I throw the pictures of us in the trash, because I looked pretty and we looked good together. However, the last straw was the letter he wrote me that said,

Shonda,

I love you. I got to have you. If I can't have you, no one will. I'd rather die than live without you. I'd rather kill you than see you with someone else.

I love you,
Mike

* * *

That was it. Atlanta and me just wasn't working out. I packed Bree and my bags, and called my Dad from the AirTran gate. In the middle of the Atlanta airport, I was on the phone crying to my daddy, telling him I was on my way home. He said I could stay at his apartment until I got on my feet. I didn't care where we lived. I was coming home with no money and no job.

We boarded the plane and the flight started off fine. Then it turned into the roughest flight in history. I am not exaggerating. The flight from Atlanta to Philly usually took about two hours max. But since we kept hitting a bunch of turbulence, our flight took longer. I was scared when the plane bounced all around the sky. The pilot made an announcement for everyone to put on their seat belts and remain calm. Bree is crying, I'm trying to calm her down, and meanwhile I'm trying to pretend I'm not scared. The plane passed the rough patches of turbulence and settled at a lower altitude. I wanted to get off that plane and get home.

My dad met us at the airport; he was so happy we were home. Bree ran up to him and gave him a kiss and said "Pop Pop our plane almost crashed."

"No it didn't. We just got stuck in turbulence."

I gave my dad a hug. It had been a few months and he looked a little fatter. I patted him on his stomach and asked him what he'd been eating.

"I got a new friend," he said as we walked to baggage claim.

"What is she feeding you, five meals a day?"

"No, but she makes some good Louisiana crunch cake." I laughed at my dad as he grabbed our luggage off the luggage belt. We walked to the parking lot where my dad's truck was parked.

* * *

12

My dad said I was lucky that one of his tenants had moved out and I could live in that apartment until I got on my feet. He then took us to the Pathmark and bought us some groceries. Then we stopped at his house and he let me borrow one of his televisions.

We arrived at the apartment: it was a small first-floor one-bedroom. My dad said a husband, wife, and two children had lived there. I couldn't see how.

"They left all this furniture?" I asked as I looked around.

"Yeah, they needed to leave something because they skipped out on their rent," my dad replied. They left a twin bed frame and futon bed frame, and in the kitchen was a tiny two-chair pinewood dinette set. Tonight me and Bree would have to rough it on the floor in our sleeping bags, I thought.

"You don't have to stay here tonight. Ya'll can have my bed and I'll sleep on the sofa."

"We'll be all right, Dad. I want to unpack and get settled."

"Well, I'll take you tomorrow to buy some mattresses for these frames."

"Thanks, Dad," I said as I kissed him on his cheek. He told me to lock the door and left.

The apartment was small but enough for me and Bree for the time being. My grandmother's sister sold my father this building for a few hundred dollars when I was younger. My dad knew a little about carpentry and plumbing and his friend Mr. Greg was an electrician. They fixed the house up and converted it into three apartments. My dad took this house, refinanced it, and bought another house. Now he has about five properties. My dad is not rich, but he is able to maintain. His tenants are usually young girls with kids that don't understand that you have to pay rent to live somewhere. I was just happy my dad let me stay there until I got myself together. However long that was going to take. In the morning I was going to call Brian and Tae and tell them we were back. But right now I just wanted to sleep.

Since it was only one bedroom, I gave Bree the room and I

would stay in the living room. After I unpacked a little, I made a list of everything that we needed. My list consisted of everything from wash cloths to sheets and food. At least my dad would give me money to get some of the things I needed. I cleaned out the refrigerator, and mopped the floor. The family who left must have been in a rush because they left all their cleaning products and even some clothes. I threw the clothes in the trash. The refrigerator and cabinet had a little food in them. I threw that in the trash, too.

The next morning, I awoke looking at the ceiling. You know how you're awake but you can't remember exactly where you are? Then I remembered I wasn't in Atlanta anymore. I was back home. My deep thought was interrupted by the sound of the doorbell ringing. I jumped up out the sleeping bag and looked out the window to see my grandmom looking up at me.

"One minute, Gram. Be right there," I yelled. I threw on a T-shirt and sweatpants and went to open the door.

"Hey, Gram," I said as I opened the door. "What brings you here?" I asked as I gave her a kiss on the cheek.

"I heard you were back, didn't like Atlanta very much, huh?"

"I guess it just wasn't for me."

"Well, either way, I'm glad to have you back, and so is your father. He was really worried about you down there."

"Yeah? I can't tell. The only thing he's worried about right now is that new woman of his that's making him fat. Have you met her yet?"

"Yes, she's very nice. He brought her past the house. Where is little miss Brianna?"

"She's still 'sleep."

"Are you still going to let her father see her? Because I would never let him see her."

"What did he do to her?"

"He never married you after all those years together. Then he marries a woman he only knew one month. If I ever see his ass he'll be sorry. You look a little down, are you all right? You're not worrying about Brian ruining your life, are you?" My grandmother rambled on. It was just like her, getting the story all wrong.

"Please, Gram, I broke up with Brian. I am feeling a little down, but not about Brian."

"What are you feeling down about? You're living, aren't you? You have a good family. Your dad gave you a nice place to live. Most people don't have that."

"I know, I just can't wait to get on my feet."

"It will happen, things happen for a reason. You know, maybe it's time to get yourself together, find a husband or go to college or something, sweetie, you're twenty-four, soon to be twenty-five. What are you going to do with your life? When I was a young girl your age, I had already bought a home and was raising a family."

"Things are very different these days."

"Well, here go some money to keep you afloat until you get where you need to be."

"Thanks, Gram," I said as I hugged my grandmother. I walked her to the door and watched my gram get into her white Lincoln Towne Car. My gram was in her sixties and still thought she was young. She traveled every summer and worked a part-time job to get out of the house.

Kimberly Vanessa Brown

In the beginning I was in denial. The first month I didn't even notice I didn't get my period. The second month I blamed it on stress and got a pregnancy test just in case.

I hate to get graphic, but every slight pain that felt like a cramp I ran to the bathroom hoping to see any shade of red, pink to maroon. I saw nothing. No blood. The cramps I think were in my mind. I felt like I wasn't ready for another child, but then again, I wasn't ready when I had my son Kevin. But I got through it. I made do. When I first learned I was pregnant for the second time, I cried. I cried so hard that I made myself sick. Malik and me were not ready for a child. We'd been having problems. I had even considered an abortion. I made an appointment. I even went to the mandatory counseling session they had before the abortion. The morning I was scheduled to go, I got up, got dressed, and couldn't make myself leave the house. At first it was that I couldn't find my keys, then it was I had to go to the bathroom, then I felt hungry, but I couldn't eat anything because of the abortion. I sat on the sofa and thought about what I was about to do. I thought about when I was a freshman at Delaware State and I became pregnant. It was horrible. Me and my roomate, Tasha were drinking in our room. Having freedom for the first time in my life. My parents were so strict on me and my sister Karen that I didn't know how to embrace freedom. Tasha invited these guys up and they brought some weed with them. We all got high. They passed a blunt around the room. When it reached me, I just followed everybody else and took a long drag. That was my first time even trying weed. My head was spinning. I was feeling light-headed. I remember more people coming in and out of the room, then seeing this guy I liked named Darius from Connecticut. He was tall, handsome, and the shade of a pecan pie. His legs were slightly bowed. The blunt came around again and I took another toke. Darius gave me some gin and juice and we started talking. I remember him smiling at me and me feeling special. Then I remember us kissing and his hands going down my pants, sticking his finger in my vagina. I remember it was feeling good. It was the first time someone had touched me. I was a virgin. He asked me to go to his room. I said no. Then he said follow him to the bathroom; I said no. My roommate left out the room and the guys went with her. I went to lock the door, and Daruis came back and knocked on the door.

"Can I come in?"

"I'm 'sleep," I said groggily.

"Come on, let me in. Let's talk," he said.

"No, I got a headache. I'll see you tomorrow." I tried to close the door but Daruis blocked me closing it with his foot. Then he came in. I was starting to come out of sleepiness.

"What are you doing?" I asked as Darius walked toward me.

"I'm about to take what's mine. You been playing all night. Now give me mine," he said as he roughly bent me over the chair. I started fighting, but he grabbed my arms and held them tightly. I tried to scream, but it was worthless. He pushed my face into a pillow. I was only five feet even, a hundred and fifteen pounds. He was over six feet and stocky. He began kissing me on my neck. They were slow gentle kisses. I was crying. I told him to stop; he didn't. He kissed me some more, then he pulled down my pants.

"Please stop, Darius, please stop," I begged.

"You want it too. You were popping it for me earlier. Pop it now, Kim. Come on, pop it." I did what he told me. I didn't want him to hurt me. My body and mind was playing tricks on me. I wanted Darius to get off me, but he wouldn't stop and for some reason it began to feel okay. Maybe I did want it. I didn't know. I started to like the way his dick felt inside me. At first it hurt, but the more he stroked, the better it felt. I stopped protesting and just let him do whatever he wanted. When he finished, he smacked my butt and zipped up his pants. He told me if I told anybody, nobody would believe me. He said that everyone saw us together earlier in the evening. When he left, I went to the bathroom. I washed up and wiped my tears away. I didn't know if I was raped or not. I wanted to call my mom, but I couldn't. I didn't tell anyone.

The next morning, I remember feeling sick to my stomach. I didn't want to tell anyone, because I did participate—even though in the beginning I didn't want it. Once it was in it felt good. I couldn't stop him, so he kept going and I let him.

I realized I was pregnant the end of my freshman semester in May. I knew I couldn't go home, so I told my mother and father I was staying all summer for classes. They thought I was enjoying school. My plan was to stay in school and not drop out. I went to summer classes and tried to finish fall. You would've never suspected I was pregnant. I gained about ten pounds, and I wrapped duct tape and wore girdles over my little belly. I went to class and was still trying to exercise. I wasn't eating properly or taking care of myself. I overworked myself. I never considered an abortion or adoption. I think I thought if I didn't think about the baby that it would go away.

I almost had my baby in the bathroom stall of my dorm, until someone walked in on me and said I looked like I was about to go into early labor. The school notified my family and I came clean. I had to leave school early and go home on bed rest. I was seven months pregnant and weighed 130 pounds. That was okay if my normal weight was not 115 pounds. I couldn't tell my father and mother that I got high and was drinking and got raped by Darius. I just told my mother I made a mistake and had a one-night stand. My mother understood. My dad went berserk. He was a Vietnam vet who had Agent Orange. He was doing okay taking his medicine and taking care of himself. But when I came home, he had to go back to the veteran's hospital. All my life my dad went in and out of his mind. But this time it was my fault that my dad was in the hospital. I made him have a nervous breakdown.

I remember coming through the door from school and my older sister Karen yelling, "We sent you away to college for an education, you bring a baby home."

My mom was my rock, being supportive and helping me deal with everything I was going through. But my dad, when he came home from the hospital, he stopped speaking to me. I guess I would stop speaking to my daughter, too, if I spent all this money on her tuition, just gave her a going away party, and sold one of my cars to send her to college and she comes back pregnant.

My dad wasn't the only person who was disappointed in me. I was disappointed in myself. The guy Darius I was pregnant by didn't even call me the whole pregnancy. He knew he raped me, he knew we had sex, but he said it wasn't his and for me not to say anything in life to him. I respected his wishes. From what I heard, he finished the semester and went home to Connecticut. Nobody really knew what happened to me except for the girl who found me in the bathroom and my roommate Tasha.

My mother took me to an obstetrician and he put me on bed rest. He said I had already dilated two centimeters and that the baby needed to stay inside for at least six more weeks. I could only take a shower every other day and was not allowed to stand on my feet or go up the steps. The doctor even wanted me to use a bedpan, but I refused. We had a bathroom downstairs so I was able to use that bathroom and wash up in the sink. I did a lot of soul searching while I was on bed rest. I was determined not to become a statistic. I was not going to let my baby stop me from accomplishing my goals in life. I was not going to be on welfare. I was not going to have another baby two years later, and I did not need a man. I was going to get an apartment and a job and finish college.

My son Kevin was born exactly six weeks later. My mother had a thing for names that began with K so I let her name him. If I could have, I would have named my son Katherine after my mom, but instead I let her name him Kevin. He was a tiny baby. He only weighed four and half pounds. He couldn't even come home for the first month. He had jaundice and was underweight. He was in the intensive care unit and in an incubator. I went to visit him every day. Seeing Kevin's frail body, his chest heaving up and down, hanging on for life, and the imprint of his rib cage against his chest, I began to feel guilty about not taking care of myself properly during my pregnancy and and I made a vow to change my life.

When Kevin was three months, I started Philadelphia Community College. I transferred most of my credits over and got an associate's degree in Business and then went to Drexel for my bachelor's. I found a job at an insurance company. It wasn't easy but somehow I managed. Now five years later I have Kevin, and I'm pregnant again with Malik's child.

Now that I have health benefits, a car, somewhere to live, even though it's small and costs too much, and a loving fiancé, why was I scared to bring a baby into the world? I wanted to kick myself for being so dumb for even allowing myself to become pregnant. I wasn't a teenager and I knew pulling out/withdraw was not 100 percent effective. I don't know why, but I was scared. Just the thought of getting up early in the morning feeding a baby is scary. Malik and me were on the verge of breaking up before I became pregnant. I just want everything to work out between us, and hopefully it will.

Chapter Two

Shonda

My grandmother helped raise me. My mother left my father and me when I was five. Most women take their kids and leave their men, but Angela did the opposite. I don't know why my mother left us, I remember that day, though. My dad was standing at the mahogany painted door with his white wife beater T-shirt, blue checkered boxer shorts, and brown slippers on. I was right beside him. I had heard some commotion that made me stop playing with my Bubba Yum doll. She blew real bubbles. I stopped doing her hair to find out what was going on. My dad was peeping through the chained door lock. My mother and the police stood on the other side. I don't know why my mother had called the police on my father, but the police were banging on the door demanding that my father let my mother in. My father was in no way a violent guy, but they were having a situation that evening. To this day, I don't know why my father locked my mother out of the house. All I remember my dad saying is, "Angela, why'd you go and get the police? Why would you do that in front of Shonda?"

Incidentally, that is the only memory I have of my parents being together. I know my parents married in 1976 and had me in 1977. I was the third try for a baby. The two before me had ended in miscarriages. My mother never came back after that night. When I got older, Gram told me my mother had schizophrenia and suffered from severe depression. My dad always called my mother a free spirit. He said she could never sit still or commit to anything.

I asked my dad when was Mommy coming home and he said he didn't know. My grandmother came and stayed with us for a little while and told me to stop asking for my mother.

When Gram stopped living with us, my dad moved this woman named Ms. Carol into our house and her two kids Troy and Tanya. I hated Ms. Carol and I hated her kids even more. Tanya was okay, but I had to share my room with her and she started messing everything up trying to play my record player and scratched up my "Hey, Mickey you're so fine, hey, Mickey" record by Toni.

Ms. Carol was so mean to me. My mother didn't eat pork and neither did my father and I was only five and didn't know any better so when she tried to feed me a bologna sandwich I had never had one so assumed it was pork.

"I don't eat pork!" I told Ms. Carol as I pushed my plate to the front of the table. She gave her daughter a peanut and jelly sandwich and was trying to feed me pork! I called my gram and told on her. I went in my room and started crying.

"Gram, she's trying to feed me pork."

"Give that hussy the phone." I ran downstairs and gave Ms. Carol the phone. The next thing I knew, Ms. Carol told me to come downstairs and she began to beat me one for not eating my lunch and two for calling my grandmother on her. I called my grandmother back. Who did Ms. Carol think she was playing with? My grandmother called my dad at work and needless to say when my dad came in and saw me crying, Ms. Carol was out of there and so were her kids. I had my own room again, and it was just my daddy and me.

Me and my dad used to run in the park and go the movies. When I was good in school, we'd go downtown to the arcade and take pictures and play games. For my tenth birthday he brought me a Polaroid Instamatic camera. I took a picture of him and me. I still have that picture in my wallet.

Kim

I worked at Renard Financial Company. My position basically was to qualify people for personal loans, or car loans. I also had to call these same people up if their payments weren't on time and make arrangements with them. My office was small, just me and two other girls. Nicole was the designated ghetto girl who loved drama. Her daughter was always going through some medical catastrophe—asthma, strep throat, fever, you name it, her daughter got it—and she had to leave work early because of it. The Puerto Rican girl Lisa, who was in between jobs and working with us until she found something better, she thought she was Jennifer Lopez, but she was more like Rosie Perez.

My mother is a retired schoolteacher. My father is a disabled vet. He was in Vietnam, and sometimes has flashbacks. As a result of the war, he has a prosthetic leg. My father goes in and out of sanity. One month he would be okay, the next seven were another story. My mother was strong, tolerating all his ups and downs. She never divorced him. I know I would have. He put her through so much shit.

Sometimes I wonder about what he saw that would have such a dramatic effect on his life. When he came home from the army he was okay. He bought a home, married my mom, and worked at the naval shipyard. He has always provided for us and never was violent, but we had to deal with alcoholism and him being addicted to painkillers. The last time my dad was home he stood on the front porch with no clothes on and said, "I'm tired of taking these damn meds. I'm not going to be a guinea pig for the United States government. I got a mission to go on for the CIA. I have to go back to Vietnam and rescue my men." To say my dad is out of his mind is an understatement. We had him 302'd and I gave up on him a long time ago.

My father to this day has resentment toward me. He's still mad at me for getting pregnant and not being married. Even though he has his own issues, he treats my sister Karen like she is a god even though she hasn't accomplished half as much as me. Karen doesn't have a degree and never even attempted to go to college. She started working at a bank as a teller when she was eighteen and she is still in the same position ten years later. She's married to a fat loser name Lonnie. He used to be a rapper/singer. He had one song in the early nineties. He used to perform and make ten thousand a show, but he blew all his money and never came out with another record. She met him on the tail end of his success. He works for Coca-Cola filling machines now, and spends every dime he gets in the studio, hoping to one day get another hit. They live in a small apartment in west Philly. They have a son that's eight named Ryan. My sister drives a raggedy Chevy Blazer, not a new one but like a '92, and yet she knows it all. We have competed against each other our whole lives. Karen beat me up every day since I could remember. She was three years older so she thought she was my boss. She would always hit me, but wouldn't allow anyone in the street to fight me. One day she would be my best friend who I could talk to about anything, and another she was my worst enemy.

My little sister Kianna, she is another story. Kianna is the baby, she's three years younger than me. And I guess the saying is true. That the baby gets whatever they want. All the rules that applied to Karen and me went out the window for Kianna. She didn't have a curfew, could buy any price sneakers she wanted, had company spend the night during the week, and she didn't have to get good grades. If she passed, that was good enough. She didn't even finish high school. She went to the Job Corps and there got her G.E.D. My sister is a flake. Every other day she got a get-rich-quick scheme. Like she asked my mother and father to loan her money for her to open up her own hair salon. Her shop was going to be called Kianna's Kreation. Then she wanted to go to nursing school, but she didn't complete that either. Every time I say something about Kianna's noncommittal behavior to everything, my mother says, "Leave her alone. She's finding herself." And talking to Kianna is like speaking to a wall. Sorry, but if she was white she would be a blonde. She is shallow and dense. Kianna's career path this year is being an actress. She's enrolled in some acting school in New Jersey. My sister actually told me, believe me or not, that now that she is in the industry, she was going to meet either a rapper or NBA star and marry them. She said because she was light skinned and had long hair, that's what they like. Need I say more?

I have been with my fiancé for almost three years. I proposed to him first. I bought him a white gold and diamond ring. I made his favorite dish, lasagna, and put my son Kevin to sleep and turned the lights out. I lit candles and put on a Maxwell CD. I poured him some chardonnay and kissed him on his cheek and said, "Malik Moore, you know I love you, right?"

"Yes, I know you love me, baby, and I love you too."

"Well, I got something to ask you," I said as I bent on one knee. "Will you marry me, Malik?"

Malik looked up at me, startled. He said "Kim, you know I love you but . . ."

"But what, Malik?" I said as I looked up at him.

"Kim, we can't get married now. No, not like this."

I couldn't believe that he didn't say yes. When I told him I was pregnant he acted excited. Now I don't know what to think. To make a long story short, Malik said we didn't have to be married to have a baby. That we were together and a ring was only a piece of metal that didn't mean anything. I didn't care what Malik said, I wanted to get married. I wanted him to marry me. I didn't care if we went to the justice of the peace and had a small ceremony. I was three months pregnant and Malik had about six months to do something, and fast.

After all that preparation, he said no. I was crushed. I almost kicked him out that night. I hardly spoke to him for a week; how could I stay with a man who doesn't want to marry me and I'm carrying his child? I thought of asking him to leave, but how would it look if I was pregnant by him and at the least not even together? So I decided I wasn't going to leave him. I knew he loved me and eventually he would come to his senses.

Chapter Three

Shonda

I had so much to do today, enroll Bree in camp, get the electric and gas put in my name, and get the phone put on. Using my cell for a house phone is not working, my bill is going to be sky high. Plus, I needed to call Sprint and get a Philly number.

I was happy to be back in Philly even under these conditions. Atlanta was nice but there is no place like home. Bree and me walked to Tae's house. It was hot as hell outside. The temperature was close to 90 degrees, but it felt like 110.

Tae is my godsister. I had known Tae most of my life. Chantae was the girl across the street from Gram's house. Okay, at five I was clueless about life and at six, this girl had her life planned. She was going to be an actress and marry Michael Jackson. She was always very direct. She came up to me as I was sitting on Gram's steps and said, "Hey, girl, want to play with me?"

"Yeah. What you want to play?"

"I dunno, maybe rope. If you walk me down the street I'll ask Ieasha if she can come out."

"Down the street where?"

"It's not far. Right there," she said as she pointed to a house a few doors down the street.

"You mean that fat girl's house."

"Yeah, her, she's nice and she's always got candy. What's your name?"

"Shonda. What's yours?"

"Chantae. Why was you crying when your dad left?"

"I wasn't crying."

"Yes you was. I saw you."

"No, I wasn't. I'll walk you down the street," I said, trying to change the subject. I didn't want her to know I was crying. She might call me a daddy's girl like Gram. From that day, it was on. Chantae introduced me to all the kids in the neighborhood and her little brother Dontae, who liked to follow us, he was only three. We caught lighting bugs and played hide and go seek. I started staying over Gram's house just to be near Chantae.

After a while, I stayed over Chantae's house all the time. We started out as best friends, then we became play cousins, but then decided that everyone was play cousins, so we decided to become god-sisters.

Tae was a year older than me, but we were in the same grade. She said that she started school late or something about her birthday came late. It was just Chantae and me from the first grade to the eighth. That's when we got separated. I wanted to go to a high school with cute boys and decent girls. Chantae wanted to sing, dance, and be an actress. So she went to the School for Performing and Creative Arts and I went to Overbrook High School. She tried to convince me to go too, but I couldn't sing, dance, or act so I saw no purpose. My goal for the ninth grade was to convince my dad to let me have some big figure-eight gold earrings and let me talk to boys.

Tae's mom, Ms. Juanita, was like a substitute for my real mother. She had Dontae and Tae, but she took me in too. I went on vacations with them and stayed over their house. My grandmother lived across the street from them so I would just run between both houses. I stayed over their house so much my dad started giving her money for me. She could use it because she didn't work. She used to work at a factory, but she had hurt her hand and got disability. She taught Tae and me everything about life. She took us to the hair salon with her, and the nail place. She made us wash out our underwear every night before bed, and made sure we tied our hair up in a scarf.

With the money my grandmother gave me, I bought me and Bree mattresses. I called my dad from the Mario's furniture store and asked him to pick up the mattresses so I wouldn't have to pay a delivery charge and wait three days for our bed. "Daddy, I'm on Fifty-second Street. I just bought Bree and me mattresses. Can you come pick them up?"

"Shonda, I'm working."

"I know, Dad; not right now. Just before they close at eight."

"I'll pick them up for you. Just tell them I'm coming. And you better hurry up and get a job so you get some money to pay me some rent by next month."

"All right Dad, bye." After that, I had exactly five dollars left. We began walking to Tae's house. I started thinking about my life again. I was not growing, I was regressing. I needed help, I needed a job, I needed to be able to take care of my daughter. Sweating and tired, we arrived at Tae's house. She was surprised to see us.

"Give me a hug, Bree."

Bree extended her arms out, gave Tae a hug and said, "Mom, can I have a water ice and pretzel?"

"Here, Bree. How much you need?" I asked as I reached in my pocketbook.

"Don't worry, I got it, girl," Tae said as she pulled out her money and gave Bree a ten-dollar bill.

"Get your mom and me one, too."

"What kind?" Bree asked.

"Give me a cherry and your mom wants a blueberry."

Bree ran out the door and returned moments later with the water ices. "Mom, can I go down the street with Brittany?"

"Go 'head," I said as I finished my conversation with Tae. Before I could get my next sentence out of my mouth, Brianna came running back in the house, letting the screen door slam.

"Mom, can I go in Brittany's house and play Barbies?"

"No, Bree. I don't know them. And stop running in and out the house before I make you stay on the steps."

The sun was starting to ease its glaze, so we went and sat on the front steps. We set on the steps and ate crabs. It was a typical sunny summer day, cars kept zooming past with loud music, guys doing wheelies on four-wheelers, and kids playing in the street. Bree continued to play rope with the little girl Brittany down the street and all these other children.

"So, what's up, girl?" Tae asked.

"Nothing, broke as shit, but I'm just glad to be home."

"I know that's right. If you would have stayed in Atlanta one more day, you would have been in your own Lifetime movie. All the good-looking men and you had to find a crazy man."

"Wasn't he crazy?"

"How you know he won't come find you like *Sleeping with the Enemy*?"

"He's not really that crazy, plus, he hasn't been back to my aunt's house since the restraining order."

"Why you look depressed?"

"I don't know. I am just broke as shit, no job and no money. Man, I'm ready to go shake my ass."

"Where you going to shake your ass at, don't nobody want to see you."

"I don't know, somewhere, my name about to be Diamond."

Tae laughed at me, but I was serious. I was so broke, I was ready to rob someone or a bank, or start a life of crime.

"I can't even get my phone turned on. They said I have to pay my whole balance; that's like three hundred."

"Can't you make a promise to pay or something?"

"No. They said I break my promises. It's okay, I'll get some money from somewhere."

"Well, if you want, you can get your phone in my name, but don't be messing up my credit."

"Thanks, Tae, that's good looking out. But I still need some money. I'm about to call Brian." I called Bree back down the street.

"Yes, Mom."

"Bree, come here and call your dad," Tae handed Bree the phone and she dialed Brian as she thumbed through her ponytail and shook in place.

"Hey, Daddy. Yes, I'm home. Can I come over?" Brianna turned to me and said, "Can I go to my dad's house?"

I told her that I didn't care.

"Mommy said 'yes'." Then she said, "Okay, daddy, I love you too. Mom, Daddy wants to talk to you," and she handed me the phone.

"Hey, Brian. We're in Philly, we got back last night. Um, I need some money." He asked me for what.

"For your daughter, that's for what," I screamed into the telephone. I told Brian I needed at least two hundred dollars.

"I can only give you a hundred. I'll give you some more later this week," he said.

"I'll see you when you get here," I said as I hit the off switch on the phone.

"That's a damn shame," I heard Tae say. I turned around to see what Tae was talking about. I saw this young girl in the door with a baby on her hip.

"What are you talking about, Tae?"

"You know, Brittany's mom just had another baby, and that makes eight."

"How old is she?"

"Like, twenty-four. How do you have eight kids at twenty-four?"

"That's messed up, and you know none of them have the same father. I feel like calling D.H.S. on her." Damn, I thought I had it bad. It was only Bree and me and I was crying broke and that girl had it way worse than I did. I don't think I could deal with two kids, let alone eight.

"More power to her."

"She needs to keep her legs closed. Matter fact, you shouldn't even let Bree play with her kids, that shit may be contagious." We laughed at Tae's last ridiculous statement.

Brian showed up, like, two hours later. He handed me a hundred dollars and I put it in my back pocket. Bree ran right up to him and gave him a hug. He told Bree to gather her things. Brianna looked like Brian, tall, skinny, and honey brown. Brian shook his head at Tae and me like we were disgusting and managed to say, "Hi, Chantae."

"What's up, Briz?"

"Briz. My name is Brian."

"Brian, really, imagine that." Chantae laughed. Brian was full of shit nowadays. Brian was Briz up until he became a cop. How I stayed with his ass for six close to seven years, I don't know. Actually, I do know how—Brian saved me. When I was sixteen years old, I went with this guy named Nard. He was a guy that always stayed in trouble and I liked him. I had to sneak to see him, because my dad said I couldn't talk to boys until I was eighteen. Nard was my first for everything. He was so cute in his own sort of way. My dad hated him and Gram didn't even tell me when he called. I think them not liking him made me like him even more.

Then out of nowhere Nard broke up with me, he never said why.

So he stopped seeing me and I was devastated; sixteen and my first boyfriend dumps me. Chantae knew everything that was going on and tried not to talk about it. She just always asked me if I wanted to go out or something.

A couple days after Nard broke up with me, Chantae invited me to a cookout with her. That's where I met Brian, Chantae's cousin Chuck's friend. Brian was seventeen and went to Gratz High School and was in the twelfth grade. He even had a car—well it wasn't his, it was his brother's, but he got to drive it, a light blue Ford Escort. Brian and me started hanging out; he was my second. I liked him. He was real fun and different. He wasn't really into the street and he took me places like the movies. We were having fun until I found out I was pregnant.

When I told Nard I was pregnant, he wanted us to get back together. He told me to meet him on the corner of my block so we could talk. He assured me that everything was going to be okay. I walked to the corner and met him. I told him he looked nice in his red and black Jordans and blue jeans, with a crisp white T-shirt. We spent the whole day together planning and daydreaming about the baby. We thought of baby names and even bought some clothes for the baby. I was so happy about me and Nard being back together. We started spending every day with each other. I even cut school on occasion to be with him. We were having so much fun, I forgot all about Brian. Brian called every day and Gram gave me his messages. I would have to call him and tell him that we couldn't see each other anymore.

The night I was about to call him and tell him that I couldn't go out with him anymore and that I was pregnant by Nard, Tae called. She said that Nard just got killed on the corner in front of the Chinese store on 58th and Landsdowne Avenue.

"What!" I said screaming. "No, no, you're lying, Tae, stop lying. Tae, this is not funny, stop lying," I said as I began crying and putting on my clothes. Gram ran in the room to see what was going on.

"What's wrong, child?"

"Gram, somebody killed Nard," I said as I ran out of the house. I ran four blocks straight to the Chinese store. All I saw was yellow police tape. There was blood-drenched white sheets laying over the bodies. I looked and saw Nard's red and black Jordans sticking out of the end of one of the sheets. I screamed "Nard!" and tried to run past the tape. A cop caught me and pulled me back. The crowd had gotten bigger. I fell out, I couldn't breathe, I couldn't see. Nard's sister Maya grabbed me and leaned me on her shoulder—she was older, like twenty-two. I just kept crying. They made everybody move so they could look for evidence.

It was so sad, I don't remember anything after that. I know we buried him. A lot of people showed up, everybody from our neighborhood and school. Everything was a blur after the funeral. His sister Maya said he was just in the wrong place at the wrong time, it was an accident. These guys from Chester Avenue were looking for Marty—he burned them out of some money. He was standing on the corner with Nard, Lil Larry, and Curtis. When he saw the guys pull out the gun he ran in the Chinese store and he didn't get shot, but everybody else did. Those bullets were meant for Marty, he should have taken them.

I didn't hear from Maya until, like, a month after the funeral. I was so out of it, I really forgot that I was pregnant. Tae and me were sitting in my room talking about everything that went down when Maya called.

"Hello, can I speak to Shonda?"

"This is Shonda, who's this?"

"This is Maya. Nard's sister. Well, I was calling you because my brother said you was pregnant by him. Are you?" Maya asked.

"Pregnant by Nard, um . . " Tae looked and me and signaled me with her hand to put Maya on hold.

"I don't know yet," I said as Tae grabbed the phone away from me.

"Tell her to hold on," Tae whispered to me as she covered the receiver of the telephone.

"Hold on, Maya, okay?" I laid the phone down on the bed. I looked over at Tae as she directed to me walk out of the room, to ensure Maya didn't hear what she was telling me in the hallway. She shut the door and said, "Look, I wasn't going to say anything but, you can't have a baby when the dad is dead. Look, don't nobody know you're pregnant. And how about if it's not Nard's and it's Brian's, you're going to have his family ready to kill you. Right."

"But what am I going to do?"

"You got to get an abortion."

What Tae said made sense. I thought about it for a moment, then with regret I got back on the phone and said, "Maya, I thought I was pregnant but I'm not."

"You're not pregnant?"

"No, umm, umm . . ." I heard her yell "She's not pregnant." Then someone in the background said, "All right, hang up." Then the line disconnected.

I never called Brian after Nard died. I didn't know what I was going to do. I was so depressed, Gram and my dad were going to take me to counseling, but I didn't feel like talking to anybody, I didn't want them to find out I was pregnant. Brian got tired of me dissing him so one day he just came up to my school and asked me where I been at and why I hadn't been calling him. I told him I didn't know why. He asked me did I want to go get something to eat, because I looked like I needed a friend.

"I got an hour before I go to work," he said as he looked down at his watch.

"I don't care where we go," I said.

I did need someone to talk to, because I told Brian everything. I felt like I could trust him. I told him about Nard getting killed, me being pregnant and not knowing if it was his or not, how I told Nard's sister I wasn't pregnant. How my Gram and Dad didn't know and how Tae told me to get an abortion.

"Do you want an abortion?" he asked.

"No."

"Then don't get one. I'll take care of the baby for you."

"Yeah, right, you going to take care of the baby."

"I'm for real, I'm going to take care of you and my baby. All you got to do is be with me."

"Be with you. Huh?"

"Yeah."

From that point on I was with Brian. He was there for me and he said he knew it was his baby because he came in me on purpose so he could have a son named Brian Junior by a pretty girl like me.

Everybody was just so happy to see me smile again. That's when I announced I was pregnant. They didn't even get really upset. I waited until October, when I was like four months, to tell my gram and Dad I was pregnant. So if they tried to make me have an abortion, it would be too late.

Brian's mom was just so happy to have a grandbaby. She didn't care that I was only sixteen and Brian was only eighteen and we were going to be parents.

Nobody questioned who the father was, they knew it was Brian. When Bree was born, I named her Brianna after him and she got his last name and we went on with life. Brian and me got together in May and Brianna was born the end of February. I don't know if she was early or late, I was young and confused. So I came to the conclusion, either I was two or three weeks pregnant when I met him, or got pregnant the first time we had sex.

The seven years we were together, we were a perfect family. We took pictures at Sears, church on Sunday, then to the movies or Penn's Landing. We went to amusement parks and even got an apartment when I graduated high school. I worked at this pizza store as a cashier and Brian's brother got him a job at the gas company.

We was talking about getting married and buying a house one day. But Brian changed when he got accepted in the police academy. He stopped talking about us. He started saying *me*. I was the one who filled out all Brian's applications, and made him go take the test. Once he was accepted to the police academy, our relationship just changed altogether. I guess we outgrew one another.

When Brian got out of the academy, he changed. He started coming home late, hanging out with his corny cop friends, and being bourgie like he had the best job ever. He went and bought a new car, a green four-door Toyota Camry. You could not tell him it wasn't a Lexus. He wouldn't even let me drive it because I didn't have a license. He told me he didn't want me talking about anything illegal on the phone. He swore the cops were listening in on the conversation. Like our phone was tapped. He talked about his job all day long. Then he started staying the night out saying he was doing overtime. I found out his overtime was a girl he met in the academy named Andrea. That was all I needed, a reason to leave him. I wanted to leave Brian years ago, but didn't know how to. I felt like I needed him.

Everyone always told me how lucky I was that Brian was young and still responsible. I was grateful that he stood by me when he wasn't even sure if Brianna was his or not. I saw what other girls went through with guys. They had to beg for milk and Pamper money, and I didn't have to do that. I felt lucky to have Brian. I never cheated on his ass, cause I thought he saved me from being alone and having Bree on my own. I felt like I owed him something, but it had been seven years now. I had paid him back. It was time for both of us to move on. I left Brian and three months later my payback was him getting married. I then decided to move to Atlanta. Before I left, I told Brian I wasn't coming back and that we should find out if Bree was his. She looks like him, but then again, she looks like me, too. Not knowing the truth was okay when we were together, but now that we broke up, I thought about it every day. He told me there was no need to.

Tae said I should go out and have a good time and on Monday start looking for a job. She called herself making me forget my worries by taking me out to the bar around the way called Johnny's. Her little brother Dontae met us there and he was a mess. Dontae can take the smallest thing and make it seem funny.

"What's up, little brother?" Tae asked.

"Shonda, what's up?" he said as he looked at me and puckered his lips out.

"Now, Dontae, you know we like brother and sister."

"I don't care, we can commit incest, baby. You ready to let me smash."

I laughed at Dontae and told him to get out of my face. Tae jumped up and said that Dontae was disgusting. She went to hit him and he flinched away, still trying to tell me that he always wanted me since he was three and I was five.

"You really like me, so you got me and Tae drinks on you the rest of the night," I said.

"Hell no, I ain't got your drinks, I was only playing with you."

I knew that would make Dontae change his tune, and it did.

"I don't give chicks none of my money."

"You don't have any to give away." Tae laughed.

Tae wanted me to forget about my worries and I sure did when I ordered a double shot of Hennessey straight with a coke on the side. I was grooving off the Henney, we was talking about old times. Dontae's fat, little black butt was making us laugh doing dumb dances and talking about people in the bar.

"You got to try this drink," Tae said as she motioned me to take a sip. As I raised the cup to my mouth and took a sip, Tae said, "It's called Hypnotique."

"It taste good, what's in it?" It was real fruity and sky blue.

"I don't know." Tae shrugged.

"Oh, look, there go Asha," I said. Asha was this girl we used to hang out with back in the day. We stopped being with her for several reasons, mainly because she was the biggest hoe in West Philly, and because she was a liar. She came walking toward us. She had an auburn wig on, a big ass Louis Vuitton bag, and blue jeans with plastic brown sandals that was supposed to match her bag, but didn't.

"What's up Tae and Shoney, long time no see." I turned around ignoring her and kept talking to Dontae.

Tae responded by saying, "What's going on Asha, money?"

Then Tae did something that made me sick. She started acting Joe. Joe meaning Joe familiar. Being on Asha's dick saying, "Oh my God, girl, that ring is the bomb," as she held Asha's ring up to the light.

Asha had this smirk on her face and kept smiling and said, "Thank you."

"So when you getting married?" Tae asked.

"In September. Are you going to come to my bridal shower?"

"Yeah, I'll come."

Asha dug into her oversize Louis Vuitton bag, pulling out two invitations. She handed one to Tae and the other to me. "Shonda, I want you to come too, it will be like old times."

Then Dontae burst out and said, "Who the hell is marrying your smut ass, Asha?" I could not control my laughter. I damned near spit my drink out my mouth. Dontae asked what I was dying to know.

"First of all, I'm not no smut and you better watch who you talking to," Asha turned around and said with attitude.

Tae broke the heat up by re-asking the question in a nice way. Dontae and me was still laughing. Asha looked over at him, and then turned away and said, "I am marrying Floyd Ruskins. He's from Philly and plays with the Detroit Lions."

"Oh, so he play basketball?"

"No, football."

"Oh, that's nice. Congratulations. You need to hook me up with one of his friends."

"I can do that, call me. My number is on the invitation."

Asha walked away and Chantae immediately smacked Dontae on his back. "Why would you ask her that? You so fucking ignorant, boy." Dontae was ignorant and has always said his mind since we was little.

"That was a nice bag."

"I know," I said.

"Yeah, that jawn cost like a gee."

"Well, why she got on a thousand-dollar bag with thirty-dollar sandals?" I asked.

"Um, I don't know. Why you hating?"

"I'm not hating. I'm just saying."

"Saying what?"

"Forget it."

After Asha left, Chantae's friend Dave from 17th Street down north Philly showed up. He came by, bought us drinks. He was a cute little boy. I say little boy because Chantae is twenty-five and this guy looked like he was about seventeen. Oh well, as long as he kept buying drinks he was cool with me. Chantae had a thing for using or getting everything she wanted from men. Maybe it was her oversize breasts or just her I-don't-give-a-fuck attitude. Whatever it was, it worked for her. We always joked that she had the chest and I had the butt—if we switched body parts one of us would make the perfect woman. Any guy she dated I rarely knew their name because she referred to them by their occupation, car, or where they resided. For example, the last couple of months Tae has dated the boah with the Benz, Septa (that's the bus driver), and the trash man. Now it was all about the young boah from 17th Street tonight. Ask me his real name, I couldn't tell you.

Chantae's friend from 17th Street gave us a ride home from the bar. We was all real fucked up. I was going to spend the night at Chantae's, but her and her friend wanted me to go ride with them to Atlantic City. I didn't feel like it. They was making too much noise and my head was spinning. I told Tae I was going home. Her friend offered me a ride, but I told him no and that I would be okay. I only had about three blocks to walk. Plus it was the summertime, everybody was still outside. I told Tae bye and began walking home.

I'll say I got about a block and half away from her house when this dark-skinned young boah with light facial hair came up to me in this blue hoodie and black jeans and said, "Listen shorty, I got a gun, where the money at?" I looked at him like he was joking. He was really serious, though. I paused for about two seconds and then he said again, "Shorty, where the money at?"

I dumped my pocketbook out and said, "Here, take everything. Here, I got a daughter, please just take whatever you want."

The guy snatched the money Brian had gave me earlier out my hand and picked up my ATM card and said, "What's the PIN?"

"Zero, Three Seven. Eight," I said frantically. Then the guy darted back around the corner. I stood there for a moment and then I saw these women across the street. I was crying and I ran over to them and told them I had just been robbed.

"Do you have a phone?" I asked them.

"No, sorry, honey, I don't have one."

The other lady said, "That's a damn shame, I thought ya'll was talking. You can't even walk the streets without somebody trying to rob you these days." The first woman continued to look across the street like the guy was coming back.

I saw another lady talking on her cell phone. I ran over to her and said, "Miss, please dial 911. I was just robbed." The lady told whoever she was talking to I'll call you back. She dialed 911, then passed the phone to me.

"I have just been robbed," I said between sobs.

"Miss, calm down. Tell me what happened."

"I was just robbed."

"What did he have on?"

"A blue hoodie and black jeans."

"Was he black?"

"Yes, he was black. Can you send the police? I don't feel safe out here!" I screamed as I looked around the dark street. The other ladies had disappeared and it was only me and the lady whose cell phone I was on.

The cop finally arrived, a thin, short white guy. With a messed-up army haircut. His blue and red lights were flashing everywhere.

"Are you the lady that called?" he asked. He pulled over and got out the police car.

"Yes, I called."

"Tell me what happened," he said as he got a pen out of his pocket and wrote down every word that I said. I gave him the description of the guy again. Then we walked across the street and I picked up my stuff. My license was still there and so were my keys.

Other cops pulled up. The first cop radioed something in, then another guy pulled up with a guy matching the description I just gave. A young guy was sitting in the backseat. They asked me to see if that was him. I told them it wasn't him. This guy was shorter, darker, and a lot younger than the guy that had just robbed me. As soon as I said no they let the guy go.

The cop then asked me could I come down to southwest detectives and give a statement.

"Can I go tomorrow?"

"You can but if you come now, I'll make sure you get home. You don't want this to happen to anyone else, do you?" The cop was right, I didn't want it to happen to anyone else, so I got in the car with him and went to the station.

The police district looked nothing like the police stations on television. The cop told me to have a seat. I had a choice of five non-matching chairs, which colors ranged from a black to a busted orange chair. The light hanging from the ceiling was dim. There were wanted pictures hanging everywhere and the tan tile floor was dirty and scuffed. I waited for a few moments and the cop came and said, "The detective can talk to you now. This is Detective Clark."

He said hi and gave me half a smile and said, "So tell me what happened." I told the detective in detail exactly what happened. He then asked me could I pick him out of a line-up if I saw him again. I told him I probably could and he said, "Then I want you to look at these photos for me. There are fifteen pages, take your time."

I looked at every picture twice and I hate to say it but they all looked the same. I mean, every guy could have been him. They were all dark skinned and had light facial hair. I didn't want to pick out the wrong guy, so I said I didn't think any of them were him.

After I looked at each picture I had to sign a statement. I had called my dad and told him what happened. My dad took me home, made sure every window was shut, gave me a good night hug and said good night, and asked, "Why didn't Tae walk with you?"

"She had company and I just wanted to come home."

"Next time call me or catch a cab. I don't want you walking. I'm going to see if Mr. Rick got any cars. You need one. I don't like you walking in these mean streets. Where's my granddaughter?"

"With her dad."

"You just got back. She should be with you, not him."

"Dad, she was with me for six months straight without break, she can be with him for a little while."

Kim

At nine in the morning, Kevin ran into the room and said, "Mom, Malik is going to get me some new sneakers at the mall. You going with us?"

"No, tell him I don't feel like it."

Kevin ran out of the room and came back a few seconds later and said, "Mom, Malik said he wants you to come with us."

"Kevin, tell him here I come." It was Sunday and I didn't feel like doing anything. Why did Malik feel as though he had to take Kevin to the mall early in the morning? He knew I liked to relax on Sunday. That was the only day I could sleep until eleven or twelve.

We drove up Route 309 to the Montgomeryville mall. The doors were just opening when we arrived. Kevin ran straight to the Foot Locker.

"Which ones should I get, Mom?" he said as he held up three different pairs of sneakers.

"It doesn't matter, whichever sneakers you want, baby," I said as I yawned. I couldn't believe they had me out here. Kevin tried on some basketball Nikes. They were blue and yellow.

"Can I wear them home, Malik?"

"Ask your mom."

Kevin turned around to me and said, "Mom, can I wear them home?"

"Sure."

"Now I can run real fast. I'm going to beat everybody in Gym," Kevin screamed as he ran around the store.

After leaving Foot Locker, Malik said, "Walk me to that store over there. I want to see something."

"Something like what?" I hissed through my teeth. I was definitely ready to go. He stopped in the Zales jewelry store and began looking around. I waited outside.

"Come here, Kim."

"What?"

"Just come here."

I walked in the store and Malik said, "Remember what you asked me the other night?"

I said "Yes."

"I didn't say yes, Kim, because I wanted to do this right. How I look having a ring and you don't?" Malik then got on his knees and asked, "Kim, will you marry me?"

I was confused and so very happy at the same time. "Malik, of course I will marry you." We hugged and I gave Malik a kiss. Everyone in the store clapped. Kevin looked around in bewilderment.

"Now, pick out your ring."

"I get to pick out my own ring?" I was crying, I couldn't barely see. But my vision was not clouded to the fact I wanted a big ass diamond to show off to my sisters and mother. We went over to the case and the lady placed engagement rings on the display case. I saw this beautiful princess cut–diamond platinum ring. I tried it on and automatically fell love with it. "I want this one, Malik," I said.

"That will be five thousand and two hundred dollars," the salesgirl said. Malik's eyes popped out of his head. My tears started flowing as I watched Malik count his money. He had a handful of twenties and fifties.

"Is everything okay, baby?" I asked.

Malik said yes and went and spoke to the salesgirl. He came back and said, "Kim, I only have twenty-seven hundred on me, so I'm just going to apply for the rest in credit."

"Malik, you don't have to do that. I can find another ring."

"No, I want you to have that one. You deserve it, baby."

I stood there glancing at my ring. *Karen is going to be so jealous*, I thought. The salesgirl continued to smile and then took the cash Malik had and gave him an application for the line of credit. Kevin asked me what was going on. I told him me and Malik were getting married.

"Yea, so Malik is going to be my stepdad?"

"Yes."

"Malik, you going to be my stepdad?" he ran over to Malik and asked.

"Yes, I am," Malik said as he continued to fill out the application. After Malik completed the application, even though they had

Malik's money and driver's license, they still looked at us like a hawk, making sure we didn't run out of that door with the ring. A few moments later the lady came back over to Malik and said, "Sorry, sir. Your line of credit has been declined."

Malik looked at me with defeat in his eyes, like he was about to cry.

"Would you like to see another ring?" the lady said as she began to reach for my ring.

"No, we are going to take this ring," I said as I pulled out my Visa card and handed it to the lady.

Malik then pulled me to the side and said, "You can't pay for your own ring."

"I want this ring, Malik."

"I want you to have it. But not like this."

"Malik, it's no big deal. You make the payments, then, okay? I know if you had it you would buy it."

"Okay, but baby, I'm going to pay for it as soon as I can."

The lady interrupted our talk and asked, "Will you be taking the ring?"

This time Malik answered "Yes."

We then celebrated our engagement with brunch at the Marker Restaurant in the Adams Mark Hotel on City Line Avenue. Malik told me that he wanted us to take our time and not get married right away. I agreed, we did need to take our time. I was happy that we were engaged.

After brunch, I was so excited I called my mother and told her that me and Malik were getting married. She screamed, "I can't wait to tell your father! Come show me your ring. Where is Malik, I want to congratulate him."

"He took Kevin to the movies. I'll be past there."

I stared at my ring every time I had a chance. I held it up to the sunlight to see how beautiful it was. I thought about us getting married and being happy. I didn't know what kind of wedding I wanted. Now that I had my rock, the justice of the peace was not that appealing. I wanted a big fabulous wedding. A lace white dress with a long train, Kevin to be the ring bearer, a big church, a choir singing, and a Cinderella carriage waiting outside for me. My sisters and mother would be in beautiful beaded dresses. The flowers would be turquoise, white, and pink. Malik would stand there waiting for me in a Mandarin tuxedo, looking good. Jarrod standing next to him as his best man. Or I could get married on the beach in the Bahamas. The water would be softly crashing against the beach as the sand tickled our feet.

My fantasyland wedding was crushed, once I reached my mother's house. I saw Karen's car and couldn't wait to flash my ring in her face because she only had a simple gold band. I walked in and my mother ran up and hugged me.

"I'm so happy for you."

"Let me see," Karen said as she snatched my hand from my mother.

"Nice," she said as she nodded.

"So, when's the wedding?"

"I don't know yet. I just got engaged."

"Well, you're pregnant and I think you better get married before that baby gets here."

"Karen's right, y'all need to get married before you start showing," my mother said.

"I know that's right. You got one born out of wedlock, you don't need another."

"I can't have a big wedding if I'm pregnant," I said.

"Why not?" my mom asked.

"Because she is going to be all big and her nose is going to spread all across her face."

"Well, your first wedding is supposed to be your big wedding," my mom said.

"That's true," Karen agreed.

"What do you mean, my 'first wedding'? This is going to be my *only* wedding."

"Hopefully it will be, but don't you know the national divorce rate is fifty percent?"

"Well, I hope y'all stay together cause I like Malik, he's a good guy."

Talking to my mother and sister was depressing, but it got worse. Kianna came through the door. My mom yelled to Kianna before she could get all the way through the door. "Your sister is engaged."

"Really? About time," Kianna said. She looked over at my hand as she swept her blonde weave out of her face. It was obvious that nobody was happy for me. I got up from my mother's table, grabbed my pocketbook, and walked out the door.

"Where are you going?" my mother asked.

"Home."

"Your sisters are only playing with you. They're happy for you. Aren't y'all happy for your sister?"

"Girl, you know I'm happy for you. Congratulations," Karen said.

"Me, too," Kianna chimed in as she poured herself some iced tea.

"I can't tell," I said as I exited the door. *Forget them*, I thought to myself. I didn't understand the point in rushing to get married. Malik wasn't going anywhere and neither was I.

A coworker of mine named Stephanie introduced me to Malik. She was having a cookout and begged me to come. She was dating this guy named Jarrod and wanted me to meet his friend Malik. Kevin was three at the time and I couldn't find a baby-sitter. I didn't want to go at all. Stephanie pleaded. So I finally went. I didn't put on anything special. Not even any makeup. I barely fixed my hair. I walked in the cookout, said hello to everyone, and made a plate and sat in the house on the sofa in the living room. Kevin was running around and pushing Stephanie's magazines off her coffee table. I went to get up and chase him when a guy was coming down the steps drying his hands with a paper towel. He was kind of tall and built, his complexion was a medium shade of brown. His shoulders were broad and he had a little definition in his arms. I looked over at the steps, then back to my child, who was ripping up all the magazines.

The guy caught Kevin and said, "Come here, little guy. Is this your son?"

"Yeah."

"How old is he?"

"Three."

"Really? He's a big boy."

"Yeah, his dad is big."

"He must be, because you are so tiny."

"Huh."

"Not like that, but you're small and petite and he is big. I mean that in a good way."

I was used to people teasing me about my size.

"I'm Malik, Jarrod's friend," he said as he extended his hand out.

"Kimberly, but Kim is fine, Stephanie's friend."

"What are you doing after this?" he asked.

"Probably putting him to sleep and then fall asleep watching *Saturday Night Live*."

"Will your man be with you?"

"I don't have a man."

"Really. So can I see you again?"

"It depends."

"On what?"

"If you write down your number before I leave. Because I'm leaving now," I said as I got up and picked up Kevin to get him ready.

As soon as I walked to the backyard Stephanie screamed, "Where are you going?"

"I'm about to leave."

"I got somebody I want you to meet."

"No, Stephanie, I got to go."

Stephanie held my arm and said, "Jarrod come here. This is Kim. Kim, this is Jarrod." We both said awkward hi's. "This is my man; I want you to meet his friend Malik," she said as she pulled Kevin and me around the party.

"I'd like you to meet Kim," she said to Malik.

"We already met in the living room."

"Oh, well exchange numbers and call each other." We laughed at her matchmaking skills.

Malik called me, we planned a date with Kevin included. We took him to the park and went to the movies. We talked a lot on the telephone. Malik told me about himself, how he was a paralegal and had an associate's degree in law. He graduated from Pierce Junior College and wanted to go back and get his bachelor's degree in Criminal Justice, then go to law school. He wanted to become a lawyer because his little brother is in jail for robbing a bank with a beeper and still got charged with possessing a gun, even though the police and prosecutor knew he didn't have a gun and he was on drugs when it happened. Malik said that he wanted to defend people like his brother. He said there was no way his brother should have gotten ten years. He was high and not in his right mind and did not have a gun on him. He also told me about his sister Nadia and his mother Gloria. His dad died when they were little and his mom raised him and his brother and sister.

We had several dates with and without Kevin. Malik and Jarrod lived together, so I visited them a lot. From the beginning, I didn't like Jarrod. He was a short skinny bum. He was always slurping down a Corona and wanted Malik to go party with him. My mom baby-sat all the time. She couldn't believe I had a boyfriend. I never really dated after I had Kevin; I couldn't trust anyone and I was focused on getting my life together.

I fell in love with Malik because he made me laugh and I felt safe with him—something I hadn't felt in a long time. I still think about that night with Darius; sometimes I have flashbacks and nightmares. I used to sleep with a butcher knife under my pillow and jump up, startled. I went to counseling, but that didn't really help. I think time and love from Malik healed me. I never told Malik about what happened. Maybe one day I will, but right now I can't.

A year after me and Malik met, he moved in with me and Kevin and we have been together ever since. From the beginning, my mother objected about me living with Malik. She said if he stays there for more than a year without proposing to you then he never will. My mother does not know what she is talking about.

The thing that is so funny, Stephanie wanted me and Malik to meet bad, but when her and Jarrod didn't work out, she called me and said that I should drop Malik. I think she was really upset that me and Malik's relationship turned into something real, and Jarrod was just having her on the side. The last time I talked to her was when I changed jobs a year and a half ago.

Now, all Malik has to do is go back to school and get his bachelor's degree, and go to law school. So we can buy our two-car garage house in New Jersey and be a happy family.

Chapter Four

Shonda

"What are you doing?" Tae asked.

"About to pick up Bree from camp. Why, what's up?"

"I know this place that's hiring, paying twelve dollars an hour."

"Where at?"

"At this temp agency downtown. They are going to place you in a law firm. They offered me that job, but you know how I do. I decided I'm not working this month."

"I don't have anything to wear."

"Well, just call."

"I will, what's the number?" I wrote the number down and decided to call. "So what's up with you?"

"Nothing, probably go out to a late breakfast with the trash man."

"The trash man. What happen to Seventeenth Street?"

"Oh, you know I don't have any time for any young boahs. I was just getting his little ass to take us down Atlantic City, but your ass wanted to go home."

"Yeah. I should have stayed. I got robbed."

"You're lying."

"No, I'm not. I'll tell you about it later. Let me take a quick nap. Then I'll call the job."

Tae can find a job anywhere. If someone was not hiring they would still hire her. She has the gift of gab. I don't think she has ever been on an interview and not gotten a job. But Tae likes to work when it is convenient and it's not summertime. The summer is her time to live off men. I called the number Tae gave me. A lady answered the telephone. "Thank you for calling Monroe Staffing. My name is Pamela, how may I help you?"

"Hi, I'm calling about a receptionist position you have available."

"Did someone call you? Are you registered with us?"

"No, I'm not, but my friend Chantae Sampson said the position was open."

"Yes, I know Ms. Sampson. Well, since you're not registered with us, you have to come to our office and take a test and fill out some paperwork. I will contact our client and see if we can set up an interview for you. If you pass the typing and spelling tests, we then will assign you. When can you come in?"

"Tomorrow."

"We have eleven-thirty open."

I told her I would take that interview time but had no intention on keeping the appointment. I can't type and I'm not taking anybody's spelling test. I called Tae back to find out why she didn't tell me about the tests.

'Tae, why didn't you tell me about the typing test?"

"Girl, it's not that bad. You only have to type thirty-five words per minute."

"Well, what about the spelling test?"

"They just want you to cross out all of the words spelled wrong. I mean, it's obvious shit like they spell 'doctor', d-o-c-k-t-o-r. They just don't want to send any illiterate people out representing their company."

"You sure?"

"Yeah, man." Tae made me feel a little better but I was still skeptical.

* * *

I decided to wear a black V-neck dress and a gray and black suit jacket with silver bangles and silver stud earrings. This is as professional as I was getting. I had to take the ten trolley into Center City. I got off at City Hall and walked to One Penn Center. I sold my car when I moved to Atlanta. How I regret my move altogether. I just wasted six months of my life and now I had to start over from the beginning.

I walked into the tall office building as I was met with lunchtime traffic. Everyone was leaving out of the building and I was trying to come in. I pushed for the tenth floor. I was greeted by the cheerful receptionist Pamela. She had me fill out a form and an application. After I gave her back the clipboard and pen, she reviewed my application and then took me into a room to take the tests. She instructed me to read the directions and take the practice typing test, and after I took the tests to notify her. She closed the door and I sat in the small office with two computers and light tan carpet. There was a container of pens and pencils.

The typing test was okay. It didn't allow me to backspace, though. When I made a mistake I had to just continue because I was being timed. The next test was a spelling test. Tae was right, it was so elementary. I had to click the mouse on each word that was spelled wrong in the paragraph. As soon as I finished the test the computer automatically printed out my score. I pulled the paper from the printer. I read my score; it said 90 percent spelling and 80 percent typing. I heard Pamela walking down the hall, so I hurried up and put the paper back on the printer and had a seat. Pamela opened the door and went straight to the printer. She took a look at my result and said, "Thank you, Shonda. What we will do is contact you if we need you." She then shook my hand and led me to the door. After my interview, I went to Kinko's and faxed my resume to a few other places.

I waited two days before I called the staffing agency back. "Hi, my name is Shonda Robinson, I was calling to see if someone was hired for the position."

"Sorry, yes, the position has been filled," she said.

I said thank you and hung up. I was disappointed, but not defeated. I decided to do follow up calls with all the places I had faxed my resume to. Everyone I contacted's voice mail either came on or they said they would get back to me. This job search shit was getting to me. My dad was going to want some rent real soon, and I needed some money. Right now I feel like a failure. If you would have asked me at fifteen where and what I would be by the time I was twenty-four, I would have told you rich and famous, not broke and jobless.

I accepted a job at a telemarketing company. I had to be at the job orientation at nine o'clock in the morning. I hurried to get myself together and Bree to camp on time. Once I got to the job, I realized it was not for me. For one, the job was paying eight dollars an hour and you had to be in the union and the union took approximately twenty dollars out of each paycheck. They didn't have benefits. No cell phones or beepers were permitted anywhere in the building. You had to leave your cell phone home and they didn't have a phone for employees. One lady raised her hand and said what if my son gets sick? How would he get in touch with me? They didn't have an answer for her. We were supposed to be in training for two days then start on the phones by ourselves. The job was advertising a pay of eight dollars per hour but then they informed us the base rate was minimum wage and the eight dollars was with your commission. If that was not enough they wanted us to call people's houses and set up appointments for them to purchase aluminum siding. After they told us all ninety million of their rules, it was time for lunch. A lot of the employees went for a smoke. I went to the bus stop. That job had too many rules. I was not feeling it. On my way, I decided that I made the wrong decision. I should have kept that job until I found another one. My dad always said you always have to have some type of income and right now I didn't have any.

My dad must have some kind of intuition, because he called as soon as I walked in the door.

"How was your first day of work?"

"It was good," I said halfheartedly.

"Really?"

"Um-hmm."

"What time you get off?"

"At four."

"Shonda, it's one-thirty now, why are you home?"

"Um, Dad, they let us leave early today."

"Well, I was just checking up on you. Call your grandmother, and give Bree a kiss."

"All right, Dad." Something's got to give. Life can't be this hard—or at least it shouldn't be.

Kim

At times I hate my job, but I have to put up with this until something else comes along, because I got bills. I have been at Renard for about a year and a half. I started in an entry-level position. I was promoted within seven months to Assistant Branch Manger, and two months later to Manager. My job is located on Cottman Avenue in a strip mall in the northeast part of the city. I should be happy, but I'm not. As the manager for the branch, I make close to $40,000 with bonuses, but it's still a struggle. My son's tuition is so ridiculous, and rent is another story. I want to buy a house, but my Malik wants us to wait. I just leased a new 2002 silver Nissan Altima and all my credit cards are to the max. I make more money than Malik. The money he makes he has to pay a car note on his Ford Taurus that is always in the shop, credit cards, and his student loans. Our rent is $900.00 a month, which we split. Then we have cable, electric, telephone, credit cards, cell phone, gas. The only thing we don't pay for is water.

After I get off work, I go pick up Kevin and start dinner. I help him with his homework, we eat, then he takes his bath and gets ready for bed. I try to read to Kevin each night, but most nights, I forget or fall asleep until Malik gets in. Malik gets in around eight, he really works hard, but until he goes back to school he's going to be stuck doing all the hard work while the lawyers make all the money. My baby walked in and I jumped off the sofa and gave him a hug. "You hungry, baby?"

"No, I ate some Chinese at the office." I hated when I prepared meals and Malik didn't bother to eat what I cooked.

"I'm going to get in the shower and go to bed," Malik said as he yawned.

"You want me to get in with you?" I asked.

"No, I'm going to get in and get out."

Sex between Malik and me is still good. But when we first met, we used to have it at least five times a day, no exaggeration. But now Malik is really consumed with work all the time and if it's not work it is some type of stupid sports game. Baseball, football, basketball, you name it. I met Malik in the bedroom when he got out of the shower. He dried off with a towel, grabbed some boxers out of the drawer and got in the bed and lay down. I tapped him on his back and he said, "What?"

"Come on, baby," I said as I began to rub his back.

"I'm 'sleep."

"Wake up."

"For what?"

"Because."

"Kim, baby, I'm 'sleep; in the morning, okay?"

I turned back over. Who feels like getting up in the morning before work to have sex? *Never mind*, I thought.

Then Malik grabbed me and said, "You want it right now, you can't wait until the morning."

"I can wait. If that's what you want," I said.

"I won't make you wait," Malik said as he began to caress my body.

At first I was not really into it. But the more Malik touched me, the more excited I became.

No matter how many times me and Malik have sex, it's like a new experience. Maybe it's because he is only the second man I have been with in my life. He flipped me on my back, pulled out all his nine and a half, and slid it in.

"Malik it's not wet yet. Get it wet."

Malik kissed me till I became wet everywhere with his saliva. Then he put me to sleep.

"Good night, baby. Love you."

"Good night."

"Baby, I said I love you."

"I love you too, Kim."

Chapter Five

Shonda

I came home and heard the lady Pamela on my answering machine.

"Hi, Shonda, this is Pamela from Monroe Staffing. We had a position open up at the law firm Demarco, Rhome, and Cooper. If you're interested, they want you to start tomorrow. The pay is thirteen an hour. Please call me back if you get this message before five."

I wanted to scream once I heard the message, but I didn't have time. I looked over at the clock and it was 4:50 P.M. I had ten minutes to reach her. The phone rang like twenty times before she finally answered. She sound pleased to speak with me and gave the address and dress code of the office. She said that the law firm's dress code was very strict and very businesslike. I thanked her and said goodbye. I began to search through the small amount of clothes I had. I couldn't find anything that looked halfway businesslike. At my job in Atlanta I wore a uniform; everything in my closet was too revealing or too tight. I wanted to make a good impression. I had to find something to wear. Tae didn't have any dress business clothes that I could fit into. So I called my last resort—my grandmother—and asked her could she loan me some money to get something to wear to work.

"Shonda, you have to come and get the money. I'm in for the evening, I took off my clothes."

I went and got the money from my grandmother, then I walked to the avenue and went to a cheap discount store. Usually I would not step foot in one of these stores, but I needed to make my money stretch. Since I was starting in the middle of the week, I needed three outfits. Unbelievably, I was able to purchase a black shirt, black plaid and gray pants, a white shirt, brown slacks, and navy blue printed pants. I had a suit jacket that I could match up with the pants. I had a few dollars left. I knew I would need that for lunch and my first day at work.

Pamela told me I would meet someone by the name of Toni and that she would be able to help me. I walked in the busy office and asked for Toni.

"You must be our receptionist," a lady with heavy eyeliner said.

"Yes, I am. Are you Toni?"

"No, I'm Monique, but I'll get her for you and her name is Tonia." She walked down the hall and brought back a heavyset woman with a nappy brown Jherri curl and bright red lipstick.

"Hi, I'm Tonia, the office manager. Are you from the temp agency?"

"Yes."

"Well, let me show you around." She paraded me around and introduced me to most of the office. I followed her but I couldn't help wonder why she still had a Jherri curl in this day in time. We walked down the hall and we stopped at three offices in the back of the hall. She said, "First, let me tell you we handle personal injury cases only; you may receive some calls about criminal cases. You can let them know we don't take those cases. This is Mr. Demarco's office, he is the main partner. He doesn't like to be bothered so transfer all his calls into voice mail. This is Mr. Rhome's office. He's never here so don't worry about him. Now Mr. Cooper, he's the one you'll see the most. He may ask you to get him some coffee but he rarely comes out of his office and he takes most all his calls. He's a sweetheart, he treats everybody to lunch once a week.

"That's the coffee room. We have a refrigerator and microwave. I ordered out as you can see, but I'm starting my diet again tomorrow." She laughed as she pointed to her gut. We walked out of the coffee room and down the hall. Then she continued and said that, "These are our paralegals, Malik and Danny. They get a lot of calls and they do most of the daily rundowns with the clients."

We came full circle and got to the last room, which was the file and copier room. There were so many boxes and files. "And you have already met Monique and that's Desiree," she said. "If you have to go to the bathroom, press the standby message on the phone. Also, you can take your lunch between twelve and one P.M." Then she showed me how to work the phone and a list of extensions and she walked away. "If you need me, I'm at extension 410." As soon as she walked away from the desk and I placed my coat on the hanger, the phone began to ring. The light on the phone on nine lines started blinking all at once. "Hello, Demarco, Rhome, Cooper."

"Hi, may I have extension 121." I transferred the call. The next line, a man with a deep Russian accent, said "Is Mr. Rhome in?"

"Um, let me see," I said as I transferred him to the extension. He called back yelling at me, two seconds later.

"I asked for Mister Rhome, is he in or not? I don't want his damn voice mail."

"One moment please," I said as nice as I could, then someone walked up to the desk and said they had an appointment with Mr. Cooper. I buzzed Mr. Cooper's office. He answered and told me to send him in.

Five o'clock came and I was ready to go. The day had been so stressful, I don't know if I'm going back tomorrow. Bree needed some summer clothes. So I guess I didn't have any choice but to return.

Bree and me needed everything. There was nothing in the refrigerator. I had to get something to wear to work. I felt like a smoker. I thought about who I could call to get some money. I had only been in the city for a couple of weeks and already my resources were dwindling. I had too much dignity to call my grandmother again, Brian just gave me money, and my dad, well, he already has done enough for me. Then I went to my jewelry box. Mike had bought me a diamond tennis bracelet. It wasn't the clearest bracelet or biggest, but I was sure I could get something for it. I told Bree to throw something on herself so we could walk to the store.

"What store we going to, Mom?"

"Just put some clothes on, it don't matter." Bree came back into the living room with green pants on and a hot pink too little T-shirt.

"Bree, that does not match."

"You said put anything on."

"All right, smart girl, just come on." I located my keys, turned out the light, and we walked to 52nd street.

Before I entered the pawnshop, I turned around to see if I saw anyone I knew was seeing me going into the pawnshop. I thought about it; how would they know I'm not buying something? They didn't know what I was doing, who cares what they think? Inside there was an old dirty man buying lottery tickets. I walked up to the counter. The man spoke to me from behind the thick glass wall and asked, "What can I do for you today?"

"I want to sell this," I said as I took out the bracelet and slid it under the opening of the glass wall. I turned to see if anybody was seeing what I was doing.

"How much do you want?"

"One hundred."

"I'll give you seventy-five."

"Okay," I said as I filled out the form.

"I need to see your license, too." I pulled out my license and completed the form, then I gave it to him. He went into his register and pulled out three twenties, a ten, and five ones. He counted them, then gave me the money and said have a good day.

We walked out of the store and I asked Bree if she was hungry. She said that she was.

"Can I have some fries and a burger, Mom?"

"Sure." I got Bree a Happy Meal from the McDonald's down the street. Then I stopped at the market and bought some groceries. I bought two shirts to wear to work the rest of the week and went into the house and got ready for the next day.

Kim

Malik went to visit his brother today. His brother was locked up in Fort Dix, New Jersey, in federal prison. He was doing ten years for robbery and a gun charge. But since he's been in jail he has accumulated more time. Malik wanted me to go with him, but I didn't want to go. I loved him but I hated visiting his brother. Every time we went, we had to give up our whole day, get searched and wait, then sit, and then they let us in. Malik thought it was his fault for his brother being in jail. He always sent him money. He believed whatever his brother said, but I thought Malik's brother was full of shit. He was always talking about the man and getting put in the hole. Malik felt like it was his obligation to take care of him since it was only him and his brother, mother and sister. Their dad died and Malik took over as the man of the family. He felt like it was his fault for his brother choosing the wrong path, like he didn't do enough for him. Malik's brother was a bum, but he couldn't see that.

Chapter Six

Shonda

My job was getting better. I finally learned to use the phone; now if I could only master E-mail. I always used a computer at all my jobs, but never had to send memos through E-mail. They had me typing, faxing, sorting mail, distributing mail, collecting time sheets, ordering supplies and floral arrangements. I thought I would just answer the telephone. But it was still very stressful. Mr. Demarco came out of his office and said, did a fax come in for him. He was a tall older white man with silver-gray and traces of black in his hair. He had on a white-collar button-down shirt and suspenders with high-water gray pants.

"No, I don't believe it did."

"Are you sure?"

"Yes, I'm sure," I said as I answered the telephone. A few seconds after, he came back down the hall and said, "I need you to make a copy of this, fax it, then scan it into the computer and E-mail it to me." I knew how to E-mail and copy, but I had no idea how to scan.

I sat there and continued to answer the phone, then he came back out of his office and yelled at me, "Did you fax what I asked you to yet?"

"No, I didn't have a chance to."

"Well, can you do it now?" First of all, who did he think he was talking to? Did he know I would walk right up out this mother-fucker? He better recognize. Instead of cussing his ass out, I went and smoked a cigarette. I hadn't had a cigarette in months, but right now I needed one. I went to the stand in front of the building and bought a pack of Salem Lights. This was a habit I didn't miss—cigarettes cost $4.15 now; that's lunch money. I lit the cigarette and inhaled. It slowly calmed me down. Who knew lawyers could be so rude.

"What you doing out here?" the girl Monique from the office asked.

"Getting away from that chaos in the office."

"The phones getting on your nerves."

"Pretty much. I thought my job would be simple just answering the telephone and taking messages. But I'm E-mailing, faxing, copying. I don't have time for this."

"You're like our third receptionist in four months. If you need help just let me know."

"I will."

The girl Monique took her smoke and then went back into the building.

Another guy, Malik from the office, came down and said, "You're not quitting already are you?"

I laughed at him and said, "No but I could see why y'all can't keep a receptionist."

"Well, please don't quit, we need somebody to answer the tele-phones," he said as he put his hands together like he was pleading with me.

"I'll try not to," I said as I smashed the cigarette into the recepta-cle and went back upstairs. I answered some more calls and the girl Monique showed me how to scan the documents into the com-puter. It was easy. I also had a memo to type and about ten faxes to send all while I answered the phone.

The girl Monique came back to the desk. "You still stressing."

"No, I'm okay."

"You want to go lunch with all us?"

"No, I brought my lunch, but thank you."

"Well, let me know if you change your mind, we leave at twelve. The company is treating. My extension is 412."

"Okay, I'll let you know."

The damn phones were getting on my nerves. I changed my mind. I would eat lunch with Monique. I called her extension and told her I was coming. She came to my desk and I put the phone on standby and grabbed my bag. We caught the elevator to the lobby and met up with three other people, the two paralegals, Danny and Malik, and the other file clerk Desiree. Monique reintroduced me to everyone. Everybody said a friendly hi and we walked out the building.

For lunch we walked over to Liberty Place, one block away from the office. It was a mini mall with a large food court. The food court had several food vendors. I secured a place for us to all sit. Saving six seats was not an easy task. There were mobs of people trying to eat lunch. I had Chick-Fil-A and everybody had an assortment of Chinese, salads, and Italian. You could tell that everybody was cool with each other, they played and joked so much.

I couldn't wait to get my first paycheck, I had so many things to do with it. I had written a list. I needed to get my hair done, buy Bree some sandals, and give my dad some money. I was going to try to buy some more work clothes, a transpass, food, and put furniture on layaway.

Payday came and I was happy. Money, I forgot what it was like to have some. I couldn't wait until the clock read five. I was going to take my daughter out. I managed to pay my dad, get Bree sandals, buy a few shirts and a little food. I didn't have a chance to put any furniture on layaway.

Monday came. I got paid on Friday, so please tell me why I am broke. I didn't even have enough money for lunch, so I brown-bagged it. Between calls I tried to write down what I had spent over the weekend. I was about ninety dollars off. I was calculating what was missing. I had forgotten that I paid my grandmother back. So now I knew why I was broke. Well, I just had to wait two more weeks to get paid again. Oh, well, maybe I'd lose some weight by not eating.

After work I was tired. I picked Bree up from camp. She had a cut on her face.

"Bree, what happened to your face?"

"That boy Najee hit me and you told me if anybody hit me to hit them back."

I did tell Bree that. I didn't play anybody messing with my child. I had to go to the camp director and get ghetto with her. I asked her why did my daughter have a scratch on her face. She said that Bree and the boy were fighting. "Was anyone watching them? How can a little girl fight a boy?" I asked.

"Your daughter has been picking with him."

"My daughter does not pick on anyone," I said, defensively.

"Your daughter told him that he needed a haircut and some new sneakers."

Bree and I walked home, and I asked her, "Brianna, why are you picking on somebody? You do not make fun of people, that's not nice. Everybody can't afford to get new sneakers and their hair done. You're lucky. I don't want you talking about anyone, you hear me?"

"Yes. Mom, he said I was ugly and tall so I told him to get out of my face. Then he called me a bitch, so I slapped him and he hit me and I hit him back and the counselor pulled us apart and I got in trouble. I don't like that camp anyway."

"Well, I don't have anywhere else for you to go."

"My dad said he would watch me. Can we call him?"

"Bree, if you don't want to go to camp, fine. We'll call him when we get in the house."

As soon as we got in the house, I called my dad, my funds was low.

"Dad, can I borrow some money, I need a transpass."

"Aren't you working? Didn't you just get paid?"

"Yes."

"They didn't pay you yet."

"Daddy, come on now. How am I going to keep my job if I can't get there?"

"I'll come and bring it to you but when I'm going to get some more rent money?"

"When I get on my feet." I am tired of asking people for money. *I really need to change my life, get myself together,* I thought.

Tae called me and asked, "Are you going to Asha's bridal shower with me?"

"I really don't want to go. That's your friend."

"Come on, go with me."

"I don't even know what to get her."

"You can get her anything."

"Like what?"

"A gift certificate or something. I don't know."

"I don't want to go to her, 'I-got-a-man party.' Plus, I don't have any money to buy her a gift."

"That's not what an engagement party is."

"Yes it is; all it's for is to show off your ice. Hold up, wasn't sister girl just checking out women, doing her both ways thing when she was dancing? Now she's getting married. Please."

"That was a rumor, she did not go both ways."

"Well, count me out." Asha was always a little whore. I didn't know anyone that was called a slut in the eighth grade but Asha.

"Come on, just go, I don't want to go by myself."

I told Chantae I would go. That's when she informed me the bridal shower was tomorrow.

Asha's place was in Center City. It was a condo by the Delaware River. If I would say her place was not nice I would be lying. Her condo was sharp, she had red leather furniture with pure white carpet. She made us take off our shoes at the front door. I thought that was cheesy. She was serving champagne and sushi. Tae and me grabbed glasses and tried to admire her place without looking too impressed. But in reality, I was in awe. Her shit was off the hook. The condo looked like a baby MTV *Cribs* or something.

As she walked over to us, she said, "So glad you could make it, ladies." She then gave us a fake hug, and introduced us to her friends. One woman was Asian and three of them were white; all the others looked like they were mixed, with something. They told stupid jokes and talked about all of their fiancés and husbands. *So what*, I thought. Tae tried to join in their shallow conversation, but as much as she tried, she didn't fit in. I went to the bathroom. On my way out of the bathroom, I caught a glimpse of their bedroom. Her bed was the size of two king beds and I saw why. I also saw that Asha had a closet full of shoes and Louis Vuitton bags. Her closet looked like a small boutique. I peeked in some more, but I didn't want to get caught snooping. I walked back in the living room and saw a picture of Asha and her fiancé. He was huge, like four hundred pounds. Asha opened her boxes. Everything was a piece of lingerie. Frederick's, Victoria's Secret, even more champagne glasses.

"Don't ruin your shape and get pregnant on your honeymoon," one of her friends yelled.

"Floyd is taking me all around the world before we have any children."

One of her girlfriends stood up and said, "Are you ready for your surprise?"

Asha said, "Yes."

"Well, get ready, girl," the girl said as she opened the door. And this tall dark guy in some MC Hammer pants walked into the room and looked around. The first thing to come to my mind was *eww* and after that it was *yuck, disgusting, and nasty.* The nasty guy came over to me and started gyrating. Everybody else was getting excited about him. Then his friend, another big muscle guy with too much stinky sweat and baby oil, and some stank musk on, came in and did backflips, somersaults, and splits. The women gave the men money and slapped them on their butts. When the guy came over to me, I just turned my nose up and then he tried to sit on my lap and I pushed him off. No, thank you. He almost fell. I told him I was sorry, but I wasn't. I couldn't wait for the party to be over because it was sickening.

Girls like me work hard every day to be committed to one man, and what do I have to show for it? Nothing. But somehow Asha had clawed her gold digger hands into the back of her soon-to-be husband and is rich. Somehow I didn't think that was fair.

We caught a cab home, which was also getting tired and really expensive. We began to talk about Asha.

"Did you know her fiancé is, like, four hundred pounds?"

"You're lying."

"No, I'm not, I seen a picture of him, he is huge. Their bed is, like, *big*," I said, as I extended my arms out as wide as I could.

Tae could not stop laughing. Then her phone rang. All I could hear her ask is, "She okay?"

"Who," I asked her.

She motioned me to be quiet and put her face closer to the phone. "That was my mom. She said Brittany's mom Michelle tried to kill herself."

"What?"

"Yeah, my mom said she left the gas on, and her kids found her on the floor when they came in from playing outside. Brittany and all her brothers and sisters got taken away by D.H.S."

"That's a shame."

"No, it's not. She didn't take real good care of them. She had too many kids. But damn, she tried to kill herself? Remember when you tried to kill yourself?"

"I did not try to kill myself. I was thirteen, and I ran away."

"You left a note that said 'I don't want to be here anymore.' "

"I did not say I didn't want to be here. Like be here in this world anymore. I wrote, I didn't want to live with my grandmother or dad anymore. I wanted to find my mother, so I ran away to the bus depot. I was going to catch the bus to Cincinnati, that's where my mother's sister lived. But before I could get on the bus, my dad found me."

"Whatever. Well, maybe you didn't want to kill yourself, but that dumb bitch did. She is funny."

"Tae, you know that's not funny."

"It is to me. That dumb bitch should have killed herself. People that keep having kids and don't take care of them properly need to die or go to jail."

Kim

The excitement was starting to overwhelm me about the baby. I couldn't wait to go shopping. I was only four months, but I couldn't help spending my lunch walking around the baby boutiques and stores. I saw everything I ever wanted, and the pink was to die for, and I saw so many beautiful shades of purple. I saw cribs that turned into toddler beds and then daybeds then into full-size beds. They were a little pricey, but nothing was going to be too good for my little princess. I didn't have any money when I had Kevin, so this time I am going all out. I didn't have that option the first time. I took whatever was given to me with Kevin. Now I wanted everything matching, my crib to match the stroller that matches the car seat that matches the diaper bag that matches the walker and playpen.

* * *

I called my mother and told her about my mini-shopping spree. "Mom, I saw all this baby stuff today. I couldn't help it, I bought a few things."

"You did what?" my mother asked.

"I bought a stroller and a few outfits."

"You don't even know what you're having, and it's bad luck to buy baby things too soon. Don't you know that?"

"Mom, that's just an old wives' tale."

"Plus, you are going to have a baby shower; don't take all the fun out of having the baby."

"Well, I can't take this back. I'll just write in the invitation what I already have."

"You can't do that. That is so tacky."

"Okay, I won't do that. I got to go back to work. Bye, Mom."

"Wait, Kim, have you talked to Malik about y'all getting married?"

"Not yet, why, Mom?"

"Well, I just think you should get married before the baby gets here."

"Mom, we will get married when we are ready. I'll talk to you later." I didn't care what my mother said. I was going to start buying my baby things, and I would marry Malik when I was ready.

I returned to the office to find Lisa arguing on the phone with her boyfriend.

"So, is it off or on." I laughed as I walked past her desk.

"It's most definitely off. Don't you know he's going to his mother's wedding in Hawaii without me?"

"Really, why?"

"Because his mom didn't invite me, because I called her a slob. So I said, if she don't like me and I'm going to be your wife one day then you shouldn't go."

"So you want him to miss his mother's wedding for you."

"Yeah, what's wrong with that?" Lisa said as she looked at me like I was on her boyfriend and his mom's side.

"I guess nothing."

"Stop it, you know it is something wrong with that, Kim. Lisa is crazy and lives in la la land if she thinks that her boyfriend should choose her over his mother," Nicole said.

"I'm not crazy. I'm serious. I mean, it doesn't make sense. She's going to die and I'm going to be here and I'll remember this."

I couldn't stop laughing at Lisa, because in her mind she thought she was right with her self-centered ways.

We made up some bad debt, that's when we got our customers to pay what they owed. I made them call everyone on the bad debt list. I even threatened if they didn't call and ask people to make payments that I was going to have them make house calls.

Nicole and Lisa got busy and so did I. We brought our bad debt for the day from $90,000 to $54,000. Not bad, we had to get our money before the holidays approached. And every ten thousand I recoup, I get a bonus. My baby is going to have the best, simply the best.

Kevin and I ate dinner. All he wanted to talk about was the baby.

"Mom, can we have a boy and a girl?"

"No, it's only going to be one baby."

"Well, I want a boy so I can teach him how to fight."

"You can't teach the baby how to fight."

"Well, when will it be here?"

"In about five months." I know it was a mistake telling Kevin. He was going to ask me every day when the baby was going to be here.

"Now get ready for bed. You have to take a shower and we have to read."

Kevin took his shower as I did the dishes. He came into the living room with about eight books.

"We're not reading all these books, Kevin, pick one, then go to bed."

I read Kevin his book—*A Lunch Box for Me*. He got in the bed, I kissed him good night, then he asked me could I tell the baby good night. I told him I would and turned off the light.

"Baby, I saw all this beautiful stuff for our baby. I even bought some things for her," I told Malik as he walked in the door.

"You mean for him."

"No, baby, it is a girl, I can feel it."

"I don't care what we have as long as it's healthy."

"Malik, my mom said that we should get married before the baby gets here."

"Kim, I told you when I gave you that ring that we were going to take our time and I didn't want to get married right away. We have to get some money up to buy everything for the baby. So don't tell me what your mother said, because I don't really care."

We need to write a list of everything. Pampers, milk, everything. Because I don't want to run to the store every other day for Pampers.

"Okay, but my mom said don't start buying the baby anything until after the shower."

"Well, just get the stuff we definitely need. I want to call Nadia to see too what we need." Malik's sister Nadia was an expert with kids because she had three of her own—all girls. "My mom really wants a grandson."

"When did you tell her?" I asked.

"The other day when I went to see Jay."

"What did she say?"

"That she wanted a grandson."

"Oh, well, y'all have to be disappointed. I'm going to get my first ultrasound next week."

Kevin came in tothe bedroom and said, "Mom, I hear stuff in my room."

"Boy, it's nine o'clock. Get your butt in the bed."

"But I do hear stuff."

"You heard what I said."

"Kim, leave him alone," Malik said as he got up out of the bed and took Kevin's hand and walked Kevin back to his room. Malik put Kevin to sleep and said I wasn't going to talk to his son or daughter like that.

"If he or she don't carry his butt to bed, I will."

We spent the rest of the night relaxing. Malik took off his work clothes and I laid on top of him and we watched *The Parkers* and *Girlfriends*. Malik wanted to watch *WWE RAW* but I could not watch that stuff. Wrestling is so fake.

"Kim, it's an important case coming up. I know you heard about the little boy whose arm got caught in the school bus door. Well we're handling that case. So I'm going to be working a lot of hours. Just for a couple of weeks until we get all the research done that's needed."

"Baby, that's fine, but I don't want you stressing yourself out. When you become a lawyer you can pay somebody to do all this work for you."

"I know. I know."

"Well, you should sign up for fall classes."

"I will when I'm ready," Malik said as he turned off the light. Malik is too smart to just sit and do research. I want him to be the man, not the man behind the man. I met the partners at his job last Christmas at their holiday party. I didn't like the way they acted. They put on airs and spoke down to me. Malik said it was all in my mind and I felt intimidated. I just want him to go to an African-American firm where he might have more opportunity.

Chapter Seven

Shonda

Istill didn't figure out how to do a mass E-mail. That guy, Malik, caught on instantly and began secretly showing me the next day. Malik sent this cute E-mail that said meet us for lunch, at 12:00 P.M. I E-mailed him back and said I will. I enjoyed eating lunch with everybody, they were so crazy, they made work fun and go by fast. They would walk past my desk and say little jokes. Monique had all the 411, D.L. (Down Low), Hot and Juicy. To sum it all up, the gossip. You know it's one person in the office that knows everything about everybody. Before the day was over I knew who was married, on the verge of divorce, broke, bow-legged, bulimic and ready to run to the bathroom to throw up after lunch. She wore way too much makeup, had a loud mouth, big chest, and skinny chicken legs, and a raspy voice. She was off the hook. Danny was this skinny white boy. He was cool as shit. He had this banging bob layered haircut. It was sickening, his hair looked better than mine. He told the weirdest white jokes. I assumed he was gay because he always referred to his significant other as his partner. Most days I had no idea what he was talking about, but I laughed. The girl named Desiree was a filing clerk, she didn't have a body, she was skinny with no breasts or butt, poor child. I was not feeling her, because she wasn't that nice to me. Actually, she gave subtle hints that she didn't like me. Like today she let the door slam in my face and the other day I went to get on the elevator and I swear girlfriend pushed the button for the door to close. I think she likes Malik and doesn't like all the attention he has been paying me. Malik gave me compliments every day in front of everybody. She probably was mad because she thought she was cute and she wasn't. If it wasn't my hair, he liked my sandals or the designs on my toes. I like everything on him, especially the way he dresses. I love Malik's shoes. They stay polished, and his pants were crisp and his shirts hung perfectly on him.

"You look nice," Malik said as he walked past my desk.

"Thank you," I said.

"So, you okay today?"

"Yeah, I'm fine."

"If you need my help, just let me know, okay?"

"I will," I said as he walked away. He turned back and gave me another smile. Monique had already told me that Malik was engaged and had a baby on the way, so I was not interested in him, but he was nice-looking and built like shit. He must work out or something. I would definitely get with him if he wasn't taken. Then she confirmed that Desiree did like Malik and had been trying to get with him for months. She said he doesn't pay her any mind, even when she tries to throw it at him on the regular.

I walked into the coffee room to get some tea. Everyone was talking about what they were going to order in for lunch since it was raining and nobody felt like going out.

"Shonda, what you getting?"

"Probably a salad. Bring the menu to my desk."

I told Monique to order me a turkey chef salad with no olives.

77

Our food arrived an hour later. The rest of the day the phones were slow and I didn't have any work to do. I searched the Internet and checked my E-mail. Malik had sent me another E-mail. He said he was just saying "Hi" and asked was I okay. I sent an E-mail back to him that said, "I'm fine." His next E-mail said, "I know that." I E-mailed back and told him that was an old line; he E-mailed back LOL talk to you later.

My dad's friend Mr. Rick had a car for sale. A 1991 Beretta. He was selling it for four hundred and fifty dollars. The only problem my dad said was that it had a little dent in the front, because Mr. Rick's wife was in a car accident. I told my dad I wanted the car but I didn't have any money. My dad agreed to buy the car for me. But I had to pay him back. He told me he would try to get it and drop it off later in the week. I thanked my dad and told him I would pay him as soon as I got some money. My dad is a good dad. He always looked out. He had to since it was just him and me. My mother was a free spirit, she was someone who could not stay in one place for a long period of time. I wondered why she left a lot when I was younger. I daydreamed in school about her. I imagined her picking me up from school, taking me to her house and baking me chocolate chip cookies. I wondered if she was dead or did she have another family. Sometimes I even felt like going on a talk show with my story and have them find my mom, but then I think it's been about twenty years and she didn't find me or my dad and we haven't moved. So fuck her, she does not care about me. Sometimes I think, what could make a woman or man just walk away from their responsibilities without a care? I would never do that to Bree.

Kim

My hopes and dreams have come true. I called Malik as soon as I left my ultrasound appointment. I had just got back in the car and was coming out of the parking lot, on my cell phone. I couldn't wait to tell him. I was so excited I almost backed up into a parked car. I asked the receptionist for Malik Moore.

"One moment, please," she said.

A few seconds later Malik answered.

"Malik Moore."

"Hey, baby. Guess what?"

"What?"

"We're having a girl."

"Are you serious?"

"Yes. Are you mad?"

"No, I'm still happy. I love you and my new daughter."

"I love you, too."

"Well, I got to get back to work."

"I'm cooking your favorite. Lasagna."

"I'll get there as soon as I can, okay?"

"Have good day. Bye, baby."

This pregnancy was going well. I was gaining weight already and I didn't care. As long as I didn't have a difficult time like I had with Kevin. I had to just start eating my vegetables, drinking milk and water, and leave the coffee alone. I had about six cups of coffee a day. It got me through the day. Lisa and Nicole got on me and tried to switch my coffee with decaf. I told them if they touched my coffee again I would fire them both. They thought I was joking but I was dead serious. The rest of the day I spent returning calls.

I was on a roll when my mother called and asked me, "Are you going to visit Daddy with me?"

"No."

"Why not?"

"Because I don't feel like it. The ride is too long. Tell Dad I said I hope he gets better."

"He will be disappointed that none of you think enough to come to see him."

"Mom, I'm tired and I don't feel like taking a five-hour ride to visit him for a couple of hours."

"Fine, then, I'll call you when I get back."

I did feel sorry for my mom. She had to take that long trip to upstate New York by herself, but she was the only one who still believed that my father could change. I had lost hope. I love my dad but I can't deal with him. The last time I visited him he stared into outer space the whole time.

Chapter Eight

Shonda

VIP is bullshit. Who invented that shit? None of these people in here are very important, at least I don't think so. Tae convinced me to spend twenty-five dollars to get in the VIP room at Cole's. This guy named Bilal she was talking to, was a promoter and telling her who he knew and who was going to be at the party. He told Tae that Freeway and Beanie Sigel were a definite and that a surprise guest may show up. He also said all these niggas from the NBA and rappers were going to be there. Once again Tae got me caught up in the hype. I was mad about my twenty-five dollars. My thing was, if that guy liked Tae why did we have to pay to get in? He said we didn't have to pay to get in, but he didn't have any control over VIP. The whole party was filled with little I-sell-drugs boys. Bilal walked around the club looking disappointed. He didn't even say a whole lot to Tae all night. It didn't matter cause Tae had met someone else anyway, this guy from Seattle, Washington.

At twelve nobody was there. Just a bunch of made-up bitches and all the I-sell-drugs boys. Then around twelve-thirty, the dance floor started getting packed and the party started to get good. I started dancing, drinking, and having a good time. I didn't know if I still had it. Okay, this guy was walking toward me. I smiled. He smiled back. I thought he was about to ask me to dance, but then he walked past me and asked the girl next to me to dance. If I said I didn't mind that everybody was dancing and I wasn't, I would be lying. Finally, a cute guy came over and asked me to dance. His clothes looked a little dated, but who cares, somebody had asked me to dance. So I still had it. We walked out on the dance floor and I lie to you not, this nigga started Harlem shaking it. He looked like he was having a seizure, people turned around to see what was going on. I even stopped dancing, looked at him and walked off the dance floor. I was so embarrassed I didn't feel like dancing anymore. I just walked to the bar and ordered a lime margarita. I waited for Tae to get back. While I waited, I ordered another margarita. It was one o'clock and I had to get up in just six hours for work. I hoped I would make it. I felt fine when I was sitting, but when I went to stand up, my legs were shaky and I almost fell. I was fucked up and I didn't even know it. I was so messed up.

I'm sorry, but I was a bad mommy today. After last night I couldn't get up for work. I called out. I didn't get up to take Bree to camp. It was cloudy and gloomy outside. I was comfortable under my covers. I got to sleep until about nine when Brianna came in the room bothering me.

"Mom, I'm hungry."

"Eat some cereal, Bree."

"There's no milk." I knew there was milk in the refrigerator. But since Brianna couldn't find it, I had to get up and get it for her. I went, got the milk, a spoon and bowl, and poured her cereal. I got back in the bed and tried to fall back to sleep. Brianna woke me up again. "Mom what do you want me to do now?"

"Whatever you want, you ate, now go play."

"Mom, didn't I have camp today?"

"Yeah, Bree, you had camp today, but I let you stay home today to get some rest."

"I'm not tired, Mom."

"Bree, I'm tired and I'm going to sleep. I don't want you to bother me unless it's an emergency."

"What kind of emergency?"

"A fire or something. Now go watch television or play with your Barbies." I snuggled back under my covers and went to sleep.

I looked at the clock. 11:45 A.M. I didn't feel like I had been 'sleep for almost three hours. I was shocked that Bree hadn't woke me up. I needed that sleep. If it wasn't so rainy outside I would take Bree to the movies or something. I took a shower, told Bree to clean up her room and fixed me and Bree a tuna fish sandwich for lunch. I wished I had my car.

Malik called me at home.

"Hey, I heard you were sick. I just wanted to check on you."

"Yeah, I'm a little sick," I said as I faked a cough.

"What's your sickness, a hangover?"

"No, I'm really sick."

"Well, I hope you feel better. I just wanted to check on you to make sure you were okay. I hope you feel better."

"Thank you. It's nice to know someone cares."

He laughed and said, "I'll see you tomorrow."

My dad got me the car. He said I didn't have to pay him back, just for me to make sure I got insurance on it and got it registered. I called around and the tags and registration are going to run me about three hundred dollars.

I called Tae to tell her the good news. I asked her if she wanted to go out, because I was about to drop Bree off with Brian. When I called her, she was on her way to Washington.

"Washington D.C.?" I asked.

"No, Seattle, Washington."

"Girl, what is out there?"

"That guy I met at Cole's, he plays for the Seattle Super Sonics and he asked me to come out there for the weekend."

"Really?"

"Yup, and he sent me the plane ticket, and you know I'm out. I'm about to be like Asha and have a baller."

"Well, be safe and call me as soon as you get there." Damn, I was jealous of the way that Tae could just get up and go. Sometimes I wondered how my life would be without Bree. What would I be doing? Would I ever have gone to college, where would I be living, and what would my life be like?

I was getting ready for the next day and braiding Bree's hair, when Tae called me.

"I was waiting for you to call. How is it? Where is he at? Does he have any friends?"

Tae kept trying to butt in. Then finally she said, "Shonda, he never showed up. I'm still at the airport."

"What?"

"Yeah, I'm here. I kept calling and he never came. I have been here for five hours. I left him like twenty messages."

"Oh, my God, girl, I don't believe he would do that shit."

"I know, it don't make any sense."

"Well, maybe something came up," I said, trying to comfort Tae.

"I don't care what happened, I just want to come home."

"Get on a plane."

"I don't have any money. He paid for my ticket out here. I only got a one-way ticket. He said he would pay for my ticket home. I spent all my money on clothes to come with."

I couldn't believe Tae was that stupid. I knew she knew better. I wasn't going to tell her how stupid she was until she got home.

Right now I had to get her home. Tae needed me to wire her two hundred dollars, and her flight didn't leave for another two hours. I wasn't supposed to drive my car, it was not registered. But I had to go get Tae. I hope I didn't get stopped by the cops, because they would give me thousands of dollars in tickets and take my car. I had to ride to the trashman's house and pick up the money for Tae. After I wired the money, I stayed on the phone with her.

I went to meet Tae at the airport. My car didn't have a radio so Bree and me made up our songs. We sang all the way to the airport. Since September 11th you couldn't park in front of the airport so I had to keep circling the airport until she finally walked out.

"Tae, how could you be so stupid? What were you thinking about?"

"Look, I'm tired, yell at me tomorrow." I don't know who Tae was talking to. She knew I was going to cuss her out, and I did the whole ride home.

"I did research about him. He really do play for Seattle and he wasn't gaming me up."

"I don't care, you was all the way on the other side of the country without any money. You know better, Tae."

Kim

"Renard Financial, this is Kim, how may I help you?"

"Yes, I want to know why y'all stole my car?"

"What is your name?"

"Bill Marston."

"One moment," I said as I researched his name in the computer. We had crazies call the office all the time. People with bad credit trying to get loans, people whose cars have been repoed, and even people that have financed furniture that want us to come and pick it up, after they chopped it up.

"Yes, Mr. Marston, I found your record. Yes, I do see that you have a past due balance of three thousand one hundred and fifty dollars. However, I don't show that we have your car."

"What do you mean you don't have my car there? Let me tell you something, I know you are one of these damn Republicans, but I have friends in high places. I'm calling my congressman in the morning. I know my damn rights."

"Really," I said with sarcasm. We were not allowed to hang up on our customers so I put Mr. Marston on speaker phone and let Nicole and Lisa listen in on the conversation. I had to push mute so that he couldn't hear our laughter.

"Are you there?" he asked.

"Yes, I'm here."

"Well, I know one thing, when I get there, you better have my car and if you don't, then I'm going to report you to the Federal Bureau of Investigation."

"Okay, well, I'll see you when you get here," I said as I laughed.

Mr. Marston showed up in the office with his wife an hour later.

"I'm Martha Marston. I'm here to pay our past due amount on our loan. What is our balance?"

"Three thousand one hundred and fifty dollars."

"Will cash be okay?"

"Yes, that will be fine."

"Don't mind my husband, he has Alzheimer's. He forgot we parked our car in the garage. We fell a few months behind because we're paying for our grandson to go to Seton Hall," she said as she passed me an envelope full of hundreds.

"Why are you giving her our money? She's the one who stole our car."

"Shut up, Bill, she did not steal our car. Our car is outside."

You can see why I hate my job at times. I have to deal with all the crazies.

* * *

Karen had tickets to a play at the Merriam Theatre. She couldn't go, so I told her I would buy them off her. Her cheap ass was going to lose her money if she didn't go. But now that I was buying them, she said she would only charge me forty-five. She paid fifty for them. I called Malik at the office and left a message telling him I had tickets for the play. While I waited for Malik to call back, Nicole begged me if I could take her with me. I told her no because I was taking Malik with me.

"You should take me with you. I need to go somewhere." She whined while I continued to take a few calls and Nicole was still talking my head off about why I should take her.

"You can go with me if I don't get in touch with Malik."

"That's a bet," Nicole said.

When Malik called back Nicole told me I had a call. I smiled at her and said, "Hey, baby, you got my message? I got tickets for the play at the Merriam Theatre."

"Babe, remember I told you it was Jarrod's birthday and that I was taking him out." The moment Malik mentioned Jarrod's birthday it came back to me that we talked about him going out on Friday earlier in the week.

"Yeah, I remember you saying that, but I forgot what day you said. Well, have a good time, and I'll see you at home, love you."

"Love you, too," Malik said and hung up.

Nicole was smiling, listening in on my conversation.

"You can go now, Nicole, he can't make it."

Chapter Nine

Shonda

I was bored in the house. Bree had gone with Brian for the night. I needed to get out of this damn house. It was Friday. I needed a drink and to sit back and relax. I called Tae and asked if she wanted to go out.

"Yo, Tae, you want to go out?"

"Where do you want to go?"

"I don't care. Bree is gone and I shouldn't be sitting in the house. Come on, let's go."

"Where are we going to go?"

"Bluzette. Look I got your drinks wherever we go."

"All right. What are you going to wear?"

"I just got some jeans on with my black shirt and black boots."

"You going to walk around here?" Tae asked.

I'm not driving again until I get my paperwork right. Yeah. I'll be around there in a hour."

I should be scared to walk in the neighborhood since I got robbed, but I wasn't. I had some Mace now. If someone thought about saying anything, they were going to get some spray right in their face. I reached Tae's house and we planned to get the party started early.

"Boy, get off the computer so I can call my cab," Tae yelled at Dontae.

"Wait, these jawns love me."

"They love you because they can't see you."

"Shonda, he be on the computer all day with girls he don't know what they look like, they probably fat."

"All my jawns looked like dimes."

"Look at this one," Dontae said as he showed us a picture of one of his chatting buddies. The girl in the picture was dark skinned, she was pretty with a long black weave, one hand was on her hip and a lollipop was in the other, and she was wearing a white bikini with her breasts hanging out the top.

"You know what, you're disgusting."

"Told y'all, these jawns want to send me plane tickets and everything, but I'm cool."

"Nobody's going to send you nothing. Mom, tell Dontae to get off the computer."

Ms. Juanita came downstairs. "Hey, Shonda, when did you get back?"

"I've been back a while now," I said as I gave Ms. Juanita a hug.

"Mom, tell him to get off now."

"God damn it, y'all are twenty-five and twenty-three and acting like you're one and two. Get off the damn computer, Dontae." Dontae reluctantly got off the computer and we called our cab. While we waited, we decided to get the party started early. Tae poured me Bacardi rum and coke and I took some sips.

The cab driver beeped his horn once and we got in.

"Third and Market," I told the driver as we pulled out of Tae's block. Our driver was an older black man with silver hair brushed to the side. He had this terrible band music on. Tae asked him could he change the station. The driver changed the station. He turned on a hip-hop station. The new Missy song "Work It" was on. That song got us right in the mood to dance and drink some more. My plan for the evening was to get fucked up. The DJ started talking over the song, saying, "Yeah, we're broadcasting live from Utopia. It's off the hook, everybody is down here. All the ballers and ballets. Celebrities are pouring in." The DJ was getting Tae and me hyped. Instead of just getting some drinks and something to eat and Bluzette, we decided to go to Utopia.

Okay, the bitch on the radio need her ass whooped real bad because we paid twenty dollars to get into Utopia and there was about thirty-five people in the club. It was not off the hook. There was nobody there. If I saw that DJ I would tell her about herself.

"You want to leave?" Tae asked.

"Yeah, this shit is corny." Even though we just paid twenty dollars, it was not worth wasting our time, cause we already wasted our money.

Mad as hell, we got back in another cab and drove to our original destination, Bluzette. Bluzette was a nice after work sophisticated crowd, no I-sell-drugs boys in sight. A guy came over to us and asked us what we were drinking. I hesitated because he was looking at Tae when he asked. After Tae ordered her cosmopolitan I then told him that I would have an apple martini. Tae's big breasts usually gets us free drinks. While Tae's friend made himself comfortable at our table, I went to the bathroom to check my makeup. There was someone already in there, so I had to wait.

"You can use this one if you like," I heard a voice say.

"Excuse me," I said in a disgusted voice. I know this guy did not just say that I could use the men's bathroom.

"No, thank you," I said, turning back around. I know as soon as I said yes he would have asked to come in with me. Then I would have to slap him or better yet use my Mace on him. When I came out of the bathroom, the guy who asked me did I want to use the men's bathroom was waiting for me.

"Listen, I wasn't trying to talk to you. I was trying to be nice."

"I didn't say you were trying to talk to me."

"Well, I just wanted you to know that I wasn't."

"Well, thanks for letting me know."

"Because if I was interested in you, I would ask your name. So what's your name?" He was short, and a little too skinny, but cute. I told him my name and he said his name was Jarrod. He followed me back to my table. The guy Tae was talking to had left. I sat down and Jarrod I just met said that he would be right back.

When Jarrod brought his friend back, to my surprise it was Malik from work. Malik looked at me then back and Jarrod and said, "Nope, man, this is my girl, she work at my job. She's off-limits." I laughed at Malik and they had a seat. They told us they were celebrating Jarrod's birthday. We all sat back and talked and ordered appetizers and drinks. When it was time to leave Malik asked, "Do y'all want anything else to drink?"

"No, we're good," Tae answered.

"How are you getting home?"

"Probably catch a cab," I said.

"You don't have to take a cab. Jarrod will drop you off."

"I will?" Jarrod asked.

"Yes, you will," Malik said as he turned back toward us. Malik sat at the table telling jokes and embarrassing stories about him and

Jarrod when they were in high school. Me and Tae could relate to
their tales, because we had just as many stories to tell.

Malik and Jarrod dropped us off at my house. "See you Monday,
Malik, thanks for taking us home."

"It's cool. Take it easy. Y'all be safe." Jarrod smiled as he rolled
up the window.

As soon as they pulled off, Chantae asked, "So what's up with
Malik, why didn't you tell me about him?"

"Don't he look good? He flirts with me all the time at work."

"He was all up on you tonight."

"Right, he always compliments me every day, but, girl, he's engaged."

"That's not married. I would holla at him."

"I heard his fiancé is pregnant too."

"Well, that's different."

"Yeah, but if he wasn't engaged he'd be mine."

Tae said, "I know that's right," as she turned out my light. She
slept in my bed and I slept in Bree's room.

Kim

Me and Nicole had a great time at the play. She wanted me to
take her to get a drink or something. I told her I was tired and
going in the house. What would I look like going into a bar with a
pregnant belly.

I called Malik to see where he was. He told me he was riding with
Jarrod and that he had to drop him off at his car. That was a couple
of hours ago. I hated when Malik went out with his friend. I called
him back on his cell phone. It's two o'clock in the morning and he's
still not home yet.

"Hello."

"Malik, where are you at?"

"Jarrod has to drop me off at my car. I'll be there in a little bit."

"It's two o'clock. You said that hours ago."

"Kim, I'll be there," he said as he hung up. Malik needs to stop hanging out with Jarrod and get his shit together and get home. Jarrod doesn't have a girlfriend or any kids. He works as a security guard and has no ambitions. Him and Jarrod have been friends since high school. But I think it's time for him and Jarrod to part ways. He is such a bad influence on Malik. I don't even like when he calls my house. I know he's out trying to get Malik hooked up with girls. Jarrod was mad at Malik when he moved out and moved in with me.

Malik came in maybe forty-five minutes later. "Malik, we barely have time to spend together during the week, so why don't you spend time with me on the weekend?"

"Kim, I only went out tonight. I had a few beers. I'm tired and I'll talk to you tomorrow."

Saturday morning I got up before Malik and Kevin. I made a big breakfast. Eggs, turkey sausage, and pancakes. Kevin came in the living room to watch cartoons. The aroma of breakfast must have gotten to him because Kevin ran into the kitchen with his Power Ranger pajamas on asking me what I had cooked. I told him and he rubbed his stomach and said, "Yummy." He went and woke up Malik and we all ate breakfast.

After breakfast I was sleepy. I cleared the table and decided the dishes could wait until later. Kevin went into the living room and finished watching his cartoons while Malik joined me in the bed. He gave me a kiss and started rubbing on my stomach. "I love you little baby girl," he said as he lifted my shirt and kissed my stomach. "You are going to be daddy's princess."

"How do you know she is not going to be mommy's princess?"

"Because I know. Our second baby can be yours."

"Our second baby?"

"Yes, our second baby. We are just getting started."

"That's what you think. I'm getting my tubes tied. Are you going to be able to go with me to my next ultrasound appointment?"

"Of course, baby, I'll be there with you, Mrs. Moore."

I loved when Malik called me Mrs. Moore. I couldn't wait to be his wife. The rest of the morning we lay in the bed, snuggled up watching a movie on cable.

Chapter Ten

Shonda

I probably said, "Thank you for calling Demarco, Rhome, and Cooper, how may I direct your call?" a million times a day. My mouth would get dry from talking so much. I wanted to get some tea and lemon for my throat. I walked into the kitchen and saw Monique. I said what's up to her and she responded with a loud, "What's up, girl?"

"Nothing much."

"You going with us to lunch?"

"No, I'll probably stay in today."

"Malik will be disappointed."

"Why you say that?"

"Um, let me stop, he's engaged and has a baby on the way. I only said that because he told me he saw you Friday. Where you see him at?"

"Bluzette."

"Who was you with?"

"My friend Tae."

"Oh, well. I'll see you later."

Bye, nosy girl, I thought. Tonia came past my desk telling me about her new diet plan. She was the office joke. She has been on

95

Jenny Craig, L.A. Weight Loss, and the Atkins Diet all while I have
been here. And I haven't been here that long.

Later I went into the coffee room again to get some tea and I saw
Malik. My heart fluttered like I was a little kid. He came behind me
and accidentally rubbed up next to me.

He said, "Excuse me."

I smiled. I knew he rubbed against me intentionally. He sent me
an E-mail saying how much fun he had the other night and we all
had to go out again. I sent him an E-mail back and said okay.

Fridays at work were usually relaxed, the lawyers were not here,
and Tonia took early days.

Malik had invited everybody out for a drink after work. At first I
wasn't sure if I wanted to go. Monique asked, "What are you doing
after work?"

"Nothing, my daughter's staying with her father, so I'll probably
stay in the house."

"Why don't you go out with us, then?"

"Where y'all going?" I asked.

She called Malik and put him on the speakerphone.

"The Black Rac. Why?" he asked.

"I'm trying to get Shonda to go," she said.

"We are you going to have a good time? Come on and go,
Shonda," Malik said.

I broke down and told them I would meet them.

"Cool, now it's me, you, Danny, and Malik. Desiree said she wasn't
sure if she was going," Monique said.

"If she goes I don't want to come," I whispered under my breath.

"I know that's right. I don't really want her to go, she is a pain in
the ass. All right, well, we all meet at nine. Malik, you going to come
and get me?" Monique asked. "My car is in the shop." Malik said.

"Your car can stay in the shop," Monique said.

"Drinks on you Malik, right?" I said.

"The first round anyway," Malik yelled through the speakerphone.

Kim

Malik was in a rush to get out of the house. I was going out with my mother and sister to dinner. My mother, Kevin, Karen, Ryan, and me went to dinner at the Olive Garden. Kianna couldn't make it because she was at a video shoot. My mother said she was going with a record producer named Greg in New York. My mom went on about how Kianna's modeling and acting career was about to take off. "Y'all know Kianna's friend writes music for Usher."

"Yeah right. You know you daughter believes anything anyone tells her," Karen said.

"I know everybody in New York thinks they are some kind of record producer. Kianna is impressionable," I said.

Whatever, I thought.

Once our food came, I stuffed myself with chicken parmigiana and a virgin piña colada. Kevin didn't eat much of his food and Karen just talked the whole evening about Lonnie and his demos.

The boys left the table and went to the bathroom. Karen then told us that her son's school was trying to put Ryan on Aderol. My mother had a fit. "You do not let them white teachers tell you what your child needs. If you have to, work with him at home. Don't put my grandson on meds."

"Karen, you shouldn't, Ryan isn't hyper. His teachers probably don't care about him," I said.

"Well, I just want what's best for him."

"I'll tutor him if need be," I said. "Plus, once he goes on the meds it's going to be hard to get him off. Ryan is not a bad kid, he is just a little hyper. I would just try to work with him and don't give him any candy. I would never put Kevin on medication."

"Ryan is not Kevin, Kim. I can't help Ryan by myself. I'm not perfect like you or your son."

"I never said I was perfect."

"Well, you think you are."

"No, I don't."

"Here come the boys. Calm down," my mother said.

The boys came back to the table and Kevin spilled his soda on me and we had to get napkins to clean up the mess. I continued to eat my food and flagged the waiter for the check. I paid my portion of the bill, left a tip and left. Everyone was getting on my nerves.

Chapter Eleven

Shonda

When I stepped out the door I was ecstatic to be child-free, it was the weekend, I could relax. I was on my way to meet up with everybody. I took a cab, I couldn't wait for the bus. Damn, it felt so good to be free.

When I got to the bar at 9:00 P.M. nobody was there yet, so I touched up my lip gloss, took a seat, and ordered a rum and coke. By 9:15 a few guys approached me. I wasn't really interested. I called Monique on her cell to see where she was. At 9:30 I sat my bag on the counter and was sipping on my second drink. By 9:45 I had given up on everybody. They made me come out for nothing. I got two numbers, paid for my drinks, and left a tip for the barmaid. I was out and disappointed—they could have at least called somebody. I left a message for Monique. "Monique this is Shonda, it's almost ten and I'm out."

I went to flag down a cab when I heard my name being yelled, "Shonda, Shonda!"

I turned around and saw Malik jogging toward me, still dressed in his work clothes.

"Hey, sorry I'm late. Where is everybody at?" Malik asked.

"I don't know but I'm ready to leave." I said, as I scratched my forehead.

"Don't leave, they'll be here, trust me—they don't miss free drinks. Let's go back up the street and wait for them. I owe you a drink anyway."

I said okay and started walking back to the bar. My phone rang and it was Desiree.

"Where you at?" I asked.

"Waiting for my baby-sitter to come; she'll be here though. Who's there?"

"Just me and Malik."

"Let me speak to Malik," she said.

I gave him the telephone. I heard him say "Okay."

"She said she'll be here no later than a half," he said as he gave me back my phone. We went back into the bar and got a table for four. If Danny or Desiree or Monique never showed up, that was okay, because Malik made me laugh and I enjoyed his company. Liquor makes the truth come out. Malik talked about his fiancée and his apprehension of being a father. I told him about my crazy ex, and my move back from Atlanta. We laughed for a good three hours. I was ready to go home.

"How you getting home?" Malik asked.

"In a cab."

"We can share one," he said and we went outside and flagged down a cab. Inside the cab Malik put his arm around my waist and squeezed me tightly. I turned to him and kissed him. I felt attracted to him since day one and now I finally got to kiss him. I asked him did he want to go to my house. He asked me if I was sure and I said yes. I gave the cab driver my address and minutes later we pulled up. Before we entered the apartment, I reminded Malik that I didn't have a lot of furniture and I had just moved in. I was ready to take care of myself and get what I needed.

I turned on my Musiq CD and sat on the sofa next to Malik. I placed his hands on my waist, turned his face toward mine, and kissed him. Then I lifted his shirt and kissed near his navel, and he let out a slight moan. Then I licked his face. I opened his shirt, and sucked his nipples. Malik was doing something to me. I didn't even care that he was engaged. He was mine tonight. We stood up and caressed each other until Malik came out of his shirt. He held me tightly, we swayed to the music as he undressed me. He unfastened my bra and gently slid my panties off. I took each leg out of my underwear, he tossed them. I unzipped his pants while he massaged my breasts. My nipples hardened from his touch. Malik pulled a condom out of his wallet. I lay back on the futon waiting for him to enter me. He approached me, I felt the tip of him ready to touch me, and Malik then jumped up and said, "I can't do this."

"You can't do what?"

"This," he said as he grabbed his shirt and put his pants back on.

I was confused and naked but I understood. He then buttoned his shirt back up and told me that he would see me later. He walked toward the door and I said, "Your loss."

"My loss, huh? I'll call you later," he said.

"Yup, have a good night," I said as I unlocked the door.

"I want to stay, believe me, but I got a fiancée."

"And—" I said with an attitude—he was starting to get on my nerves. I figured I had one last chance to make him change his mind. So I took his hand and placed his middle finger in my mouth and sucked his finger. And Malik instead of falling into my trap told me good night. He left and I felt played.

The next morning I heard my cell phone ring. I searched around until I found it. "Hello," I said as I came out of drunken sleep.

"It's eleven, why is your ass still 'sleep?"

"I went out last night. Um. I'm home, call me on the house phone."

Tae said okay and called me back and asked, "Who did you go out with?"

"That guy Malik?"

"Oh, for real. So what happened?"

"Absolutely nothing."

"What do you mean, nothing?"

"Something was about to happen but he gained a conscience midway."

"Stop. Oh, well, his loss."

"I know, that's what I told him. I'm not worried about him anyway. What's up?"

"I called to tell you that Dontae got this girl all the way from Wichita, Kansas, sitting in the living room. One of the those girls he was chatting with actually bought a plane ticket and came to Philly."

"Is she crazy?"

"No, she's actually nice and she's not ugly but he went to get a haircut and I'm stuck with her until he gets back."

"Take her to the mall or something. When does she leave?"

"Tomorrow."

"You'll find something to do with her. Have fun, I'm going back to sleep."

The next day Malik called me and said that he was sorry for sending mixed signals but he didn't want to take advantage of me. He asked could he take me out to make up for the night before. I told him that I was cool and I didn't have time for games.

"I know I left you in an awkward situation last night but please let me make it up to you. Let me take you to Jillian's."

"No, thank you. I really don't feel like it."

"Okay, well, I tried. I guess it is my loss after all. I'll see you," he said.

I hung up the phone and laughed at myself. I knew I wanted to go with Malik so bad. I have been thinking about him all day. I couldn't believe he had the audacity to leave me last night. Malik was a nice-looking guy but it was something more than looks that drew me to him. I liked his demeanor and personality and plus I never, ever in my life have been that snubbed. I was going to give Malik another chance, but he was going to play by my rules now. I called him back and said that he could come and get me at three. Without hesitation he agreed. I made Malik take me to the movies and then to dinner. When it was time to drop me off I asked him if he wanted to come in.

"Sure, I'll come in."

"Do you know what you're getting yourself into if you come in?" I asked.

"I think so."

"Well, come in and let's begin where we left off yesterday."

I waited for him to please me this time. Malik kissed all over me. I quivered as he licked all over my body. Malik ripped the condom package, put it on, and before I knew it, me and Malik were one. He was on top and I was on the bottom. His touch was smooth and gentle. He moved slowly inside. Then Malik sped up his motion. He picked me up and flipped me over. I bent over and rested on my elbows. He began stroking faster and faster. His hands clutched my waist. He pounded my body against his with all his might. He let out a few moans and was breathing heavy, then he let out a loud moan and collapsed, pulling me with him to the sofa. I was completely satisfied.

"Now what?" he asked as I walked to the bathroom.

"What do you mean?" I asked.

"I don't want everybody in our business at work."

"How will they know? I won't say anything. We'll just tell them that you met up with your friend Jarrod and I left, if anyone asks."

Kim

When I returned home from dinner, I noticed Malik was still not home. I looked down at my watch and it was 11:30 P.M. Once again he was probably somewhere having a drink with Jarrod the bum. This shit was going to have to stop when we had our baby. I am not playing him going out all times of the night. I want him in the house playing the fatherly role, not roaming the streets. I undressed, showered, and waited for Malik to come in. While I waited, I decided to put a load of clothes in the washer. I separated my dark from my white clothes. I checked my pockets, Kevin pockets and Malik's pockets. I usually find anything from money in Malik's pockets, to candy and crayons in Kevin's. I didn't want any of the above messing up my clothes. As I searched Malik's pockets, I found a plastic bag and assorted-color ribbed condoms. I waited until he got in the bed before I asked him about the condoms.

"I don't have any condoms. What are you talking about?" He acted like he didn't know what I was talking about, so I went into my dresser drawer and pulled them out and laid them across the bed.

"These are the condoms I'm talking about, Malik."

Then he said, "Oh, those. You know the city health workers give them out at lunch time, downtown. I didn't know what they were at first. You see, they are still in the bag. Come on, baby."

I knew that was bullshit. "So you shouldn't have taken them or said 'no, thank you.' "

"Kim, be for real. I said they gave them to everybody."

"Whatever. I'm tired, just turn out the light."

Chapter Twelve

Shonda

Baby, baby, baby you like the lighter cigarette, let me smoke. Sing Ashanti, I feel you. Malik makes me feel good all over. I hate to admit it but I'm really liking him. I was still thinking about the weekend when we were dancing. Our bodies so close, the heat, our cab ride and my apartment. Umm-hmm, I love me some him. Every time I think about him I feel this tingling sensation rush through my body. I try to shake it off but it's hard. Malik is just so refreshing. I was tired of messing with guys that didn't have my best interest in mind. Malik asked about my future, what I wanted to do with my life; he even explained the stock market and financing out to me. I never had a suit-and-tie type. I didn't even know what a 401K plan was. Brian was always acting like a tough guy. Malik was attractive because he had masculine confidence. His hands are so soft and he always smells so good. His abs were tight like he did hundreds of crunches each morning. It was hard to ignore him at work. I tried to act normal, but what is normal now?

Lunch went as normal, we all laughed. Danny asked about Friday. I stuck to the story that Malik met up with Jarrod, I had one drink and then I left. Nobody was none the wiser. Everything was really the same, well, until Desiree was smiling in Malik's face. Last week that wouldn't have bothered me but today—hands off. He's mine, at least while we were at work. We tried to keep our relationship a secret, but after a while it didn't matter if anyone knew that I was dating Malik. Instead of taking lunch as a group, me and Malik started going as a duo.

Tonia told me that the office frowned upon interoffice dating. She was just mad because her fat butt wasn't getting any. I know the only person that told her was Desiree, she was heated. She wanted Malik and could not have him. That probably tore her up inside.

I'm not sure how long me and Malik will last, but right now I'm living in the moment. Tae told me not to get caught up with Malik. I'm trying, but it is hard because me and Malik have spending so much time together. Right now I'm going to take it day by day.

Kim

Malik is changing. I've been finding condoms, he's been staying out late and just being mean to me. If I didn't know better, I'd swear Malik finds a reason to argue with me. Malik is here every night, but I don't think he wants to be here. It's like I don't have any control over him. Like last night was the ultimate—he went to sleep at the other end of the bed. He claimed his back was hurting but I think he just didn't want me to touch him.

I want to make it work with him, but honestly, right now I hate him. It's just like anything he does right now is irritating. For one, he comes home, turns on the ceiling fan and changes the channel on the television no matter what I'm watching. I hate him. He is ugly and I hate him. It's like I lost my power. I used to have control over our relationship. Now my threats don't work and Malik doesn't care if I'm unhappy. I wish I wasn't pregnant. I wish it was just Kevin and me. I didn't realize how good it was when it was just him and me. I wondered why I didn't see how wonderful and pretty I was. Why didn't I ever date anyone else? I mean, Malik's not the worst person in the world. I never, ever really caught him cheating, but I've always had my suspicions about him. He's always been so sneaky. The only time I somewhat caught him is when he was living with Jarrod. Something told me to ride past his apartment building. I called Malik and said, "Hey, baby, you just waking up?"

He yawned and said, "Yes."

I was like, "What are you doing?"

"Walking Jarrod's dog."

"Really?"

"Where you at?"

"Across the street from the house."

"That's funny, Malik, I'm in front of your building and I don't see you."

Malik said, "Huh?"

I repeated that I was in front of his door and for him to come out now. He hung up on me and didn't come out so I went up to the door and banged on it. His phone must have accidentally dialed mine back. Because I heard him running around. And I saw him peeking out the blinds. I bammed on the door and heard the banging. I know Malik was inside that apartment and someone was with him. But he managed to run out the back of the apartment and came running up the street with the dog. He must have come down the fire escape in the back. So I never actually caught him, but I still know what I heard. He said he was never in the apartment and he was walking the dog.

And if Malik and me don't work out, what kind of future do I have to look forward to? Who is going to want me with two kids and two baby fathers? I would feel better if me and Malik get married for a couple of years and then divorce, because at least I would be divorced and not just another single mom, but me and Malik are so up and down right now, I don't know.

Chapter Thirteen

Shonda

Today was a bad day. It was raining hard and my umbrella kept blowing up. I was happy I didn't have to take the bus because I finally registered my car. I walked seven long blocks to where I parked my car and saw a white ticket on the front. It was a ticket for twenty-five dollars. I had parked after five. Well, it was only 5:08 P.M. I wish I could catch the bitch that wrote the ticket. I took the ticket off and dug in my wet pocketbook to find my keys. My keys were all the way at the bottom, I had to damn near dump my bag to retrieve them. I got in my car and what do you know, the shit wouldn't start. I left my lights on all day. I was ready to cry. I was tired and had cramps and just wanted to go home and get in the bed. I thought about calling my dad but he might ask for his rent. I dialed Malik's phone but it rang once and then his voice mail came on. I almost cried. I started to search around the car for change. I found seventy-eight cents. I needed two dollars to get on the bus. I just wanted to pick up Bree and get in my bed.

I found some more change and got on the bus and I felt a headache coming on and my nose was running and I didn't have any tissue. I tried to sniff the nasal liquid back up. I fell asleep all the way to my stop. I walked, got Bree, and we walked home in the rain. I took off my soaking wet clothes and pulled the bed down. The phone rang. It was Malik.

"Hey, what's up?"

"Nothing."

"I called your cell phone back, you didn't answer it."

"Really. I didn't hear it ring. Call it again."

Malik then clicked to the other line and dialed my phone. I jumped off the sofa to see if I heard it. I didn't. A few seconds later, I heard a little girl's voice say, "Hello."

Malik said, "Excuse me, you found a cell phone today and I'll give you a reward if you return it."

The little girl started laughing and said, "When you lost the phone it was yours, but now that I found it, it's mine, so stop calling my damn cell phone," and hung up.

We called again and the little bitch said, "Listen, I told you not to call my damn cell phone no more you punk ass bitch."

Malik laughed and I was beginning to become upset, because the shit wasn't funny. Malik told me not to worry about it and that he would buy a new phone tomorrow. I told him that wasn't the point. That little girl was pissing me the fuck off. That little bitch played too much. I wish I could find her.

The next day, after work, Malik and me went to go get my car and to buy a new cell phone. I was thankful. He called AAA to get a jump. We sat in the car and waited for them to arrive.

"You don't have a radio."

"It didn't come with one."

"Well, get you a radio when we get the phone."

We rode to the Best Buy and Malik bought me a little hundred-dollar radio. I was just happy that I had a radio to listen to. Making up my own songs was getting old. We then went and had dinner and drinks at a little bar-restaurant on Main Street. I told Malik I was going to the bathroom. He said that he was going to join me. I thought Malik was playing at first when he said he was going to come in the bathroom with me. But then he came in and I smelled a light scent of alcohol on him, but what the fuck, I smelled like alcohol, too. We kissed and then I began to ride him as I looked in the mirror and saw our reflections. I licked my lips and told him to hit it harder, and deeper. "Bang that shit in there," I screamed. Malik began to bang his body harder into mine, swaying faster and faster until he came.

It was the best sex I've ever had, but how do we get out of the bathroom now without anybody seeing us? I tried to take some towels and rinse off. Malik peed in the toilet. I exited the bathroom, then he followed. Malik took me home and I wanted to beg him not to leave. I hated when Malik left. I wanted to say, *Malik please don't leave me. Please stay with me, I'm tired of you leaving me.* Instead of saying that I said, "Bye, baby," when he kissed me on my cheek.

Bree was spending so much time over Brian's house I was beginning to feel guilty. I couldn't help it, though, me and Malik were having so much fun together and I really didn't want Bree around another man, 'specially under me and Malik's circumstances.

I hadn't spent time with Bree, so I decided it was not going to be any Malik today—just me and my daughter. I took her to the hair salon with me. The girl pressed her hair and gave her twisties and a pony tail. Then we went shopping and got some clothes. I asked Bree if she wanted to go skating or to the movies. She chose the movies, so we went to the movies then got pizza afterward.

"Mom, am I'm going to live with my dad?" Bree asked.

"Why are you asking me that?"

"Because Daddy and Ms. Andrea asked if I wanted to live with them. I like going over Daddy's house but I don't want to live with them."

I told Bree she didn't have to live with Brian and that she was only staying over his house a lot because I was working so much.

Kim

I was so tired after work I just wanted to go to sleep. This baby is draining me. My prenatal vitamins were not giving me any energy. All they were doing were making me feel sick and nauseous. I cooked, helped Kevin with homework, and then did the dishes. Malik came in and laid right in the bed.

"How was your day?" he asked.

"It was alright. Malik, can you rub my back? It hurts really bad."

"Kim, I'm tired. I got to get up early in the morning."

"Please, Malik. It really hurts."

"Damn Kim, turn over," he said, as he grabbed the lotion and rubbed it on my back.

Malik gave me an unenthusiastic, five-minute rub.

Physically Malik is here, emotionally he is not. He is not the same man I fell in love with. That man would do anything I ask. He was there for me. Malik is a selfish bitch. I love him, but lately he is trying to start arguments on purpose. He is acting real funny. God, I hate him sometimes. My back was still hurting, so I went and got pillows off the sofa and propped them behind my back. I turned on the television and watched the ten o'clock news.

"Kim, can you turn the volume down?"

I turned the volume down a little. I could barely hear the news, so I turned it off. I tried to go to sleep, but my back was still hurting and I couldn't get comfortable. I finally got comfortable and I was halfway asleep when I heard Malik's cell phone ring. He jumped up out of the bed and went to answer it in the bathroom. I couldn't make out what he was saying because he was whispering. I wanted to know who he was talking to at 11 P.M. at night.

"Malik who are you talking to?" I asked. Malik didn't answer right away, so I got out of the bed and walked into the bathroom. When I walked in the bathroom, Malik jumped like I startled him. I asked him again who he was talking to. He said, "Just Jarrod," and told Jarrod he would talk to him tomorrow. I went to get back in the bed and Malik followed.

"What did Jarrod want this late at night?" I said as I turned my back towards to him.

"Nothing much," Malik said as he gave me a kiss, turned towards me and snuggled me.

Chapter Fourteen

Shonda

Iknew it was late and Malik told me that his fiancée was starting to trip on him. He asked me to call him only before ten. I didn't want to get Malik in any trouble at home, but I needed to speak with him. It was after eleven and I was bored. I needed to speak to him before I went to bed.

Malik answered on the first ring. He whispered "Hello."

"Can you talk?" I asked.

"Not really."

"Oh, sorry. I just wanted to talk to you before I went to sleep," I said. Then I heard a woman's voice ask Malik who he was talking to. Malik responded "Just Jarrod," and then he said "Well, all right man. I'll call you tomorrow."

I just hung up after Malik said that. I felt like a fool. I don't think I'm pushing myself on Malik, but I'm starting to like him too much. We have been going out to the movies, dinner and everything else in between, but I just don't know. I don't like the fact that I can't even call the man I'm dealing with, when I want. I don't know what I have gotten myself into.

I was running late for work. I couldn't find a parking lot to save my life. It was 8:40, and I was still circling around. I thought I saw a parking space, but it was in front of a fire hydrant. At 8:55, I decided I was just going to have to pay for parking. I was about to turn off my cell, when Malik called.

"Hey, babe, what's up?"

"Nothing, about to go into the building."

"Don't go in."

"Why, babe, what's wrong?"

"Walk around the corner."

"Why? What's wrong?"

"Nothing, just come around the corner."

"Okay, which way?"

"Down Seventeenth Street. I'll meet you on Chestnut."

"I'm going to be late."

"Don't worry."

I walked down the street and saw Malik in Kim's car. It was a brand-new silver Altima.

"Get in."

"I'm not getting in that girl's car."

"Look, just get in. Look, Shonda, Tonia doesn't work today so call out, and say you're sick."

"Why?"

"Because I have something planned for us."

"Really? What?"

"Just call out first, it's a surprise."

I called and left a message on Tonia's voice mail that I was not feeling well and I wasn't coming to work today.

"So where we going?" I asked as I gave Malik a kiss on his cheek. He put his finger up to his lip to signal for me to sit back and enjoy the ride, which I did. The car had leather in the interior and a banging sound system. He was listening to the radio. I pushed my seat back and sat back so I could enjoy the ride. I thought Malik was taking me to Delaware; then we went past a toll, and I noticed we were passing the Maryland Welcome house.

"Okay, Malik, where are you taking me, baby?" We drove for another hour and then he stopped.

"I'm lost. I got to get some directions." He stopped at a gas station and then got back in the car and said, "Shonda, I wanted us to have a day to ourselves, just me and you. I want to be able to sit back and relax with you."

I was surprised as shit that Malik had actually planned something for us. That something was a day with just me and him. I guess Malik was trying to prove to me that our relationship was more than fucking. Malik drove to Maryland and got a room at the Marriott hotel a few blocks away from the Baltimore harbor. Malik checked us in the hotel and got our key. While Malik went to the front desk, I fixed my makeup. I lined my lips and applied some MAC lip glass. Change fell out of my bag. I went to pick it up when I saw a picture envelope. The negatives fell out and were stuck between the seats. I looked up to see if Malik was coming, then I tried to slide my hand under the seat to get the negatives. I slid back up and looked again to see if Malik was coming. He wasn't, so my curiosity got the best of me. I held the negatives up to the light. I could figure out that some of the pictures were Malik and some had to be Kim. I was dying to know what she looked like. I took the negatives out of the sleeve and put them in my bag. Malik returned to the car and kissed me on my cheek. We parked and walked toward the elevator. Before I could push the UP button, Malik was all over me.

"Stop, baby. That's why we got a room." Malik ignored me and started pulling up my skirt. He bit my leg, then my inner thigh. I laughed and moaned at the same time. "Malik, we can't, it's cameras, let's go upstairs," I said.

"There's no camera by the elevator," he said.

As soon as he said that a white couple walked toward the elevator. If I would have let Malik start they would have seen everything.

Ding, the elevator finally came. Malik glanced down at the key and read the room number, then pressed eleven. The white couple boarded the elevator.

"Hello," the old white-haired cheery man said.

The most I could get out was a "Hi." I stood next to the glowing elevator buttons. Malik stood behind me. He was still putting his fingers up my skirt.

"Stop," I whispered, as the couple exited the elevator, "Malik, you know they saw you."

"So what, maybe they'll get the idea to go and do something."

"Something like what?"

"What we're about to do."

Malik opened the door. I opened the curtain. The sun filled the room with brightness. I could see the harbor from the window, it had calm waves in it. I was so happy I was with my baby. Malik pulled a bottle of red Alize out of his bag. He probably would have gotten himself some white wine, but he knew I liked Alize. He then went to get some ice from the ice maker in the hallway. I checked myself out in the mirror and had to smile. I was impressed with Malik and all he did. I assured myself that it was going to work out with me and him. One day he would leave Kim and it would be just me and him. Malik came back in the room and gave me a hug. His cologne smelled so good, I just inhaled it.

"Shoney, baby, you want something to drink? Now or later?"

"Now."

"Um, baby, you look good."

"I do," I said as I took a sip of my drink.

Malik went back over to his bag, pulled out flowers and a CD player. He put in Carl Thomas, "Summer Rain." We danced side to side. Malik just held me so tightly, letting me know I was the one. After our dance, I sat on the edge of the bed.

"You look so good, Shonda," Malik said as he got on his knees and started biting my inner thigh again. My panties were still on but Malik kissed through them. I felt his tongue; it was so wet, he was making me wet. Then he slid my panties to the side with his hand and inserted his finger inside my body. He twisted in and out as he kissed me. I was about to go off just from his finger but he took turns with his tongue and finger caressing my clit.

"Uh, Malik, uh, baby." At that point I was satisfied. It was my turn to please him. So I took off my skirt and wet panties slowly and seductively as Malik sat on the bed watching. He bit his lip. I blew a kiss and stood up on the little wood table by the window. I was working, and poking my ass out like I was an exotic dancer. I put my finger inside myself and was giving Malik a show. Malik came closer. And then I fell. Ask me how, I don't know. I knocked over the Alize and ice and my leg was bruised.

"Are you okay, baby?" Malik asked.

"Yeah," I said and we both started laughing. How am I going to try to be sexy and then I fall off the table?

Malik picked me up and put me on the bed. We finished our session by Malik entering me from the front. Even though I fell, a few strokes after his entrance, Malik was done. He must have been as worked up as I was. I wasn't mad at him. I was just happy to be lying beneath my baby. We both fell asleep.

Once we woke it was 2:00 P.M. We took a shower together, then I went to check out while Malik got the car. The counter person asked me how was my stay.

"Good," I answered as I grabbed some candy off of the counter. She handed me the bill and said, "Thanks for staying with us, Mrs. Moore." I started to correct the desk agent but I smiled and folded the bill up and placed it in my pocketbook instead.

I met Malik in front of the hotel and we rode down to the harbor and parked again. We got something to eat at a place called Phillip's All-You-Can-Eat Buffet. We fed each other crab and shrimp. One of the things I liked about Malik is that I didn't have to front. We both went up to get more crab three times. I sucked butter off his lip and he fed me crab.

After our meal, reality was setting in. It was time to get back onto 95 North and go home. Malik grabbed my hand as we walked back to the harbor parking lot. "Did you have a good time today?"

"Yes, baby," I answered.

"Well, what's wrong? Why do you look so sad?"

I didn't want to start. I was trying not to start, but I couldn't help it. "Malik, it's just that I wish every day could be like this."

"I wish it could be like this too, but it can't right now. Let's just enjoy today, and worry about tomorrow later, okay."

Back on the highway we cruised to Jill Scott. I dozed off into a peaceful little sleep. I jolted up when I heard Malik's cell phone going off.

"Hello," Malik answered nervously. "Huh, what are talking about? I was at work today. You didn't come up to my job. Well, if you did, I was at City Hall with Demarco. All day. Kim, listen I'm not with no other woman. I love you, baby. . . . Don't say that. Stop crying. Listen, I'll talk to you when I get home. Then I'll come to your mom's."

Malik looked over at me. I pretended to be 'sleep until she called for the second time. I could hear her cussing him out. I stayed silent but I could not take it anymore. I tapped him and lip-synched, *Malik, you got to do something.* Malik pressed mute on his phone as Kim rambled on.

"Shonda, what can I do? You know the situation."

"I know the situation? What does that mean. How long am I supposed to tolerate this shit? Huh, Malik?" He signaled for me to be quiet, then he just hit the SEND button on his cell. Kim called back but he didn't answer. I felt tears streaming down my face.

"Shonda, stop that, stop crying."

"Malik, pull over. I'm getting out."

"Shonda, you can't get out."

"I can't go through this with you. I love you, but if I can't have you, I'll leave you alone. You have to do something." I tried to open the car door. Malik grabbed my hand and began speeding so I couldn't get out. My head jerked back from the acceleration.

"Y'all driving me crazy!" Malik screamed.

"What, you got to be kidding. Malik, you really got to be kidding. You know what, as soon as this car stops I'm out of here." Malik continued up the highway, and we didn't speak the rest of the ride.

Kim

I tried to go to work today but my stomach was killing me. Malik had just dropped me off in my car, his car wouldn't start this morning. He needs to get a new one, but is scared of the higher payment. I went into the building, got to my desk, and realized I had to go throw up. I just made it to the bathroom, when all my breakfast came up. I kept spitting up a clear liquid. Nicole came into the bathroom and asked me if I was okay. I told her no, and she said she would call Malik for me.

"No answer," she said once she got back.

He must be at a case today, I thought. I was so sick, I had to leave the office. So I decided to catch a cab. I got in the cab and realized I didn't have my house keys. Oh, my God. I had no other choice but to ride to Malik's office. I tried calling, but no one answered the phone. I went to the office and it was total chaos. I stood in the reception area of the office as everybody walked past me rapidly. I said "Excuse me, hello," but no one stopped. I guess they didn't see me. I saw a very busty, thick girl with too much makeup on and too little clothes.

"Hi, I'm looking for Malik Moore. I'm his fiancée."

"Really. Nice to meet you. I'm Monique. Um, I don't think Malik is here today."

"Are you sure? Can you check?"

"There isn't really a way to check because our receptionist does the time cards, and she's not here, she's sick today."

"Someone has to know whether or not he's here, right?" I asked desperately. *Where the hell can Malik be?* I thought while the girl picked up the phone and asked someone was Malik in the office. Okay, I heard her say, then she placed the phone back on the receiver.

"Um, I'm not sure if he came in today and everybody is really busy. Do you want me to leave a message on his voice mail, or maybe call his cell phone?"

"Thank you," I said as I walked out of the office. I pressed the down button at the elevator bank. I then decided just to go to my mother's house. I called Malik all day; he did not answer his phone. I wanted to know where he was. My mother wondered where Malik was—I had to answer her nosy questions all day.

"Doesn't he have a cell phone?"

"Yes, Mom. He does have a cell phone but it's off. They don't allow cell phones in the courtroom."

"Well, he should be here, you're sick."

"I'm fine now, Mom."

I kept calling Malik all day. Finally at 3:30 P.M. Malik answered the phone.

"Hello."

"Yeah? Where you been at all day?" I questioned Malik.

"Huh?" Malik said.

"Malik, you heard what I said. You think I'm stupid? You were not at work today. I'm at my mother's house, sick all day and you are nowhere to be found. Who were you with all day?" I asked him, and then his cell phone went dead.

Malik pulled up at my mother's house. I stormed out of the door. I got in the car. He was acting nervous at first, and I didn't say anything. Then, "Where the fuck were you all day?"

"I was at work."

"You were not, you lying motherfucker. I'm sitting here all day, sick, and God knows where you were all day."

"I told you I was at work."

"I called your cell phone all damn day and you didn't answer."

"I was at court with Demarco. Look, I'll call him if you don't believe me." Malik started dialing the law firm.

I closed his cell phone and said, "Malik, you don't have to do that. I just want to go home."

Chapter Fifteen

Shonda

I was not in the mood to cook. I ordered Bree a turkey hoagie and laid across my bed. The phone rang a couple of times, but I didn't feel like answering it. It was probably Malik trying to apologize to me.

"Hello."

"What's wrong with you?" It was Tae.

"Malik."

"What happened?"

"I don't know where to begin. We had a nice day, we went to the Marriott in Baltimore, had lunch, everything was going great until his little bitch started calling his phone and he started acting scared like she was going to hear me or something. Then he tells me I know the deal."

"No, he didn't."

"Yes, he did."

"What was that supposed to mean?"

"Exactly. I mean, Malik is cool, we have a good time, but you know in all my relationships I always came first, so what I look like playing second?"

"Fuck him. We'll go out this weekend and we're going to meet us some new men."

"I just want to chill. I don't have time for any men. I'm not fucking with Malik anymore or any man."

"Look, it's only two ways you will end up by the time you're thirty—with a husband that's cheating or cheating with somebody's husband."

I think Tae was right.

Calling out was not the best idea at work. Especially since I just called out about a month ago. Then for Malik not to show up either, that was dumb. Malik is dumb. I didn't even speak to him when he walked in the office this morning. His ass was late. His bitch probably was cussing his ass out last night. Who cares, I'm done with Malik. Fuck him. I put his negatives in the one hour this morning. At lunch I'm going to pick them up and laugh at him and his big pregnant bitch. Soon as I saw that big goofy smile on Monique's face, I knew she knew that me and Malik called out together.

She walked over to my desk. "So, what's up?"

"Nothing."

"Um, guess who came up here yesterday."

"Who?"

"Malik's fiancée. She was mad she couldn't find Malik."

"Really," I said, unsurprised.

"That's real special."

"So what's so special about that?" I said as I became annoyed.

"Oh, nothing. It's just coincidence that you and Malik both weren't here and she couldn't find him, that's all."

"Yeah, that is a coincidence. But these phones are ringing off the hook so I'm going to answer them. I'll talk to you later," I told her, so she could walk her nosy ass away from my desk.

Malik left Maxwell's "A Woman's Worth" on my answering machine and sent me white roses. If they weren't so pretty, I would have thrown them in the trash. Of course, Monique wanted to know who sent them to me. I told her in a nice way to stop being so nosy.

At lunch I ran to the Rite Aid pharmacy. I couldn't wait to look at the pictures. I got the shock of my life. Malik's fiancée was not fat and she was not ugly. Most people when they see their competition they find something wrong with them. I couldn't really say anything bad about the girl. Well, her nose was kind of big, but she was still pretty. Her hair was sandy brown and she had a glowing, creamy brown complexion. She looked like she was from the Caribbean, with a nice tan. And Malik actually looked happy. It was her in the picture with her son, I guess, and Malik. They looked like a happy family. Then some of the pictures were just her and Malik. I stared closely at the photos. I wondered where they were taken. I wondered if they were in Malik's house where he lay every night. A tear ran down my cheek. I don't know why I was crying. It just didn't seem right though. I would never have Malik to myself. I mean, why did I have to meet Malik and he be perfect for me and at the same time be somebody else's. Life is not fair.

I was walking to my car and my phone began to ring. It was Malik.

"Baby, I'm sorry. Shonda, you know how I feel about you. I'm confused as shit right now. I never cheated on Kim. Now, all of sudden you're giving me doubt about the way I feel about her."

"Malik, I can't handle this right now."

"Can you at least talk to me? Where are you at?"

"Walking toward my car."

"Where are you parked?"

"Sixteenth and Pine."

"I'll be right there."

Malik met me at my car. "I'm sorry, baby, okay?"

"Okay," I said as we hugged. "I see you got your car fixed."

"Yeah, that's why I was late this morning. Do you want to go to the movies or something?"

"I got to get Bree." I thought about it for a moment and then told Malik to give me a moment. I called Brian to see if he would pick up Bree. He said that he would.

"I can go; you want me to follow you?"

"No. Park and ride with me."

I rode with Malik. We went and got something to eat and then we stopped over Jarrod's house. Jarrod was cool, he was silly as shit. After Jarrod's we went and walked by the river at Penn's Landing. We just talked and held each other. Malik told me how he felt about me. How he had never been more confused in his life and that he felt like I was on his side and had his back and it was me and him against the world. Malik then grasped me tightly and began kissing me all over my neck and ears and face, and on my shoulders. I returned the favor and sucked all over his neck and then he stopped me and said, "Shonda, stop. You know you can't do that."

"Why not?"

"You know why."

"You're my man and I'll do whatever I want to you," I said as I continued to nibble and suck on his neck. I rested in his arms as we watched the city lights. I wanted to stay in his arms, they were warm and serene. We knew we both had to get ready for the next day, but we still couldn't leave each other.

Kim

I think Malik is cheating, but I'm too tired to catch him in his lies. Malik says he's with Jarrod lifting weights and he doesn't come in until 2:00 A.M. and I'm supposed to go for that. I don't know what to do. I'm not sure if he is actually seeing somebody. Malik never really cheated on me. At least, I never caught him. I think if he ever did that it wasn't more than a date or two. I mean, he used to always come in the house on time and now he doesn't. And he is still standing by his story that he was at court the other day. But I'm not buying that shit. He was out somewhere doing something he had no business doing, but right now I don't have any proof so I can't say anything. I was asleep when Malik came in. I woke up and noticed red marks all over his neck.

"Malik, what is that on your neck?"

"What is what?"

"That red mark on your neck. Malik, you have a passion mark."

"Kim, I don't even let you kiss on my neck, how am I going let somebody suck on my neck?" Malik said, as he got up from the bed and felt his neck.

"Exactly. I don't suck on your neck."

"I got a haircut yesterday. The barber shaves all over my face and my neck."

"Malik, you are the worst, the fucking worst. Um-hmm."

"You think I believe that?" Malik was getting out of hand. I was trying to deal with him working late and his going out with Jarrod every night of the damn week, but I know what I was looking at on his neck was not caused by a damn pair of barber's clippers.

Chapter Sixteen

Shonda

I bought Malik and me some Sixers tickets to make up for me acting like a fool. I know he loves me. I decided it was not my place to worry about Malik's home situation. That was between him and his woman. My only concern was with him being good to me. I told Malik I bought us Sixers ticket. You would think his ass was grateful and happy. But he said that it was too many people at the game and he could not risk running into anyone.

"Anyone like who?" I asked.

He said, "Anybody, Shonda. That's just too wide open, somebody might see us."

"Well, what am I supposed to do with the tickets, Malik?"

"Sell them and I'll take you out."

"No, that's okay," I said.

Malik asked me was I mad. I told him I wasn't, but I was. I can't keep going through this with him. I called from work and asked Tae if she wanted to go to the game. I told her Malik said he couldn't go with me.

"Why?"

"Because somebody might see us. So you want to go?"

"I don't have anything to wear. But I'm sure I can find something."

"The game starts at 7:30 P.M., be ready. I don't want to miss the tip-off."

I went home and got dressed for the game. I tried to do something with my hair, but I really couldn't. I decided to rock a hat and just put on my number three Sixers jersey. I had to call my dad, because I noticed the toilet was running. I left a message for him and finished getting ready for the game.

If I said Tae acted like a damn fool at the game, it would be an understatement. As soon as Tae saw Allen Iverson run onto the floor she screamed, "A. I., I love you! I love you, A.I. ! Let the haters hate because you are great!"

I told Tae to calm down, she was acting like a twelve-year-old, getting into the game. Then the Orlando Magic came onto the floor.

"Oh, my God, look at Tracy McGrady! He looks good! Oh, I love him too!"

She screamed "Defense, defense!" She didn't even know what that meant, but still she went along with the crowd. People were turning around, looking us.

"Shut up, Tae. People are staring at us."

"I don't care." Tae screamed so much that she was hoarse. Halftime couldn't happen fast enough. I couldn't enjoy the game, I was truly embarrassed. I tried to concentrate on the game, but couldn't. Every other minute she was asking all these questions. What does that mean? Why is that a foul? Blah, blah, blah. She had no understanding of the game whatsoever. My dad took me to games all the time. We went to games back in the day when Dr. J played. I had no choice but to like sports. My dad made me watch it and understand it. If I knew Tae was going to act like this, I would have brought my dad instead.

At halftime, I bought an overpriced hot dog and soda. Tae needed some water for her throat.

"Y'all all right?" two guys asked us.

"We're fine, " I said.

"We don't need to call the paramedics or nothing for your girl-friend?"

I ignored the rude guy's next comment and went and stood next to the wall while Tae talked to the rude guy's friend. I sipped my soda and watched people walking past. I had to go to the bathroom but decided to wait for Tae. The rude guy then leaned against the wall, too. We were standing there awkwardly. I didn't have any-thing to say to the guy. I just wished Tae would hurry up. The guy then turned to me and said, "So, let's start over. How you doing?"

"I'm fine."

"I see your friend is enjoying the game."

"Yeah, she is. I'm not."

"Why not?"

"Cause I can't get into the game with her loud mouth."

"How about we trade seats, then?"

"Huh?"

"Your girl sits with my boy and he can explain the game to her and I'll sit with you."

I told him that that was okay and I would be all right. He told me his name was Carl. He wasn't really my type, short and too skinny. He appeared to be a baby thug. He had a Boston Celtics green throwback jersey on with a matching hat cocked over his eye and his braids were hanging out. I took his number, but I didn't give him mine.

Once the game was over, Tae and her new friend went to get drinks and I said good-bye. I turned my cell phone on and checked my messages. Malik had left several messages. The first message was, "Hey, baby, it's Malik. Um, I can go to the game. I'll go." The sec-ond was, "Call me back and I'll meet you at the game." The third was, "Shonda, it's almost eight. I don't know if you left already, but

I wanted to go. Have a good time, babe, have fun. Call me when the game is over." Malik left a total of four messages on my voice mail.

I dialed Malik back and got his voice mail. As soon as I was beginning to leave a message, my other line interrupted. I answered the other line and it was Malik.

"You okay?"

"I'm fine."

"Sorry I couldn't go with you."

"That's okay."

"Did you have a good time? Are you on your way home?"

"Yeah."

"I'll meet you there."

By the time I pulled up, Malik was already sitting on my steps. He came up to me and asked me if I was mad at him. I told him I wasn't mad at him and we went inside the house. He asked me about the game and I told him how Tae performed. We settled on the sofa watching the news. Around twelve I looked at the clock. Malik had fallen 'sleep. I thought about telling him to get up and go home. But the selfish side of me decided to snuggle back up next to him and go to sleep. I knew if he stayed out enough nights, his fiancée would have to catch on if she's not dumb and kick him to the curb. Then me and Malik could go ahead with our lives. I dozed back off into a soothing, relaxing sleep when a blaring ring at 2:27 A.M. disturbed me. Malik's cell phone kept ringing and ringing. It was ringing so loud my neighbors probably could hear it. I don't know why he was acting like he didn't hear the phone. He jumped up and said, "What time is it?" He looked down at the phone and said, "Oh, shit, it's Kim and it's two-thirty."

"Answer the phone."

"I can't," he said as tried to fix his clothes and find his shoes in the dark.

"Well, do something, cause I'm trying to get some sleep," I said as I got an attitude.

He continued to search for his shoes. He located one and slipped it on. Malik started breathing heavy and acting frantic. His phone rang again and again. He was even talking to himself saying, "She's going to kill me."

I thought to myself that his girl got him uptight and has a strong grip on him that I would never be able to break. I was tired of sharing him. I was tired of him leaving me. I then began to feel a little guilty. His pregnant girlfriend was home alone trying to reach him, and all I could think about was myself. I should have woke him up, because Malik really looked scared. I saw his face as I turned on the light to help him find his other shoe. He looked like a shook ghost. I then felt so guilty. How something so innocent as office flirting, lunch, then drinks and dinner had turned into this.

Finally reality set in. I was sleeping with someone else's man and no matter what I did, he would never be mine. Malik found his other shoe on the other side of the living room. *Malik, how long will I have to put up with you leaving? How long*, I wanted to ask him. But instead, I blocked the door and said, "Malik, please hold me. Don't leave me. I get tired of you leaving me in the middle of the night."

"You only like me because I'm with someone."

"No, you're wrong. I like you for other reasons."

"Like what, Shonda? You love me because you can't have me the way you want to. I got to go."

Kim

"Mom, Aunt Kianna's on the telephone," Kevin screamed from down the hall. My little sister never called me unless she wanted something. Either it was money, clothes, or she wanted me to rent her a car or something. So I answered the phone in an annoyed tone.

"Yes, Kianna, what do you want?"

"Dag, why you got to be like that? I don't want anything. I got to tell you something. "

"Tell me, then."

"Well, you know Nora from when I was going to nursing school? You know the one with the big butt who use to pick me up every morning?"

"Yeah, I remember her. What about her?"

"Well she be hanging out with my girl Kira. So anyway, her and Kira was on the Internet checking out some dudes on black-planet.com. Guess who they saw thinking they decent, smiling, and what not?"

"Who?" I said, as I dreaded to hear her say Malik.

"Lonnie, his name on the page is lonniegetmoney."

"Lonnie! I can't believe that."

"Well, believe it. He got pictures and everything. Talking about he's a rapper and singer and he's trying to holla at all the fine honeys out there."

"Oh, that sounds just like Lonnie. So, did you tell Karen yet?"

"No. Well I wasn't sure what to say. So should I tell her?"

I thought about it for a minute and decided that learning about Lonnie from Kianna would not be the most compassionate way to find out her man is cheating. "I'll call her and tell her. I'll call you back." I hung up the phone.

I didn't call Karen right away. I wanted to check out the Web site for myself. I had to make up a screen name, then I was able to log in. I typed in the screen name Kianna gave and lo and behold I saw Lonnie. He looked so ridiculous. He had all his back in the day photos of him and famous people. He was such a has-been. To say the least, Lonnie is disgusting, he has a wife, and he's still trying to meet people. Please. I called Karen immediately.

"Hey, Karen."

"Hey, what's up?"

"Um, Kianna just called me."

"She did? What she want?"

"She called to tell me she saw Lonnie on blackplanet.com."

"What's that, some kind of music Web site? He is so pathetic. He's on all those can-I-get-a-record-deal Web sites."

"Well, on blackplanet.com he wasn't talking about music on this page."

"Well, what was he talking about?"

"He was trying to meet someone. You can go to the Web site. Get on your computer and type in blackplanet.com, make up any screen name, and type in 'lonniegetmoney.' "

I heard my sister typing, then I heard a sudden gasp, and Karen said, "I'll call you back."

I don't know what made me start thinking about the future. But I realized I was twenty-five and didn't have anything in life I wanted. I was pregnant and had no investments. Malik and me had an apartment, we paid rent, and had no house. I probably can pay two mortgages with nine hundred dollars a month. I mean, I know I need to plan for the future. If something happens to me, I have practically nothing in the bank, nothing for my kids, and hardly any money to bury myself. My mother and sisters would have to have a collection if I died. I got to get myself a house, and invest my money. I should have never bought my car. It rides so nice, though. But I want to be able to pay for my children to go to college. I don't want them to have to work. I want to be able to buy Kevin a car when he turns sixteen. It was time to start planning.

Sunday morning I got up and went to the market. I looked in northeast Philly for "For Sale" signs on houses. I drove around for about an hour. I saw about eight houses for sale. I was going to call tomorrow and get the prices. At one of the houses, I even got out the car and walked around the back. It was nice and had a deck and large yard. There was even a swing set. I imagined Kevin pushing his baby sister on it and having a barbecue in my yard. I needed a house. Malik may not be ready, but I am. I brought the discussion up to Malik over dinner.

"Baby, when I went out to the market this morning, I saw a lot of houses for sale."

"Really?"

"I mean, what we pay in rent, we probably can get a nice house."

"Kim, I'm not ready for a house. I mean, the baby is enough. Have you thought about day care, Pampers, and milk? We have a lot of bills and I still got to make payments on your ring."

"Well, I think we can afford it, and I'm tired of living in a damn apartment. This apartment has two bedrooms. Where is the baby going to go? On the top bunk of Kevin's bunk bed?"

"Here you go again, Kim. Starting your shit," Malik said as he got up from the table.

"Where are you going, Malik? I'm only talking."

"Well, right now I don't feel like hearing your shit. I'll be back," Malik said as he grabbed his coat and went out the door.

Chapter Seventeen

Shonda

Malik is cool. I like him, but it's not going to work out between us. I keep thinking that what I'm doing with him is wrong. I mean, morally, he isn't married, but sometimes I sit back and think about what his pregnant girl is doing at home while him and me are at the movies or when he has his face between my thighs. I feel a little guilty. But my guilt always lightens when I hear his voice.

"Hey, Malik. What's the deal?"

"What you doing?"

"Nothing, sitting back getting ready for tomorrow."

"You want some company?"

"That sounds good."

"Open your door. I'm outside."

I liked the way Malik asked did I want company; he didn't assume anything. I went to the door and gave him a kiss. His leather jacket was still cold from outside. Malik pushed me up against the wall and brushed my hair back with his hands.

"I missed you, Shonda. I was thinking about you all day."

"No, you wasn't."

"Yes, I was. I don't know what you doing to me."

"I'm not doing nothing to you," I said as I walked Malik over to the sofa. I offered him something to eat. He said he had already eaten and asked me to turn the television on. I did, and we sat back on the sofa as he played with my hair. A knock at the door startled us. I went to peek out the blinds and it was my dad and a lady. I answered the door.

"Hey, Dad, what are you doing here?"

"Coming to fix the toilet and introduce you to my friend." My dad came in and the woman followed. "Shoney, this is Ms. Marjorie."

"How you doing?" I said.

"Hi."

"You can have a seat." She sat down next to Malik. My dad still didn't notice Malik was here until he turned around and Malik stood up and went to shake my dad's hand.

"Dad, this is Malik. This is my dad Harold."

"How you doing, Sir?"

"Fine, just fine," my dad said as he looked Malik up and down, probably wondering why he was dressed up. After my dad finished appraising Malik, he told Marjorie, this won't take but a minute. Marjorie told him to take his time. I asked her a few questions, then I went to join my father in the bathroom. My dad was kneeling on the bathroom floor examining the toilet, when he asked me, "How long have you known this guy, Shonda, and where does he work?"

"He works at my job and I've known him a while."

"Really. How do you like your job?"

"It's going good."

"Well, you know you're not supposed to mix business with pleasure."

"Daddy, it's not like that."

"Where is my granddaughter?"

"With Brian."

"Shonda, you need to spend some time with that girl and stop shipping her away. I didn't do that to you."

"Please, he needs to spend time with her."

"Well, tell her her Pop-Pop is going to take her shopping Saturday for school clothes."

"Dad, she wears a uniform."

"Well, I still want to get her some clothes and toys," my dad said as he flushed the toilet and grabbed his tools. He got up to rinse his hands off in the sink and said, "Well, call me if you need anything."

"I will."

My dad then walked into the living room, said good night to Malik, and he and Marjorie left.

Kim

My baby was kicking all around today. This was the first strong kick that I had felt. Whoever said being pregnant was fun lied. I have no idea how anybody can do it more than twice. I had a few stretch marks from Kevin, but now I was getting more. The stretch marks were covering my brown belly like a spiderweb. The new marks were a dark purplish and red color. I had nothing better to do with my time than eat ice cream and watch *A Baby Story* or *A Wedding Story* on The Learning Channel. But the worst show for me to watch was *Maternity Ward*. Seeing those babies come out and all the pain the women went through frightened me. The woman on the show that didn't have a horrifying natural labor, had C-sections. I couldn't even imagine going through labor again. I just hope this time I go full term and Malik is standing by my side. I don't want any complications or problems. I had enough of that last time. I look at Kevin sometimes and think that he is a miracle baby. I think this baby is, too. After everything I have been going through, it will be worth it to see my daughter. I want to tell my daughter everything about the world. I want to protect her and teach her about everything. Warn her about men and drugs. School her on boys and sex. I can't wait to do my daughter's hair and teach her to drive. My mom was a great mom, but I don't think she prepared me for the streets. I learned the hard way that people are mean and deceitful, that everybody does not care about you. My mother was strict, but she also sheltered me, Karen, and Kianna from the real world. That's why Kianna is delusional now. I won't raise my daughter like that. I'll give her her own space, but to a degree. My daughter will learn from all the mistakes I made in my life. She will cross every bridge that I build for her. I know Malik will be a good daddy to her, he is a good man.

Chapter Eighteen

Shonda

My father had left me a message saying it was important. I said I would call him back after I helped Bree with her homework. I knew all he wanted to talk about was me paying some more rent. My dad walked in my door without knocking. That was not cool.

"Dad, how you going to just walk in here. How about if I had company or something," I said.

"Brianna, do you want to go with me?"

"Yes."

"Well, go to your room and get your stuff, cause I have to talk to your mom," my dad said.

What was so important that my dad had to talk to me about?

"Sit down." My dad grabbed my hand and said, "Shoney, baby, you know that guy Malik you've been dating is engaged and his fiancée is pregnant?"

"Where did you get that information from?"

"Marjorie told me."

"Daddy, it's not like that."

"Baby, yes it is."

"Marjorie's sister is a close friend with that girl's mother. He is not a good man."

"Dad, let me make that decision."

"I'm telling you, baby, leave him alone. Shoney, you deserve better."

"Dad, it's not like that."

"Well, I don't want to see him around here and I'm very disappointed in you." He called for Brianna and told me he would bring her home tomorrow when I got off work.

"Dad, I am grown and I can make my own decisions. Don't tell me how to live my life."

It hurt real bad for my dad to talk to me that way. He has never said he was disappointed in me. After he left I called Malik. I cussed him out so bad on his voice mail. I left a message that said, "Malik, you fucking bitch, I know you recognized my dad's friend. You should have said something. Now you got my dad mad at me, saying he is disappointed in me, and that you are engaged. When you get this message, give me a call."

Malik called me back and said, "Shonda, calm down. I didn't recognize that lady."

"You calm down. I can't take this, Malik, you make your decision right now. Either it's going to be me or her. If you're engaged be engaged, I can't take this anymore."

"Shonda, you know I can't do that. I can't leave her right now."

"Well, leave me alone right now," I said as I hung up the phone on him.

Malik called me back later that evening and asked me to meet him. I was still mad at him but I agreed to meet him. It was raining. I turned on my wipers. I didn't know what to think or what to say. I practiced different lines, anything to make him leave that woman alone. What could I say? I saw Malik pull up.

"What's up?" he said as he got in my car.

"Nothing. I wanted to talk to you." As much as I wanted to be Miss Hardcore, I couldn't. I broke down, tears started streaming down my face, and all I could mutter was "I want to be with you, Malik, but not like this."

"Shonda, I love you, girl. You know that," he said as he pulled me close to him. He turned toward me and I saw what I thought to be rain was an actual tear. Malik was crying too. I couldn't believe we were sitting in my car crying for each other, for our relationship, in the rain at 1:00 A.M. in the morning. We were hugging and holding each other between the console. I scraped my arm on the emergency brake, that's how hard I was holding onto my man. I don't know what I'm going to do about Malik. I can't take his situation, but I can't be without him either.

Kim

I was 'sleep when Malik came in the house. I looked over at the alarm clock and it read 1:30 A.M. It was the third time this week. I heard him lay his keys on the table, then go into the bathroom. I heard the toilet seat go up, the toilet flush. The water started running and the bathroom door opened back up. I saw him turn the bathroom light out, then the hallway light. He came into the room, took off his shirt, and placed it on the hamper. Then he sat on the bed and took off his pants, placing them over his shirt. Malik only had his boxers and T-shirt on. He got under the covers and turned on his side and plumped the pillow under his head. I guess he thought I was 'sleep.

"Malik, where were you?" I asked him.

"With Jarrod."

"It's 1:30 A.M."

"Yeah. Come on, Kim. I'm tired, don't start."

"I'm not starting, it's just that you don't act like you love me anymore. And I don't feel like you behave like someone who is about to get married." The more I spoke, the more enraged I became. I sat up and said, "Malik, you don't want to be here or marry me?"

"That's not true," Malik said, finally responding to my questions.

"But you know what, Malik, it's okay. Because I don't need you. You don't have to be here. I can do this on my own. I did it before," I said as my tears soaked the neckline of my nightgown.

"Where is this coming from, Kim?"

"Leave, Malik." I couldn't believe I had said that, but I meant it and I said it again. "Leave, Malik. Just leave." I pulled the cover off him. I took off my engagement ring and threw it at his head. I then began punching him in his back. "Go, be with your bitch, Malik."

"What bitch?"

"The bitch you stay out with until one-thirty in the morning," I said as I backed up off him. He then stood up, grabbed me by my arms, and told me to sit down. He turned on the lights, got some tissues and wiped my nose, and said, "Listen, Kim, I don't want anybody else but you. I'm not leaving you. I'm not Kevin's father. I won't leave you like that. You're the one, that's why I gave you a ring. I love you. I asked you to be my wife. You're about to have my child," he said as he searched for the ring on the bed. Malik located the ring and tried to put it back on my finger.

"Malik, why you keep cheating on me?"

"I'm not cheating on you."

"Yes, you are, Malik, I can feel it. I know you have been cheating. I can feel it and it hurts. It hurts real bad, Malik. Why can't you just be happy with me? Why can't we be happy? We used to be happy," I said as I slumped against the wall, crying. Malik came next to me and kissed me. I tried to get him off me. I told him to leave again and again but he wouldn't.

"I love you, Kim. I'll never leave, you hear me? I love you. You're my wife."

He helped me off the floor and put me back in the bed. I was still crying and he held me tight. I felt safe and secure.

Chapter Nineteen

Shonda

I asked Malik, after lunch, if he wanted to go out. He was a little hesitant and said that he had to pick Kim up from the hair salon, but after he dropped her off he would be available. He said that would be around 7:00 P.M. I don't know what hair salon she goes to but I knew she would never be out of there by 7:00 P.M. So I called Moviefone and checked to see what movies were playing around 9:30 P.M. That gave Malik plenty of time to pick me up. I wanted to maybe get a drink and get something to eat.

Malik called me around 10:00 P.M. and said he had to cancel our date. He claimed something came up. I know he somewhere chilling with his fiancée, but that's cool. I got a good mind to call that bitch right now and tell her everything. Not to get her back but just because she possessed something I could not have. She slept peaceful, while my sleep was restless, wondering when I would see him again. I hate him so much. I wish I was her.

Kim

Malik and I have been so busy. I decided to plan a getaway weekend for us. My mom said Kevin could come over for the weekend. I was so excited I bought strawberries, whipped cream, and honey. I booked a room at the Feather Nest—it was a theme room hotel. Our room theme was the Tahitian Hut. The room had mirrors on the ceiling, and a small waterfall by the Jacuzzi. I wished I could drink, but I couldn't. It took a half of day of work to continue to plan our weekend. I was so excited. I bought a black lace thong nightie and some champagne for Malik. I bought a dozen red and pink roses. I picked the petals off the roses and spread them all over the bed. I put the champagne in the mini refrigerator.

I dropped Kevin at my mother's. I parked my car at her house and she dropped me off at the salon. I planned on just getting my hair wrapped, but when I walked in, I saw a girl with blonde streaks. I thought that new hair would be good for me. At first Natalie wouldn't color my hair because I was pregnant. But I convinced her that my baby would be okay. I told Malik to pick me up around seven. He sounded a little disappointed because he said he was almost there. I told him I had a surprise and he said what?, and I told him I'd tell him when he gets here at 8:00 P.M.

My hair turned out so pretty. Those little streaks gave my hair the lift that it needed. Natalie finished my hair around 8:15 P.M. I waited until 8:30 P.M. before I called Malik. He didn't call me back right away. He showed up at 9:00 P.M. I wanted to cuss him out, but I didn't. I still tried to get along with Malik.

"Hey, baby, you ready for your surprise?"

"What's the surprise?"

"Let me drive," I said.

At the first red light, Malik pulled over. I tried to slip over to the other side of the car, but my belly prevented me. I got out and walked to the driver side. I got in the car and immediately adjusted the mirrors and seat. Malik kept asking where we were going.

"I got us a room at the Feather Nest."

"What! Kim, why would you spend two hundred dollars on a room?"

"I just wanted us to have some alone time."

"You know we got to get ready for the baby, Kim, you shouldn't have done this without consulting me."

Malik was a real asshole, I didn't complain that he was almost an hour late picking me up. I haven't said anything about what he's been doing lately. I tried to still be hopeful that our night would be good. I parked and opened up the room. Malik seemed unfazed, like his mind was somewhere else. I poured him a glass of champagne and went into the bathroom and changed. When I came out Malik was lying naked on the bed, with the lights dimmed. *That's what I was talking about*, I thought. I filled the Jacuzzi with water and turned it on. Malik ate all inside my body, and he hasn't done that in the last four months; it felt like the first time. Then he tried to put it in, but it wouldn't rise to the occasion. I sucked on it. It wouldn't get hard. I played with it. Nothing worked. I rubbed him down. Licked him everywhere. I was working for him to get it up, but it never happened. He blamed it on the champagne; he did have about five glasses. I was jealous, he was really buzzing. I blamed it on him not being interested in me. Maybe it was because I was pregnant. I don't know. I began sucking on him and I felt his dick getting hard. I thought it was working, but when I went to put it in I heard a snore and realized Malik had fallen 'sleep on me. He fell the fuck to sleep. There once was a time Malik and me had sex three to four times a day, no lie. Now he falls 'sleep. Malik's mind was not with me. He did not enjoy our night. I cried in the bathroom.

In the morning, Malik woke up and kissed me on my cheek and said thank you for the room. He asked me what time check-out was. I told me 11:00 A.M. He said sorry for falling asleep and let's enjoy

the room before check-out. Last night I would have loved his en-
thusiasm, but at seven in the morning he can kiss my ass. "Malik,
I'm 'sleep."

"Okay, baby, well, I'm getting in the Jacuzzi."

"Well, I'm getting some rest." Fuck Malik.

Once we checked out of the hotel, Malik must have realized he
had a hangover. He was shunning the sun like a vampire. I didn't
even ask him if he needed some aspirin. I had to pick up Kevin from
my mom's house and look at some houses.

Malik slept the whole day. He had a really bad hangover. I never
gave him any aspirin, Tylenol, or nothing. Fuck him. I hoped he'd
die in his sleep. I went to look at some houses with the realtor.
Kevin went with me and was very excited. He couldn't wait for the
baby to arrive and to have a new big bedroom.

When I came back from looking at houses, Malik's ass was still
on the sofa 'sleep. When he saw me he asked me what time it was.

"It's almost seven o'clock. I know you haven't been on the sofa
the whole day."

"Yeah, I have. I'm going to get up now. I have to make a run."
Malik went and got in the shower and got dressed. I told him fine.
I don't even care anymore. He left. I called Karen to see how she
was doing. She said Lonnie was still denying that he was on black-
planet.com. Then he confessed that his brother was playing a bad
joke on him. Karen said that she didn't believe him and was even
considering leaving him.

"Karen, you know you can't leave him over some Internet shit."

"I know, but I'm tired of Lonnie's ass."

"Well, I'm tired of Malik. He has changed. Last night I got us a
room, and he went to sleep."

"You're just pregnant and moody. Anything Malik does right
now is going to get on your nerves."

"It's not because I'm pregnant, it's Malik. He is changing."

"Well, I tell you one thing, if he changes, you change too. You're pregnant; tell Malik to kiss your ass. Make him sweat you. See, he thinks he has you because he gave you a ring and you're pregnant. But let him know, 'Malik, I don't need you. You are going to marry me or you can get out.' The best way to have a man sweat you and get what you want is to tell a man to kiss your ass."

Karen was right. I usually wouldn't listen to her, but what she was saying was making sense.

Chapter Twenty

Shonda

Malik makes me so mad. He's probably somewhere chilling with his bitch again. He called me this afternoon and said he couldn't make it last night, but he would definitely make it up to me tonight. It's 8:00 P.M. and he still hasn't called me. It's bad enough he stood me up last night, but I refuse to get played again. I'm not going to let him be chilling at home with her and I'm sitting home being bored and miserable. I called the guy Carl I met at the Sixers game.

He asked me out. I told him I had my daughter and she was 'sleep, but that he could come over and watch a movie. We sat on the sofa and talked a little. Then the bell rang. I jumped up. I peeked through the blinds and who did I see? Malik. I thought, *oh shit*. I told Carl my friend was outside and I would be right back. I slid out the door. Malik tried to come in and asked, "What are you doing?"

"Nothing."

"Why we out here?"

"Because I have company."

"Company?"

"Malik, yeah, company. I'm tired of waiting on you. You stood me up the last couple of days. Was I supposed to continue to sit by the phone? You're not home alone."

"You're right," Malik said as he turned away. I stood in the doorway with my arms crossed. Malik turned around and said, "I guess I'll call you later."

He started walking toward his car, when I said, "Malik, hold up. I'll make him leave."

"No, you don't have to do that."

"I know I don't have to, but I will."Malik looked at his watch, then said he would go get something to eat and come back.

I closed the door and looked at Carl, who was sitting there with his hands in his lap trying to figure out what was going on. "Um, Carl. Listen, something came up and I got to go. So I'm going to call you later, okay?"

"Yeah, all right. I see what kind of games you're playing," he said as he picked up his coat and headed for the door. As soon as he got in his car and sped off, Malik pulled back up. I left the door open and had a seat on the sofa, waiting for Malik. Malik walked in shaking his head. He closed the door and said, "I don't believe you, Shonda."

"Believe what? That I'm tired of you taking your time to make up your mind? How you going to be mad at me for having friends when you still live with her? You don't even know what you want."

"I know what I want."

"Evidently you don't, Malik."

"I do, Shonda, you just don't know. I got to go." I couldn't believe I made my company leave for him to argue with me and then leave again.

I couldn't let Malik leave. I stood in front of the door. I broke down and begged Malik not to leave.

"Please, baby, I'm sorry. What did you want me to do? You still home with her. You're not home alone and you want me to be home alone worrying about you all the time?"

Kim

Talking to my sister got me hyped. She told me the best way to have a man kiss your ass is to not pay him any attention. I planned on doing just that. If Malik wants to act like he doesn't want me, fuck him! I was so tired of Malik and his shit. Either he was going to set a fucking wedding date and act right or he was going to get the fuck out. Nobody has time for him. Playing games with my life. He is useless here. He is here every night, but it's like he doesn't want to be here. It's like I lost all control over him. He just doesn't care anymore. Me and my children will be okay. Either we're going to be together or not. I'm tired of crying, I'm tired of being depressed. I'm just tired of Malik. He got to get his shit together. He used to love me. I've been calling his cell phone and he hasn't even called me back. At one point in our relationship all I would have to say is "Baby"and Malik would be here. Now I'm lucky if he answers the telephone when I call him. Like I have been calling him for the last couple of hours.

Malik walked back in the house close to 10:00 P.M. His face looked like someone just died. I didn't care. I was going to tell him how I felt. Kevin was watching a SpongeBob Squarepants video on the television. I ordered him to his room.

"What's wrong with you?"

"Nothing. What'd you cook?"

"I didn't cook anything. When I do cook you don't eat." I had had enough. For once and for all, I was going to tell Malik how I felt.

"Malik, I feel like you don't want to be here with me, I have my doubts about you right now. You demand and demand. But I don't think you give me as much as I give you. I don't like you not answering your phone. I don't think you are very supportive of me, I need my back rubbed, my feet massaged, I'm pregnant. I need you to take care of me in every way. I just feel like you don't care."

"It's not like that."

"Yes, it is. If I say white you say black, if I say cold you say hot. All of your actions have been suspect lately. I feel like I got a man, but then again I don't. Malik, what's wrong with you? If you're not going to be here for me and this baby, and you don't want to marry me, then you're useless."

"So what are you saying?"

"Maybe we need a break from one another. I don't know, but I'm tired of getting treated like shit."

"I don't treat you like shit, Kim, I do the best I can for you."

"No, you don't, Malik, you don't even try, and I'm tired of tip-toeing around your ass. You want to see what's out there? Go right ahead. I don't need you. I'll be okay without you. Leave, Malik. If you don't want to be here, get up now and leave. I'm tired of the way you're treating me. I cook your food. I wash your clothes. I'm having your fucking child, but do you rub my back, do you ask me about my day? No, Malik, all you do is talk about your cases and your life. I got my hair dyed and you didn't even notice."

"If that's what you want, fine." Malik walked in the kitchen, reached in the cabinet, and grabbed the trash bags. He then walked into our bedroom. I followed him. He started grabbing all his clothes out of the drawers and throwing them inside the bags. Then he went into the bathroom and grabbed his toothbrush and deodorant and colognes and threw them in the bag, too. I watched silently as he emptied out his half of the closet. I didn't say anything. I went and had a seat on the sofa, to calm myself down. I could feel the baby tensing up. I was out of breath.

"Malik, leave. I thought I couldn't be happy without you but you can leave, Malik. I'll survive without you." And with that, Malik slammed the door and left.

I couldn't believe he had actually left. I thought about getting off the sofa and calling him, but decided not to. I walked into my bedroom. I looked in the closet and it looked just how I felt, empty. He didn't even make any effort to talk to me. He must not want me anymore. I called Karen and told her that I kicked Malik out. Karen asked me was I crazy.

"I couldn't take it anymore."

"You think I don't get tired of Lonnie's ass sometimes? You think Mommy and Daddy haven't ever gone through anything? But you never give up. You don't kick your man out. When you kick your man out, the first place he runs to is another woman."

I didn't care what Karen said, I had to put my foot down. Malik had gone too far.

Chapter Twenty-One

Shonda

When I saw Malik with two green trash bags, standing at my door, I didn't know what to think at first.

"Can I stay here tonight?" he said.

"What's wrong, baby?"

"I left Kim." One part of me was screaming, yea, yea, I won! I knew it. I knew he would leave her one day. Yes, yes I got my man. But the other was like, what now? I hope Malik didn't think he was staying with me, because I wasn't ready for that.

"You going to let me in?"

"Yeah, baby, I'm sorry. I'm just surprised."

"Yeah, me too. I just couldn't take her shit anymore. I was going to stay with Jarrod but I can't find him. I hope you don't mind."

"Malik, you know I don't mind. Come on in." I grabbed one of the bags and Malik followed me into the living room.

Malik took my hand and said, "Shonda, I realized when I thought about you being with someone else, I couldn't deal with it. I want to be with you and you only." He looked in my eyes and said he meant every word that he said. "I know what we have is real, Shonda, you made me realize that I was living a lie with Kim. I was going to marry her for all the wrong reasons."

Every word he said let me know I was the one. We talked for a little and then we got in the shower. The water was warm and I told Malik that I had to get my own place soon, because my dad was getting on my nerves. Malik agreed. After the shower, we dried off and lotioned each other down, and held each other. I fell asleep in Malik's arm. The fresh smell of Zest deodorant soap and baby oil mixed. I was so happy to have Malik with me, but I didn't know how long it would last. He might decide to go home at any time, but for the moment I was enjoying his company. It was the first time we spent the entire night together.

Kim

Malik will probably be back, he always comes back. He'll stay with his mom for a couple of days or go over Jarrod's. We've had arguments before, no big deal.

He'll probably call me today when I'm at work.

Malik hasn't even called me yet, it's one day later. I don't know what is going through his head and he is not at his mother's. I think this time it might really be over. In over three years I never let more than two days go by without speaking to him. Now I'm pregnant with his child and he doesn't even call me. That's some bullshit.

I looked at my cell phone; it read 3:27 A.M. I heard a banging noise. It scared me. The wind was blowing outside my window. It made a whistling noise. Trash cans rumbled down the street. I heard another noise, like it was in my apartment. I jumped up and peeked out my door and grabbed the cordless phone. I pressed the *on* button. I heard the dial tone. I dialed 9 and 1. If someone was in here I would press the other 1 and kick the intruder's ass until the cops arrived. My mother told me if you dialed 911 and hung up, the cops would still show up. The noise sounded like it was coming toward me. I was sure it was someone in the house. I was too scared to call the police, but I wasn't sure if it was somebody in my house. I wished Malik were here with me. I hate being alone. I was scared somebody would get me. I called Karen and told her that I thought someone was in my apartment and could she hold on until I searched the apartment. She agreed. I searched the apartment. I checked the closet, Kevin's room, my room, all the windows and doors. Nobody was in the apartment with us. I thanked Karen and went into Kevin's room, locked his door, and turned on the television and tried to go to sleep. I missed Malik so bad. I was so scared. He was my protector.

I was watching *Access Hollywood*. They were talking about celebrity couples vacations. I thought I heard Kevin call me, so I pushed MUTE on the remote.

"Kevin, did you call me?"

"Yes," he said as he came running into the living room with his black remote-control truck.

"Mom, um, where is Malik?" What was I to say to a five-year-old? Malik and Kevin were close, very close. I never thought about how this breakup would affect Kevin. I never let Kevin call Malik Dad, but he was the only father figure Kevin has known besides my dad.

"Malik is tired and he needs some time to himself."

"Is he coming back?"

"Yes."

"When."

"Soon."

"Can I call him?"

"No, he is really tired."

"Please, Mom."

"No." I thought about it. I decided to let Kevin leave Malik a message.

"Hi, Malik, this is Kevin, where are you? Why haven't you been home? I miss you. I love you, bye. Call me, please." Kevin ran back into his room. I finished watching television and got my clothes ready for the next day. I decided to call Malik's mother.

"Ms. Gloria, have you talked to your son."

"I talked to him yesterday, why, what's wrong?"

"Well, he moved out."

"He did? What, are y'all having problems? I'm going to call my son. I did not raise him like this. Give me your number again. I misplaced it." I started to give my number to Ms. Gloria, when she said, "Hold up, honey, I have to get a pen." She came back on the phone, I gave her my number, and she said that she would call me back.

My mother found out that Malik left, courtesy of Karen, I'm sure. She called me at work to see how I was taking it. My mother asked me what did I do to make Malik leave me.

"Did you chase him away, Kim?"

"No, I didn't do anything. Mom, he left on his own."

"You did something to him. Let me call Malik and see what is going on."

"Don't call him Mom, we just need some space. I don't really feel like talking now. I have work to do. I'll talk to you later."

A few minutes after my mother hung up, Lisa said that I had another call. I answered the call and it was Kianna.

"Big sis, I need a favor."

"Hey, Kianna, what is it?"

"Um, can I hold your car?"

"For what?"

"I got a video shoot in New York, they just called me and said they wanted me there. So can I hold your car?"

I thought about it for a minute and then I said, "Sorry, Kianna, no, I need my car and if something happens you can't pay me."

"You have insurance and nothing's going to happen. I'm going to go and come right back."

"Let me think about it. I'll call you back," I said. Kianna didn't give me a chance to think about it because she called me back and begged some more. I finally agreed. My final words to Kianna were to be careful.

They say you should always trust your first instincts. My first instincts told me not to let Kianna hold my car, and I should have listened to it. Because about four hours later, after giving Kianna the keys to my car, she called me saying, "Kim, listen, it wasn't my fault."

"What wasn't your fault?"

"I was in an accident. Mommy is on her way to come and get me. I was on the New Jersey Turnpike, near exit 8, and this van just came behind blinking his lights, trying to make me get out of the fast lane. I went to go over, and then he did too, and slammed right into the back of me, but I'm okay."

"I knew I shouldn't have let you hold my car. What does my car look like?"

"It's just a little hit in the back."

"Did you get a police report?"

"Well, that's the other thing, the guy kept going."

"What?"

"Yeah, he kept going. But Heather wrote down half the license plate number."

"Heather? I thought you were going by yourself."

"I was, but then I didn't want to drive by myself."

"Kianna, you are a fuck up," I said as I hung up the phone.

I woke up this morning pissed the fuck off. As of right now I was carless. I had to call my insurance company and figure everything out. The person I spoke to at insurance company told me I had a seven-hundred-dollar deductible and said that I could get a rental car. But I had to get a ride to the insurance company and to the rental car location. I called my mother's house to see if Kianna was home. She answered the phone.

"Kianna, my deductible is seven hundred dollars. Do you have it?"

"Yeah, I just got to go to the bank and get it."

"Well, I'm about to catch a cab over there." I said, relieved she had the money. I got myself dressed and got in the cab to drop Kevin off at school. I got to my mom's house and she was cooking breakfast.

"You want some coffee or something?"

"No, I'm mad, Mom. I wish Kianna would hurry up."

Kianna called from the bank and said that the line was long and that she would be there. When she finally arrived, she handed me $350.00 and said she would have the other $350.00 in two weeks.

"What do you mean you'll have my money in two weeks, I need my money now. I let you hold my car and you crashed it."

"I'm sorry, but, look, that's all I have."

"You better get the rest of my money, Kianna," I said as I walked up on her.

"I don't have it."

"Well, you better find it," I said as I stood up and pointed my hand in her face.

"Either you take what I have or you're burnt."

"I'm what?"

"You're burnt. I don't got it and when I get it I still don't got it."

"I got your burnt, bitch, don't talk to me in your little ghetto ass talk. You going to give me my money."

My mother interrupted us, "I'll pay for it. I'll write you a check. Kianna, get my pocketbook," my mother said as she tried to come between us.

"No, Mom, she is too irresponsible. She really needs to grow up."

"I don't have to do shit, you miserable pregnant bitch. Don't get mad at me cause your man left you." I stood in shock for a moment, then I went to swing on that little bitch.

"If you wasn't pregnant, I'd kick your ass."

"Kianna, what do you mean if I wasn't pregnant? I'll kick your ass now."

"You better get out my face before I kick you in your stomach."

My mom stood between us. I tried to kill Kianna as she dodged away. I picked up the mug off the table and threw it at her. The coffee spilled out onto my mom, Kianna ducked and the mug broke.

My mom started crying. I comforted her and she said, "Why can't y'all get along? We're all we got. This is how y'all going to act if something happens to me." I got my mom off the floor and she said she would drive me to the rental car. Kianna left and my mother went upstairs and changed her clothes. While I waited for her, I called the rental car agency and made a reservation. My mother came back down and told me to relax, that I was upsetting the baby by acting crazy. I told my mom that she was hurting Kianna by letting her get away with so much. She dropped me off at the rental agency and said that she would talk to Kianna.

There were about seven people ahead of me. I stood in line behind them. My head was still racing. I felt my stomach tightening. I wanted to kick Kianna's ass. My mother let her get away with too much shit. Once I reached the rental desk, one of the two agents decided it was time for her lunch, while the other talked on the telephone. At first I didn't say anything. But after five minutes of standing there and no one to help me I said, "Excuse me."

The lady looked up from the phone and said, "I'll be right with you."

Five more minutes went past. It was obvious that the agent was not on a business call. I said again, "Excuse me."

She said, "Girl, let me call you back, I got customers."

She asked me my name and for my reservation number. I told her that I had just made reservations a few minutes ago on the eight-hundred number.

"Well, I don't see your reservation. Do you have a confirmation number?"

"No."

"Well, you can have a seat and it may appear in the next few minutes." Then she rudely said, "May I help the next person, please." Any other day I would have taken a seat and waited for my reservation to appear.

"Listen, I just made a reservation, look in your computer and find it. I'm not having a seat." At first the girl gave me a look like, *who are you talking to,* but then someone came from out the back that appeared to be the manager and asked was there a problem. I explained that I had been waiting for a while and I need to go and his agent was not helping me. He gave the agent a grimace and said that he would help me. He went right on the computer and found my reservation. He said for my wait that he would upgrade me to a midsize vehicle. He gave me my keys and I said, "Thank you."

I was used to my spacious car. The car rental people's idea of a midsize vehicle was a Dodge Neon. To me, that was a compact car. My short legs barely could fit in the car, but at least I was driving. It could be worse. I could be walking.

After I left the car rental place, I went to see my car at the repair shop. I know you can't take material possessions with you to the grave and that they don't mean anything, but when I saw my car, I burst out into tears. I couldn't believe it. The whole back of my car was smashed in and the back window was shattered. I wanted to kill Kianna. The car looked like whoever was driving it should have been dead.

The repair guy walked over to me and said, "It's only a car, Miss. When I get finished with it, you won't even know it was in an accident. Okay? I'll make it real pretty for you. When it's ready I'll call you to pick it up."

"Okay," I said as I calmed down and got myself together. It was almost time to pick up Kevin and I didn't want him to see his mother like this.

Chapter Twenty-Two

Shonda

The first couple of nights felt so good I couldn't care less about Kim and that she was pregnant. She should have pleased her man. I was so happy Malik was with me. I mean, everything was going perfect. We worked together and Malik stayed with me. And when he wasn't with me, he was over Jarrod's. He couldn't stay here all the time because I never knew when my dad would come over and become suspicious, and he would probably double my rent if he knew I had a man staying with me, even if he only suspected they were spending the night. Malik was supposed to be getting his own place, but he never did. He just stayed between Jarrod's and my house. After a while, I stopped worrying about Malik going back to Kim. She called him every now and then, but he never answered his cell phone. My, how the tables have turned. Oh, well. Take care of your man or someone else will.

"Brian, when are you going to bring Bree home?"
"She's not coming home tonight. She wants to stay with me."

"She has to go to school."

"I'll drop her off at school."

"Brian, bring my daughter home."

"I'm not bringing her home, she's already in bed. I want Bree to live with me permanently."

"Did you forget she might not even be your daughter?"

"Whatever, you know she is my daughter."

"There is a possibility she might not be."

"Really. Well, she has my last name, I'm on the birth certificate, and I have been taking care of her since the day she was born, and paying child support. No court is going to deny me my child. Pick her up from school."

Brian was trying to keep my child from me. "Brian, bring my damn daughter today."

"Plus, Shonda, I have papers that say she is mine."

"Whatever. You can't get a test without me."

"All I needed was someone who looked like you and had your ID."

I called my dad and told him that Brian wouldn't bring Brianna home. His response was "What do you want me to do?"

Kim

The repair guy called me and said that my car was ready and to come and pick it up. At my lunch, I went and dropped off the rental and picked my car up. The repair shop did make it look like new. You couldn't even tell that my car had been in an accident. I was happy to have it back.

I went and picked up lunch at the Chinese restaurant. When I came back from lunch, Lisa said that Malik had called. I was so re-lived, he finally called me. I knew Malik was going to come around. With everything going on, I really needed to speak with him. It took a while, but he finally called me. I was so happy to hear his voice. I didn't care that he had not answered his phone or returned my calls. I was ready for him to say, *I'm sorry, let's get married, baby,* but Malik said something that stabbed my heart. Literally, I felt like Malik had stabbed me.

He said, "Kim, I'll be there tonight to give you my key and get the rest of my stuff." Malik didn't ask, can he come home, was I all right, how was the baby? No, that bastard said he was coming to get the rest of his stuff.

"Where have you been staying, Malik?"

"That's not important, Kim."

"What do you mean, that's not important?"

"It's not. I'll see you this evening."

As I placed the phone on the receiver, my legs began to tremble. I tried to control my composure; I tried but it was real hard. I couldn't. Tears just continued to come down. I grabbed another tissue and looked out at the traffic. When Lisa came over to me and started patting me on my back, she said, "Let it out. Don't keep it in, let it out. Let it out. It's not healthy for the baby." And I did just that. I let it all out.

Nicole brought over some tea for me. I drunk a little of it. Then I got up and went to the bathroom. I couldn't get myself together so I took the rest of the day off. I got in my car. Malik wanted his clothes, I was going to give him his clothes. He didn't have to wait until after work, he could have them now. I opened my door and grabbed my suitcases, and went into the room and grabbed everything that Malik ever bought into my apartment. Everything from his ties to a box of Fruit Loops cereal. I took it all and packed it up. Tears still ran down my face. I got back in my car. I got on the Expressway and drove to the Broad Street exit. There was a lot of traffic and I beeped my horn every other minute. I was steaming hot and wanted everyone to get out of my way. I drove right up to 1600 Market Street, double-parked right in front of the sign that said No Parking Any Time. I didn't care if I got a ticket. I popped my trunk open with my car key remote and grabbed the suitcases. I marched right into the building. I waited for the elevator. I got a few strange looks. I guess I looked like a mad woman, but I didn't care. I got back on my cell phone and called Malik's office.

"Demarco, Rhome, and Cooper."

"Malik Moore, please."

"Who's calling, please?"

"This is his wife."

"His wife."

"Yes, his wife," I said as I stepped off the elevator.

Malik's voice mail came on and said, "Yes, this is Malik Moore, I'm not in the office. Please leave a detailed message."

I hung up on his voice mail and walked into the reception area. I got immediate strange looks. I walked over to the receptionist.

"Yes, I just called for my husband and you transferred me to his voice mail."

"Yes, he's not in his office. Would you like me to get him for you?"

"No, I'll find him."

"I can't allow you to do that."

"Excuse me?"

"If you want Malik, I will get him for you and you have to wait here for him," she said as she stood up and tried to dial his extension. "Malik, there is someone in the reception area to see you. Your wife," she said as she glanced up at me. I didn't like this woman. She sounded a little too comfortable talking to my man. She told me I could have a seat. I continued to stand with my arms crossed. When I saw Malik walking down the hall toward me, I reached into the hallway and rolled all of Malik's belongings into the reception area. I wasn't going to leave my suitcases with him, so I took everything out and threw the things all over.

Malik said, "What are you doing?"

"Giving you the rest of your stuff. I thought I would save you a trip," I said as I zipped my suitcases up and walked away. I had embarrassed the shit out of Malik. Everyone in the other offices had come over to get a look at the scene I created. Malik was on the floor gathering his belongings. Then I walked back in the reception area and said, "Malik, fuck you and your bitch."

Chapter Twenty-Three

Shonda

No, she didn't. No, she didn't. The crazy bitch did the unthinkable. She came to the job and damn near got Malik fired. Tonia saw what happened but the lawyers were out. I don't know what Malik said to her but whatever it was, she did not like it. She came in the office looking like a madwoman. She didn't even look like she was seven months pregnant. She really didn't look pregnant at all. She was so tiny.

First she called and asked for Malik, saying she was his wife, and then she showed up at the desk seconds later. I almost shitted. I didn't know if she wanted me or what or if she even knew who I was. I kept my composure and buzzed Malik again. He came out and that's when the bitch dragged and dumped all his belongings into the reception area. When she left she said *fuck you and your bitch*. Well, since I was there and Malik was there and half of the office was there, even though she had no idea who I was, everyone automatically assumed she was speaking about *me*. I mean she was speaking about me but she didn't know she was speaking about me. Someone called security. I got some clear trash bags out of the coffee room and helped Malik get his stuff.

Danny said, "Damn, girlfriend was mad," as he snapped his finger in a half circle. Everyone started laughing. Even me until I saw Malik's face: he wasn't laughing. He was embarrassed. I helped him take his stuff down to his car.

The rest of the day I tried to go on like nothing happened. That was very hard. Because every other half a minute, someone in the office had an instant replay for those who didn't see what happened. And then she was like this, and then Malik was like this. If I wasn't in the middle of it, It would have been funny. I mean you have to admit, it was funny as hell.

Kim

The parking lady was writing me a ticket when I walked over to the car. She was just putting it on my windshield. I snatched it from her, got back in my car, and called Malik. I hoped he was happy. He made me do it. He should have done right by me. I know I made a fool out of myself. I shouldn't have went up to his job like that.

"Demarco, Rhome, and Cooper."

"Malik Moore."

"Mr. Moore is out of the office. I can forward you to his voice mail."

"No, I need Malik to get on the phone now."

"He's not available."

"Listen, put Malik Moore on the phone," I shouted, running a red light.

"He's not in." And then she hung up on me. And then it all clicked. The fat bitch in the office was the one that Malik was seeing. She had to be. Because why wouldn't she give him the telephone?

I called her back and said, "Are you the fat bitch fucking with my man?"

"Who the fuck are you calling a fat bitch?"

"You, bitch."

"Well, your man don't think I'm fat and you wish your skinny ass body looked like mine. Yup, I'm the one fucking your man and it's real good and that's why he left your pregnant ass." When she said that I did a U-turn in the middle of Broad Street and headed back to the office to whoop that bitch's ass. Who the hell was that bitch talking to? I started getting so upset. She was right in front of my face. I could have killed her then but didn't know it was her. When I went to walk back into the building, security stopped me. Malik called me on my cell phone and asked me to please stop it. He said that he almost lost his job and that he couldn't support the baby if he got fired, which was true. So I won't go back up there, but I'm going to fuck that receptionist bitch up.

Chapter Twenty-Four

Shonda

People were still talking about the whole Malik situation. Monique came up to the desk and told me that Desiree was in the back telling everyone that I was a hoe and that I was a home wrecker and I was getting what I deserved. No, she wasn't talking about me. She was just mad that I had Malik and she couldn't have him. I put the phone on standby. I got up from my desk and walked to the coffee room. I walked up to Desiree and asked her why was she back there running her mouth about shit she didn't know about.

"Desiree, did you have something you wanted to say to me?"

"If I had something that I wanted to say to you, I would have said it." Then she turned back around and took another sip of her coffee like I was not even there.

"Well, just to let you know, if you had something you wanted to get off your chest, don't say it behind my back. Step to me like a woman."

I was satisfied that I put her in her place. I got halfway out the door, when I heard the bitch mumble, "Like I said, your ass is getting played by Malik. Don't get mad at me because his woman was ready to take it to you."

I turned around. "What did you say, bitch?" I asked. I don't know what came over me but I mugged the shit out of that bitch. I made her neck snap. After that I felt like I damn near tried to kill that bitch. I punched her right in her mouth. How dare she tell me I'm getting played, and I'm a hoe? Bitches always want to be in your business. Her rumors were ridiculous. I felt like a fool instantly. Everyone came in the coffee room. Tonia called me in her office and asked me what happened. I explained that I went back and asked Desiree did she say that I was getting played by Malik.

Tonia made a call, stood up and said, "Shonda you know I like you. But this is business and I'm going to have to let you go. We can't have employees fighting each other."

"What about Desiree?"

"She's being sent home as well, but you are a temp, so I'm going to let you go permanently."

I went to my desk and emptied everything out. Tonia instructed me not to come back and that they would mail me my check. I had to be escorted out of the building by security. I can't believe I let another man fuck my situation up again. I guess I did let my heart play me. I mean, I still have Malik, but damn, I didn't have a job again.

All the drama of today, and can you believe Brian called me and asked me who my boyfriend was? I told him what did it matter to him. For the most part, I tried to keep Brianna and Malik apart. They rarely saw each other.

"Shonda, I don't want my daughter around all these different men."

"Don't tell me how to raise Bree, and I don't have her around 'all these different men.' When you start paying my bills then tell me how to live my life."

"Bree already told me how your boyfriend in Atlanta tried to kick in the door. You need to get your shit together, Shonda."

"Whatever, Brian. Again, live your life and I'll live mine."

Kim

Today I couldn't help but break down. It dawned on me that I was pregnant. I realized Malik was really gone. That me and my baby was over. It was scary. I wished I could go back to that night and take everything I said back. I looked at me and Malik's vacation photos last year. We looked so happy when we were in Miami on the beach. With Malik gone, it was still hard to sleep. I was used to having his warm body next to mine. Even if we weren't cuddled up, I would feel his leg against mine or something. I just could feel his presence. Not being with him or knowing where he is or what he is doing is driving me crazy. I asked myself, *did I drive him away, did I put too much pressure on him? Was it the baby, or me wanting to get married?* I know before this baby we were on the verge of breaking up, but I thought we were going to be able to work it out. When I cussed him out, I didn't want him to leave. I wanted him to get his act together. Now I think Malik hates and resents me. I called him a couple of times and he won't even return my calls. He didn't even call to check on me. I left a message for him saying to call me because I had an ultrasound appointment and I would like for him to be there.

Malik never called me back. I had to go to my doctor's appointment by myself. At first I was okay. I took off early from work. I was in the waiting room when a couple with a stroller walked in. The couple was smiling and the woman's stomach was round and firm like a basketball. They looked so happy. I smiled at them and continued to read my newspaper. I looked back over at the couple. The man played with their baby and they just looked like a happy family. Their happy family made me depressed. I got up and left the waiting room and went in the bathroom. I started to cry and cry some more; after a while I couldn't stop crying. I sat in the stall and wondered where I went wrong with Malik. I asked myself, *why didn't I have an abortion? Why didn't I make Malik marry me right away?* I tried to gain my composure, but my tears wouldn't stop coming. He promised me he would never leave me. He promised me, and now he was gone. I wiped my tears away and went back to the waiting room.

I saw my baby. It was a tiny little baby. The technician took all the measurements and tests that she needed. I asked her how did everything look. She said the baby looked healthy. My baby was healthy, that was good news. I was going to do this. I had to be strong for my daughter and my son. I have to get my kids somewhere to live. I decided I had to buy a house before my daughter got here and I had to be strong and I only have three months. It was time for me to get myself together instead of being the depressed miserable person that nobody wants to speak to. I can't be that person who only focuses on the negative, being mad and depressed about something. I had to be positive. Who would ever think I would be twenty-five with one son and another baby on the way; no husband and two baby fathers and unaccountable heartbreak. I did not see this coming at all. I stopped feeling sorry for myself and called the realtor.

Chapter Twenty-Five

Shonda

Surprisingly, Malik was not mad at me for stepping to Desiree. He was more upset that I didn't have a job and that Kim was cussing me out on the phone and came up to the office.

"I can't believe that Kim would act like this. Now we got to find you another job. We'll get the Sunday paper and we'll find you another job."

"Malik, it's no big deal, I'm cool. I'll find another job."

"I just wish none of this would've happened."

"Baby, it's okay, because punching Desiree's ass was priceless."

"Well, she got fired too! They called her at home and told her not to come back."

"That's good." I laughed.

I picked up my mail. I saw nothing out of the ordinary, bills, shut-off notices, and more bills. When I get my first unemployment check, I'm going to pay my bills. Malik has been a help to me, but he really doesn't have any money and I found out why. Can you believe him and that girl are broke up and he is still paying for her ring? I told him, if y'all not together then you're not for responsible for that ring. I need that money. I mean, if he's paying for the ring now, when the baby gets here, she's going to want money for that, too. She is not going to be dogging my man out. From what I know about her, she is a manipulator and selfish. I kept thinking about Malik for a moment until I saw a letter from Philadelphia Family Court. I opened the letter and it read that I was subpoenaed to court for a custody hearing. I couldn't believe Brian did this to me. Or at least he was trying to do this to me. He cannot have full custody. Bree will not live with him and his wife. I balled the letter up and called Bree's school. I advised her school that I was going through a custody battle and that she was not to be picked up by anybody but me. I then called Brian; he didn't answer his phone so I left him a message:

"Brian I don't know what kind of bullshit you're trying, but it will never work. You can't see your daughter at all, now that you tried to get custody. Sleep on that you dumb ass."

I tried to call Malik at work to tell him. He didn't answer. I got his voice mail. The phone rung as soon as I hung up on Malik's voice mail.

"Hello, Malik?" I asked.

"No, this is Brian."

"Brian, why would you try some dumb shit like this?"

"Shonda, you're not a responsible person. You move Brianna all over the world, you go out almost every night, leaving my child anywhere. My daughter told me you don't have a job. You deal with all these different men that beat on you. Now you got one living with you. My daughter needs stability, and you are not stable."

"What! Brian, you don't know what the fuck you're talking about and I don't get beat. I don't have to explain shit to you." I slammed the phone down. I called my dad and he said that I was grown and I could make my own decisions.

* * *

Malik took me and Bree out to Chinatown and we got Chinese food. We tried to talk in code about what Brian was attempting. I confessed to Malik that Bree might not even be Brian's.

"Malik, what are you doing?" A gray-haired woman asked, approaching our table. Malik turned around, startled, and said, "Mom."

"Who is this, Malik? Why did you leave Kim?"

"Mom, let me talk to you," Malik said as he excused himself from the table. Malik left out of the restaurant with his mother. When he returned, I asked him what happened. He told me his mom was getting on him for leaving Kim and for being with somebody else so soon. His mother was not even interested in meeting me.

Kim

Kianna called me and said that she was sorry. I said she was forgiven, but deep down I still wanted to kick her ass for calling me a miserable bitch. Maybe she was right, I think I am miserable without Malik. Lately I've been feeling like I was a fat pig and that nobody would ever want me. I am so depressed with Malik gone. I look so ugly. I hated the person I was becoming. I was the person you hate to talk to because all they do is complain about their job, kids, and man. It was time to get myself together, even though I was pregnant. I wanted to buy myself some new clothes and look like something. Back in the day when I was in high school, I used to keep myself up. I never wore the same outfit twice in a month. I even kept a calendar of what I wore so I would make sure I didn't have a repeat. I was really into my look then. Now my look is whatever I throw on and it is really a mess. I'm busting out of my clothes.

* * *

I made spaghetti. I broke the spaghetti noodles in half and tossed them in the boiling water. I poured a little salt in the water and stirred them so they wouldn't stick. My ground turkey was almost done. I seasoned the turkey with seasoning salt and put the lid on the top. I know Kevin should be tired of spaghetti. I make it at least once a week. All the other days, I either make fried chicken, or baked chicken. I'm always cooking some kind of chicken or spaghetti. When I get my house, I'm going to buy some cookbooks and take my time and cook some new, different kinds of food. Until then, we will eat spaghetti.

I called another realtor when I came in from lunch. She said that she could show me several houses on Saturday. I set up the appointment and told her I would meet her at the property.

She asked, "How is your credit?"

"My credit is excellent," I said with confidence. I gave her my social security number and information and said I would see her on Saturday. That was one of the things my mother instilled in me and that was to pay your credit cards on time. She said without credit you could not buy anything. Keep your credit good.

I had to see if my mom would watch Kevin so he wouldn't get in my way while I was looking around. Lisa, as usual, was on the phone arguing with her boyfriend. Nicole was reading the latest *Enquirer* with Whitney Houston on the cover. Nobody was doing their job. I stood up and said, "Okay ladies, listen. Our numbers are down for this month. I need y'all to get on the phone and make some calls for the rest of the afternoon." They both looked at me like, *You're slacking yourself. How can you tell us to do our job?*

Saturday came and I waited in front of the first house. The realtor was late. I called her on her cell phone and she said she was running a little behind and she would be there shortly. I was tired of waiting for her, so I got out of my car and began inspecting around the property myself. I peeked into the basement and around the back of the house. I saw slight cracks in the foundation. I would have to ask about that later. Then I was startled by the door opening. It was a petite old white woman.

"Hi. Our realtor said you're coming to see my house,"she said as she held her dog.

"Yes, I'm waiting for the realtor."

"Well, honey, you don't have to wait outside, come in."

"Okay." I came inside and the lady told me to have a seat.

"I'm Margaret Winner. I lived here for fifty years, me and my husband," she said as she pointed to a picture of her husband.

"My husband passed about fifteen years ago. I'm moving with my daughter to Florida."

"Really, that should be nice."

"You can look around."

"Thanks," I said as I stood up and inspected the dining room. The house was spacious, but everything was old as hell. She had green velvet wallpaper and an ancient green stove and refrigerator to match.

Someone was knocking on the door. It was the realtor Claire. The woman let her in.

"Sorry I'm late," she said as she took off her coat. "Shall we begin?"

I followed her upstairs. The house had three bedrooms. The master bedroom had lime green and blue flower wallpaper, and bright blue carpet. The second room had lime green carpet and the third had pumpkin pie carpet. If I bought this house I was definitely going to have a lot of work to do, mainly stripping all the carpet down. I fell in love with the bathroom. It was black and white, I could see that it would be easy to accessorize. Claire then showed me the basement, which was large and finished. And then the backyard. I had seen enough. I asked Claire, "How much is she looking for?"

"Her asking price is $65,000, but we can offer her $60,000."

"Well, I want to look around."

Claire showed me other houses in the neighborhood. The rest of the houses in the neighborhood were nice, but more expensive. I decided to go with the first house I saw. Claire made Ms. Winner an offer and she accepted.

I was on the line with a customer when I got a call from Claire.

"This is Kim Brown. How may I help you?"

"Hi, Kim, this is Claire."

"Yes?"

"Uhm, they're trying to get you approved for your loan. There is a problem with your Visa card. You've been late the last two months."

"No, that's impossible. I pay all my bills on time." Then I remembered my Visa. Malik was supposed to be paying for my ring.

"Claire, let me call you back, okay?"

I called Malik and asked, "Malik, why haven't you been paying on the Visa card?"

"I have been making the payments."

"Well, you haven't been paying on it properly. If you're not going to pay for it let me know. I'm trying to buy a house," I said as hung up on him. I called my credit card company and gave them a check by phone, to bring my account up to date. I called Claire back. She said that one thing may prevent me from getting my house.

One thing after another was going wrong. Today I got the news that Lisa had finally found another job and then corporate said that our bonuses were stopping until further notice. So that meant my paycheck was getting cut almost in half. Just what I needed, when I was about to buy a house and have a baby.

Chapter Twenty-Six

Shonda

I never thought finding a job would be so hard. One job I called was only paying $7.00 an hour and another wanted me to go to training in Pittsburgh for three weeks. Just for a customer service position. My unemployment was denied, so I had to find a job and quick. I highlighted and circled jobs in the paper. I was in the A section of the paper when I saw an ad for automotive sales. The ad read, *make five hundred dollars per week, company car and benefits*. I called the dealership and set up an interview.

I went to the Lincoln Ford dealer. There were hundreds of shiny new cars lined up. The lot was huge. As soon as I got on the lot, a guy walked up to me trying to sell me a car. I parked and told him I wasn't here for a car. I was there to meet Tony Mancinni. He pointed in the direction of the office. I went to the receptionist's desk and asked for Tony Mancinni again. She told me to have a seat. Once I had a seat, a young guy with a Caribbean accent approached me and asked me could he help me. I told him no. After he knew I wasn't interested in a car, he asked me for my phone number and said he'd like to take me out. I said no to both, then he walked away. Soon a heavy-set white guy with a couple of stomachs came over to me and introduced himself as Tony Mancinni. He asked me if I had ever sold anything. I told him no. He then asked, what made me think I could sell a car. I told him because I was a woman and people would trust me because I was not intimidating. He must have liked my answer because he said, "You're aggressive, that's what I like. When can you start?" he asked.

"Today," I answered.

"I'll see you tomorrow."

Selling cars was not as easy as I thought. As a matter of fact, it was hard. I thought this job was going to be sweet. And I would get a company car immediately. In order to get your company car, you had to be there sixty days. I guess my car would have to hold up until then. Another thing I didn't like about the job was the long hours. If I wanted to impress my boss and sell a car, I had to wait around nine to nine. So I had to ask Tae to pick up Bree. Some nights she even spent the night. I was ready to quit. I could not sell a car to save my life and it had been almost two weeks. The men that worked there laughed at me. None of them had mercy on me. They were all ruthless, they sold cars by any means necessary. Tony Mancinni pulled me to the side one day at work and said, "Shonda I want you to follow Lester today. I want you to see what he does and listen to how he approaches customers."

"Okay," I said, as I looked over at Lester. I couldn't imagine what he could teach me. Lester looked like a drunk. He had a salt and pepper mustache, cheap plastic, brown shoes with a white shirt and black slacks. He was supposed to train me? Great, I get to smell the lovely smell of alcohol all day. Mr. Mancinni called Lester over to us. "I want you to train Shonda."

Lester looked over at me and said that I was about to be trained by the best and for me to get a pen. "If you listen to me. You can make a lot of money."

Whatever, I thought.

He waved his hand for me to come over and take a seat. I sat down and he told me to "Write these five rules down. 1. Meet and greet, 2. Land them on a car, 3. Take a test drive, 4. Show them the safety features, 5. Close the deal." After he finished explaining each rule, he saw a couple entering the showroom doors. He went to approach the pair, and I walked behind him.

"Good afternoon, how's everybody doing today? My name is Lester. Welcome to Mancinni Ford." The couple said good afternoon back.

"What kind of car did you come to buy today?" Lester asked. The man said he didn't know.

"Well that's what I am here for; let me show you a few cars."

"Okay," the husband said, as they followed Lester out of the door. As they walked up to a Ford Expedition, Lester asked the husband was his wife, his daughter. The woman blushed and said, "Oh no, I'm his wife."

"Really, you look so young," Lester said. I was now witnessing Lester's game in action. We all got in the Expedition and took a test drive. During the ride Lester noticed the husband's Yankee hat. "They had a great season, didn't they?" he asked. The man agreed and they discussed sports the rest of the ride.

After the test drive, Lester showed them the safety features and said how he had just bought his wife the same truck. I knew that was a lie, because Lester was not married, but his game was working. After a hour of being fake and telling stories Lester had them in a brand new car.

Then I saw this young couple walking toward the dealership. Nobody else saw them. I knew if they were walking, they needed a car.

"Hi, I'm Shonda. Welcome to Mancinni Lincoln Ford. How can I help you?"

"I need a car," the man said.

"Okay, what do you want your monthly payments to be?" I asked him. For some reason, everybody's favorite payment was either two hundred or two hundred and fifty. This guy said five hundred. I showed him this Ford Explorer. Modeled it, showing him all the safety features, tires, trunk, and then asked him if he wanted to take a test drive. He said yes and we pulled off and almost hit a truck. I turned around to his wife and said, "Is the baby all right?"

She said that she wasn't pregnant.

Well she looked like she was six months pregnant, so then I tried to clean up my error by saying, "well, some of us have a gut after we have a baby."

Then she said, "I don't have any kids."

Okay, I knew they weren't going to buy a car from me. I had put my foot in my mouth twice. We turned back into the lot. I didn't even say anything. They got out of the truck, looked it over, and said they needed a few minutes to talk. I waited by the stairway to the dealership. They began walking toward the steps and said, "We'll take it."

I wanted to jump up and down, but I said, okay, very confident like. I brought them in the building, filled out the paperwork, and sold them a car. I felt real good about myself. They rode off in their new car.

After the first time selling a car, it got easier. I sold four cars the next week. When I got my paycheck it was twelve hundred dollars. *I could get used to this*, I thought. I was working hard but I missed my daughter.

Kim

I was so worried I wouldn't get approved for my house but Claire called me and said that everything looked good and I just needed to sign a statement about my Visa credit card and I should be looking at a closing date of November 15, 2002. I was happy about the news, because the baby was due December 30, 2002. I would be able to move in and set everything up before she got here.

The day of closing I was nervous. I thought for some reason something was going to go wrong. I went to the bank and got a cashier's check. I picked up my mother because she wanted to go with me, and waited at the realtor's office. The whole process took less than forty-five minutes. I signed on the dotted line fifty times and Claire handed me my keys and said, "Congratulations." The lady Margaret Winner had tears in her eyes and told me she hoped the house would make me as happy as it made her for the last fifty years.

I paid for a professional moving service to come and move everything. I thought moving was not a big deal, but it was a big deal. The only time I had ever moved before was when I moved out when Kevin was a baby. We didn't really have anything to move, just a crib and a bedroom set. Now my whole apartment was filled with furniture. I knew I had come so far. But I was still so down, because I always imagined me and Malik moving into our first house, not me alone.

The movers charged me eight hundred dollars. That was a lot of money, but I didn't have a choice. I couldn't lift anything, neither could my mother, and Karen wouldn't. They did come and help with the little stuff. Karen told me she was really proud of me and wanted the number to my realtor. She said I inspired her to get a house and she was tired of living in an apartment, throwing her money away each month.

I had a house but I was really broke. I had never been this broke ever in my life. I didn't want to ask my mom or Karen for anything. After all our boxes were moved in, and everyone left, it was just Kevin and me. I made up the mattress, and we slept on the floor. Lonnie was coming over the next day to put up the beds.

Lonnie and Ryan arrived bright and early to put my beds up for me. I asked him if they wanted anything to eat; he said they had already eaten and they were fine. Lonnie walked around the house and admired it.

"This is really nice, Kim."

"Thank you."

"I see why Karen came home last night saying she wanted a house. This house has so much potential."

"I know, I just want to rip up the carpet, and paint."

"Well, while you got me here, why don't you use me?" Lonnie got the boys and had them thinking they were his little helpers. They pulled up all the carpet in the house. To my surprise there was hardwood floor in perfect condition underneath. They rolled the carpet out into the backyard. After seeing how little effort it took to change a house, I decided I was going to go to Home Depot and buy paint. I wanted my daughter's room pink and Kevin's room blue and off-white for my room. Lonnie said he would paint for me, too.

Lonnie and Ryan came over the next day and painted. I was happy he was being so helpful. I tried to pay him but he told me not to insult him. Even though Lonnie wasted a lot of money on studio time, he was still a good father to Ryan and a somewhat good husband to Karen. One thing is for sure, he never left Karen on her own, and was still hanging in strong after nine years.

I let Kevin and Ryan run freely through the house and play in the back. Then Kevin ran in and said there was a big dog in the yard.

"Did you close the door?" I asked. Kevin said he did and I went to the door to make sure it was locked and saw the neighbor smiling with this hefty black dog the size of a horse.

She waved and said, "He doesn't bite. Tell them don't be scared." I hate when people have big dogs and tell you "He doesn't bite." I wasn't buying that "he doesn't bite" bull. I made Kevin and Ryan come in the house for the rest of the day.

* * *

My mom had invited me and Kevin to dinner. She said she was cooking fried fish and crabcakes. She knew I was getting big and tired of cooking. She told me I needed to slow down and rest. She said I was doing too much and my baby was going to come out running. I took her up on her offer to cook dinner for Kevin and me. She was right, but there were so many things I wanted to do, I couldn't rest.

I came in the house and all I heard was, "Surprise!" I looked around and saw so many people, I broke into tears.

"Don't cry, baby," somebody said as I entered the house. Pink and blue streamers were hanging along the ceiling. I stopped crying and asked whose idea it was.

"Mine," Kianna said as she helped me take off my coat.

"Have a seat," my mom said as she came over and sat me down on a chair that was decorated with baby everything, streamers, rattles, bottles, and bows all in pink, white, and blue. My mom then gave me a kiss on my cheek and asked me if was I surprised.

"Yes, I am," I said as almost everyone came over to say hello. My mother, friends, some of the neighbors off the block, even Nicole and Lisa were there. I couldn't believe it. My biggest shock was seeing Stephanie. She introduced me and Malik. I should kill her.

"Oh, my God, what are you doing here?"

"Your mom invited me." I hadn't seen or heard from Stephanie in more than a year, since changing jobs. I got up and gave her a hug.

"Look at your little stomach. I know Malik is so happy."

"Um-hmm," I said.

"You got to give me your number before you leave."

"I will."

Everyone came over and congratulated me and rubbed my belly. I made myself a plate and ate. My mom had made tuna macaroni salad, seafood salad, fried chicken, barbecued chicken, macaroni and cheese, and pies and cake. She had really outdone herself. I opened all my gifts. I received so many things, I knew I wouldn't be able to take all of them home. I got two strollers, three high chairs, a bassinet, clothes, Pampers, bouncers, walkers, tubs, car seats, and baby lotion and powder. Kianna had bought the baby a washed white wood crib and dresser. Now all I needed was to get my milk and get another case of Pampers and I would be set. I thanked everyone and then we played silly baby games. Everything was going so great until it was time to cut the cake. I read the writing on the cake and it said *Congratulations Malik and Kim on your new little bundle of joy.*

My mother does a lot of things to save face. And she was definitely trying to save face. I don't know why she wrote that, she knew Malik was not coming.

After I cut a few slices of cake, I pulled my mother to the side and asked why she had put that on the cake. She told me she spoke to Malik yesterday and he said he was coming. I was upset at my mom for interfering but I was also shocked that Malik was actually coming. This I had to see.

Malik showed up right on time. Everyone was ready to leave as he came in. All the women came up to congratulate him and he thanked everyone. Malik put on a great show for everyone. Malik loaded everything that could fit into my car. I rolled my eyes, left, and didn't even bother to say thank you.

I wrote out thank you cards and sent them out. I went to Babies 'R' Us and picked up last-minute things I didn't get at my shower; like onesies and undershirts. I picked up some Dreft detergent and diaper wipes. I bought two cases of Pampers because they were on sale. I was trying not to go to the market every week to run and get Pampers like I did with Kevin.

Chapter Twenty-Seven

Shonda

I had to take a day off from work to go to the custody hearing. The day of court I almost passed out. The thought of actually losing my daughter to Brian made me cringe. I entered the court building on 34 S.11th Street. I walked through a metal detector and showed my subpoena. The guards directed me to the elevator. I took the elevator up to the third floor. I signed in and I was told to have a seat until my case was called. I read the newspaper while I waited. Brian walked in a few minutes after me. He was accompanied by a young black woman, nicely suited. I rolled my eyes and looked down at my paper. The young woman opened her briefcase and pulled out documents and eyeglasses. She put her glasses on and began going over them with Brian. That's when I knew I was in trouble. The young woman was Brian's attorney. I should have listened to Malik when he told me to get an attorney. I thought Brian was too dumb to have one, someone must have got in his ear. I nervously waited about half an hour for them to call me. My hands were sweating and my stomach was bubbling. They called our names and I walked into the tiny courtroom.

As soon as the proceeding began, Brian's attorney assaulted my character. She portrayed me as an unfit mother. Brian lied on me and said that I was on drugs and had domestic issues with all the men in my life. I wanted to get up and smack the shit out of him. She also said that Brian was a police officer and had an immaculate record on the force. The judge asked if he had any documentation to support those accusations. They didn't. I had to represent myself. I told the judge the truth, that we had been sharing custody since I returned from Atlanta in May and that Brian was upset because I was in a new relationship and he didn't feel like my daughter should be around my boyfriend. I told the judge I was not on drugs and did not have a domestic violence history. I also let the judge know that Brian may not even be the father. I felt confident with everything I said when Brian's attorney presented my restraint order from Atlanta. She also had records from Bree's after-school program with a three-month record of pickups that showed who signed Bree in and out. Out of seventy-five times, my name was on the list only twenty times. Then his lawyer presented something that stunned even me. She had a paternity documentation with my name on it that proved 99.9 percent that Brianna was Brian's. I told the judge that the form was a fraud and the signature on the form was not mine. For a moment I thought that Brian was getting custody of my child. I thought it was over with all the information that Brian's lawyer submitted, but in the end, the judge didn't care that Brian was a cop or that I moved Brainna twice in the last year. She knew I had a job and I wasn't on drugs. She also knew that I had custody of Brianna since we broke up. She denied Brian full custody and gave him partial custody pending another paternity test. Brian's day to have visits with Bree were Sunday, Monday, Tuesday. I would have Bree on Wednesday, Thursday, Friday, and Saturday. Brian also had to pay me child support of one hundred thirty-five per week.

It was definitely a victory. The next paternity test proved that Brian was Bree's father. I'm just glad this whole custody battle is over, because it was draining me. I know one thing though, I was recommitted to my daughter and was not going to ever let anything come before our relationship. My twenty-fifth birthday was in a couple of days. I did a lot of soul searching. I had no clue what I wanted to do. I know I was definitely treating myself to the hairdresser and go out to dinner with Malik.

Kim

I was packing my bag for the hospital. All the magazines I read said you should have your bags packed by your eighth month. I couldn't believe my due date was really approaching. I had almost one month to go and my body would be mine again. I cannot wait to be able to lie on my stomach and stretch out comfortably.

Stephanie called while I was packing my bags. We said our hellos and I asked her where she saw my mom.

"You know I ran into your mom at my job."

"Where are you working now, Stephanie?"

"At Macy's."

"Macy's?"

"I'm between jobs. I was in Columbia, South Carolina, working at this radio station, but that didn't work out."

"Well, we have a position opening up at my job."

"Really?"

"You know I'll give you the interview, and I'm in charge of hiring and firing."

"So what's Malik been up to and how is Jarrod?"

"Girl, Malik left me."

"What!"

"Well, I kind of kicked him out. But he wanted to leave. Actually, I think he's staying with Jarrod again. He's messing with this fat-ass receptionist from his job."

"You serious. How long have you all been broke up?"

"Almost three months."

"Oh, my God, girl, I know it's hard."

"It was, but you know, I say fuck Malik. I've been through worse and if he thinks it's somebody better than me, then go out and be with that."

"Keep in touch, I'll take you to lunch or something."

"Yeah, girl, and you got to come and see my house."

"Stay strong."

"I will."

"And you got to let me be your baby's godmother. What are you having, anyway?'

"A little girl."

"Give me your address. I'll stop by sometime this week and we can set a date for the interview."

Kevin kept asking me all week, could this little boy named Brandon come over after school and spend the night. I told him to wait until Friday. I hoped he would forget, but he didn't. After school, Kevin had the little boy Brandon and his mother waiting for me.

"Hi," I said to them both.

"Hi, I'm Claudette," Brandon's mom said.

"Is your son spending the night at my house?"

"Well, yes, that's what he told me. They said you were going to take the boys to the movies."

"I didn't say that, but I can rent them a movie and bring him home later this evening."

"So he's not going to spend the night?" she asked. First off, she must be trying to get to the bar. Because what mom would allow their child to spend the night over someone's house they do not know.

"No, he can't spend the night. I have a lot of running around to do. But he can come over for a little while. I'll bring him home around eight."

The boys got in the car. I told Brandon's mother I would see her at eight. I told the boys to put on their seat belts and I drove to Wendy's. I ordered chicken nuggets and fries for them and grilled chicken for myself. Then I took them to Blockbuster and let them pick out two movies.

When we came in the house they ate, then went upstairs and watched the movies. I sat downstairs and relaxed. It was the first time all week I had a chance to take it easy. After I ate my sandwich, heartburn started to kick in. My throat felt like there was a lit match in it. I went to get some Tums out of the medicine cabinet. I went in to the kitchen and got a glass of water. Then I felt a little pain on the side of my stomach and water trickling down my legs. I knew what that meant. I was ready to go into labor, but I was only thirty-six and a half weeks. I told the kids to come on and turn the movie off and let's go. We all got in the car and I asked the little boy Brandon where did he live? He said, "I live on Chelsea Street."

"What is your address?"

"I don't know."

The I asked him "What's your phone number?" Once again he said that he didn't know. I knew I had to get to the hospital, but I had to take this little boy home first. I decided that I would just drive to my mom's house and let them stay there and get in touch with his mom later. I was about to get on the expressway when he said, "That's my block right there," as he pointed to the block.

I made a quick right turn and asked, "Which house do you live in?" I asked as we drove slowly down the block.

"The green and white house."

I beeped the horn and his mother came to the door.

"You're back early."

"I'm going into labor."

"Really. You shouldn't be driving. Pull over and I'll take you."

"That's okay. Can you watch Kevin for me?" I thought about what I asked her for a minute. I glimpsed over at her house; from the outside it looked okay.

"Sure," she said as she took the boys out of the car.

"I'll send my sister for him." I got another sharper pain and asked her if she could write her address and phone number down. She did and I sped off.

The hospital was only, like, fifteen blocks away so I didn't want to wait for an ambulance. I got caught at a red light and got the biggest crippling pain in my life. It was like a Mack truck slammed into my side and back. I pulled over, called Malik and his voice mail came on. Then I called my mom. She said she would meet me at the hospital and for me to hang up and get to the hospital.

I ran red lights trying to get the hospital. I wished a cop would stop me. Maybe he could help me get to the hospital faster. My contractions were coming pretty frequently. I took deep breaths and kept driving. I pulled up in front of the emergency room entrance of the hospital. I got out of the car and waddled to the nurses' station on the labor floor. "I'm having my baby," I told the nurse. She ran from behind her station and got me a wheelchair. The nurse asked me my name and who my doctor was, while she pushed me to an examination room. The nurse helped me get on the bed, undress, and put on a gown. Immediately doctors ran in and examined me. They hooked me up to an oxygen mask, I.V., and my stomach up to a heart monitor. A doctor informed me I was at six centimeters and that my baby would be arriving in the next few hours. The doctor asked me would I been getting an epidural for pain. I definitely needed something for my pain. I shook my head yes. They gave me a form to sign, I was almost out of it. The anesthesiologist stuck me in my back with a big, long needle.

My mother ran in the room, grabbed my hand and asked was I okay. I told her I was fine and that I needed her to move my car. She said okay and brushed my hair off of my face. "Where are your keys?" she asked.

"In my pocketbook."

"Do you want me to call Malik?"

"No, mom, don't call him. I called him already. Call his mother," I said.

An hour and a half went past and Malik and his mother still didn't show up.

My mother spoke with Malik's mother. She said she was on her way and that she would try to get in touch with Malik.

Malik didn't show up at the hospital. My mom was in the window sobbing, trying not to let me see her cry.

"Mom, are you all right?" I asked through the oxygen mask.

"I'm fine," she said as she shook her head.

"Are you sure?" I asked my mother. I knew she was not okay. I knew she was thinking of when I had Kevin. *I* was thinking about when I had Kevin.

"I told you not to stay with that no good ass nigga more than one year if he didn't marry you, Kim. Now you're about to have two kids and two different fathers and you're still not married."

"Mom, do I really need to hear this right now? I'm in pain. I can't make Malik be here and do whatever I say." As soon as I got the last word out of my mouth an excruciating pain hit my side and back. A nurse ran into the room and said that my baby's heartbeat was decreasing and I needed to calm down.

"Sit back," the nurse demanded.

"I have to go the bathroom," I said.

"Sit down," she said, again.

"I have to get up."

"Please, sit back, your baby is coming. You feel the pressure of the baby's head."

My mother walked over to the bed and grabbed my hand. "I'm sorry Kim. I didn't mean what I said. I just want the best for you."

I knew my mother meant well, but I didn't have the time to pay her any attention because I was in so much pain. I wanted to get this baby out. Malik was supposed to be here. He was supposed to be here. I was in all this pain by myself. All I heard was the doctors and nurse screaming, "Push!"

I was grunting, pushing, breathing, and screaming all the while I yelled for them to get this baby out of me. I couldn't believe I was going through this shit again, without the father of my child. He was supposed to be here holding my hand. My mother called his cell phone again and he still didn't answer. Karen and Kianna made it to the hospital. Kevin was with Ryan and Lonnie—they picked him up for me. My mother was still crying, trying to hide her tears. I couldn't concentrate on her, I had to concentrate on me.

"Push, push!" the doctor and nurse yelled.

"I'm pushing!" I screamed.

"One, two, push!"

I was sweating and pushing and sweating some more. Finally, the doctor said, "Here it comes." They pulled the baby out. I heard a cry. I looked over to my baby. I saw something dangling from my baby. At first I thought it was the umbilical cord, but it wasn't, it was a penis. I had another son. They cleaned him off and wrapped him up. As soon as I looked at him my first thought was, he looks just like Malik. Most babies don't look like anyone. But my son looked just like Malik. My second thought was, what am I going to do with a pink room?

I left another message for him. "Malik, this is Kim. You have a son. You weren't here to see his birth. You could at least come and see him."

Chapter Twenty-Eight

Shonda

Do you have days you just want to kill somebody? Today, on my birthday, was that day.

I went to the hairdresser Tae told me about. First of all, I made an appointment with this stylist three weeks ago and once I arrived at the hair salon they told me she had an emergency, and had to leave. But that this other chick named Shay something could do it fine. I mean anybody can do a wash and curl, right?

Any licensed stylist couldn't fuck up a wash and curl. At least that's what I thought. I would have looked better if I let my Aunt Grace who's ninety-six do my hair. It was horrible. I almost wanted to cry. I showed this bitch a picture and she still fucked it up. She said I needed my ends trimmed and cut off about four inches of my hair. She had me looking a mess. I didn't even want to pay her, but I did reluctantly. My birthday was becoming more and more fucked up by the minute.

Huh, I had to go home and recurl it myself and tied it down with a scarf so I wouldn't look like a big puffball. Malik met me at my house and said it didn't look that bad. I wanted to smack him. Then he turned around with tears in his eyes and said some bullshit on my birthday, that he had to go because the baby was born. I said, "Malik, why are you crying?"

"My son was just born and I wasn't there. I got to go to the hospital."

I was in shock. I wanted to say, *Malik, what about me? What about our plans? It's my birthday.* Instead I said, "Malik we can celebrate my birthday anytime, go be with your son."

He got his jacket, gave me a kiss, and said he would be right back. As soon as he left, I called up Tae.

"Tae, girl, that baby was born."

"Really, what she have?"

"A fucking boy."

"Um, that's deep. I thought she was having a girl."

"That's what Malik told me."

"You know a son is different from a daughter. Right?"

"I don't know about all that, but I do know Malik was in here crying because he wasn't there when his son was born."

"Ah, that's a shame he missed his baby being born."

"What's a shame about it? The baby won't remember that he wasn't there. If he would've been there, he would've been comforting her not the baby."

"You're right. So what are you going to do?"

"I don't know, but I'm going to call you back," I told Tae. I shouldn't have to spend my twenty-fifth birthday alone because he wants to rush down to the hospital. It's bad enough this bitch fucked my hair up. *Spent all my money for what?* I thought as I looked into the mirror.

Kim

Malik's sorry ass finally showed up. He gave me a kiss on the cheek. I wiped it off. He said hello to my mother, she shook her head and sat in the chair next to me.

"Malik, where the hell were you when my baby was having your baby?"

"I didn't know she was in labor. My phone was dead," he said as he turned to me and said, "Where's my son, Kim?"

"In the nursery."

"Can you have them bring him in?"

"I don't feel like it."

"Kim, I want to see my son."

"Well you should've been here about an hour ago when he was born if it really was that important to you."

My mother stared Malik down. Then Malik walked to the nursery. I could get out of the bed, but my mom went to the door. I could hear Malik ask the nurse to bring in the baby boy Moore.

When the nurse brought in the baby Malik fell in love. He said, "Look at my boy, you look just like me. I love you."

"What did you name him?" Malik asked as he turned to me.

"I haven't decided yet."

"Are you going to name him after me?"

"I don't know Malik. I'm tired, I just had a baby," I said as I went to walk in the bathroom. My mom and him had words while I was in the bathroom. When I came out he was sitting in the windowsill with the baby. His mother Ms. Gloria and sister Nadia showed up.

"You made it huh?" Ms. Gloria said as she opened her arms to grab the baby. "Hold up, let me wash my hands first," she said as she went into the bathroom. "So how'd it go, son?"

"Malik just got here," my mother said. His mother looked at him in disgust, then she washed her hands. My mother said she was going to get something to drink and left the room. Malik stayed with the baby for about three hours. His sister and mom left. His mother told me before she left that she would get the baby some clothes.

* * *

Six o'clock in the morning they brought the baby into the room so that I could feed him. The nurse asked me had I decided whether or not I was going to breast-feed. I knew it was the healthiest decision, but who had the time? I knew my body would go back right into shape if I did it, but also, I didn't want my chest leaking. I had to return to work and I don't think it would be right to start the baby and stop the breast-feeding within six weeks. My paid leave was only six weeks and after that I was on my own. If Malik was a real man, I wouldn't have to rush back to work, but since he's not, I do.

Chapter Twenty-Nine

Shonda

When Malik came in from the hospital, I didn't know what to say to him. I had been waiting on the sofa for him.

"How is your son?" I asked.

"He's fine. I'm sorry I ruined your birthday."

"It's okay, baby, your son is more important."

"My son looks just like me, Shonda. He's a handsome little boy. I don't deserve him. I'm a deadbeat already," he said as he sat down and put his head on my lap.

"You're not a deadbeat. You didn't know he was coming today," I said as I stroked Malik's face to comfort him.

"You're right, I didn't know, but I still should've been there."

"You'll be there for everything else. Malik, maybe you can start getting him."

"I don't think Kim will go for that. She barely let me hold him today. Maybe she'll change when he gets a little older. I don't know."

The rest of the night I tried to assure Malik that this situation was going to be temporary. I tried my best to comfort him. I even offered to take him to dinner, but he preferred for us stay in the house. Nothing I could say was going to ease his mind. I rubbed his shoulders and temples. We watched *Law and Order* and laid on one another the rest of the night.

Kim

My mother drove me home from the hospital. Before we left, I had to choose a name for my son. I named him after his dad. She didn't agree or think he deserved that honor, but he looked just like him and I couldn't take that away from him.

Kevin was so excited to see his little brother. I was exhausted. My body was aching. My breasts were like a 44 DDD and they hurt like hell. Karen came over to help me. I couldn't even take a shower. Even the water touching my breasts hurt. I slept the rest of the afternoon. The phone kept waking me up, friends and family were calling to see how I was doing. Karen told everyone I was resting. Karen put Kevin to bed and cooked me dinner. When they left, I was all alone, just me and my boys. I couldn't believe I had another baby. Kevin was five, almost six, and here I was doing this all over again, by myself.

Little Malik woke up at least five times a night. He liked to cry. He was driving me crazy. It was just me, all by myself, getting up and feeding him. I still wasn't used to my house and I was scared to go downstairs and make bottles.

Chapter Thirty

Shonda

The next day I got up and couldn't sell a car to save my life. I had too much on my mind. I kept thinking about Malik and his situation with the baby. I wished I could talk to Kim woman to woman. I wanted to go over to her house and say, "Listen honey," on some Jill Scott shit. "He was your man but he's mine now. What y'all had was good, but you getting in the way of how I'm feeling." That would be the bomb. She had Malik's baby, but I had his heart and I was not letting it go. It had been a week since that baby was born and she wouldn't let him see him. Making my man depressed was putting a damper on our relationship. He was really upset about not being in his son's life and I couldn't take him being depressed.

"Robinson," I heard my name being called by the manager.

"Here I come,"I said, turning around, letting him I know I acknowledged him. "Yeah, what's up?"

"What are you doing?"

"Nothing."

"You going to sell some cars today?"

"Yeah."

"Sell me two today and you can go home."

"That's a deal."

"You won't sell two cars today. It's too slow. But I do need you to sell at least three cars before the end of the month. All right?"

"Sure."

"And stop daydreaming out the window before I start treating you like a woman again. And you don't want that. You know women get the coffee and cream," he said with an ignorant, yellow-stained-teeth-from-smoking laugh.

Whatever, I thought. I got bigger and better things to do than walking up to complete strangers and introducing myself and conning them into paying $600 a month for a car. Unless they look like they're real sweet targets, like the old man walking through the showroom doors.

"Well, hello, handsome, how are you?" I said as I put my hand out for the older man to shake. I continued with, "I'm Shonda, welcome to Lincoln Ford. What car can I put you into today?"

"Hm," I continued, looking the old man up and down. "I think you'll look good in a Lincoln Continental with a soft leather interior and a CD changer. Yeah, you look like an Al Green man, your wife, she's into Frankie Beverly." This guy was following me out of the showroom like a puppy.

Within an hour I had that man signed to a three-year lease without his wife's consent and driving down the street. It couldn't have been easier.

Right after Mr. Sweet-as-Candy left, a hippie white couple came strolling in. I had the perfect sell for them. These people kill me, going on the Internet thinking they're doing research, taking measurements and all that shit, just to buy a car. For what they know, they need a minivan for all of your kids from your second and first marriages. I sold them a Ford Windstar, red, 35,000 miles on it. I sold them on safety and economy, needless to say, in less than three hours. Shonda made herself $1,100 in commission and had her manager on her, well, you know he was all up on me. And I was walking out the door going home early because I had sold two cars.

Kim

Little Malik was one week old and I forgot how hard it was to have a baby. I love little Malik, but whoa, someone should have reminded me about the nighttime feedings, Pampers, and the crying. My baby is going to grow up and become a singer because his little lungs put out the loudest cries. He wants to be held all the time. I can't even put him in his bouncing chair without his little butt crying. Even the happy big brother Kevin told me to make that baby shut up. I wish Malik was here to pull some of this weight, but he's not and I have to learn to deal with it. He's been calling me, but I don't want him to know where I live, so I don't answer his calls. He can see Malik when Malik is four and he can tell me where Malik took him and what happened. Until then, I'll send him a picture.

Chapter Thirty-One

Shonda

Malik is still "down in the dumps" about his son. That bitch Kim won't let him see his son. I understand that she doesn't like me, and she's probably hurt, but she shouldn't be taking it out on Malik just because he doesn't want her. Malik was acting like a bitch, he needs to grow some balls. Malik asked me to go to the mall with him. I agreed reluctantly and rode to the King of Prussia mall with him. I thought he was getting something for me, but he said he wanted to pick up some things for the baby.

I picked out little Malik's clothes. The Gap had so many adorable denim outfits and shoes that match. The little girls' clothes were better, but the boys' stuff was nice. After the Gap, we went into a few other stores. I was calculating how much Malik had spent so far and I was up to about four hundred.

"Baby, what else do you think he needs?" Malik asked me.

"I don't know, when was the last time I had a baby?" I said, as I shrugged my shoulders.

"I mean, you're a woman so I thought you would know."

"Call her and ask her." That's when Malik said she still wasn't talking to him. I told him he would have to go to court and get some papers filed for joint custody, and to drop the stuff off at her mother's and keep all his receipts for when he goes to court.

"Shonda, you know I know about the custody stuff and law. I'm not trying to go there and have the courts tell me how to handle my affairs with my son."

"I feel you Malik, but this is not making any sense." Already, I didn't like the way this bitch was pulling along my man.

Kim

"Kim, how are my boys doing?" my mother asked.

"They're okay."

"How are you doing?"

"Fine, a little tired."

"Well, baby, maybe I'll try to get them this weekend."

"Thanks, Mom."

"I called you to tell you that Malik left a few packages here for the baby. He asked me for your address."

"I don't care, I don't need him."

"You do need him and, well, he's sitting here in the living room. I'll put him on the phone."

"What do you want Malik?" I asked. At first I didn't hear anything. Then Malik stuttered, "Yeah, Kim, can I see my son? I bought him some stuff."

"No, Malik, you can't. He doesn't need you." I hung up the phone.

My mother called me right back and was whispering at me in a hard voice, "Kim, you let that man see his child. Whatever happened between him and you is just that. Between him and you. You are never supposed to deny a man the chance to be around his child. Kevin doesn't have his father. I don't like what Malik's done, but at least he's trying."

"Mom, I hate him."

"Kim, don't use your child as a pawn. You and Malik are over; let him have a relationship with his child. I'm giving him your address."

"Mom, don't." She hung up on me. I guess my mom was right. If Malik wanted to be a part of little Malik's life, I shouldn't try to stop him. I should use it to my advantage.

Malik knocked on my door. He had cases of Pampers and Carnation Good Start milk, and about six bags from Macy's, Baby Gap, and The Children's Place. I still was not impressed. I left the door open and Malik walked in. I went upstairs and got the baby and brought him downstairs. Malik had a seat on the sofa and reached out for my son. I told him to go wash his hands. He got up off the sofa and walked into my kitchen.

"This is a nice place, Kim."

"Thank you," I said as Malik came back in the living room, drying his hands off with the towel. He placed the towel on the table and took Malik from me.

He said, "What's up, son. How you been, Daddy missed you."

I left them alone and went and made a bottle. I heard Kevin run downstairs. When he saw Malik, the first thing he said was, "Malik, where have you been. I missed you. I didn't have anyone to play basketball with."

"I missed you too, Kevin."

I heard Malik ask Kevin if he had been practicing. While they talked I stayed in the kitchen and listened. I came out of the kitchen and grabbed the camera and took a picture of Malik, Kevin, and little Malik.

When it was time for Malik to leave, Kevin started crying. Malik told me he would call him tomorrow and told me if I needed anything to call him.

The next day Malik called me and asked me could he come and get Malik. I told him no. He asked for Sunday and I said no. Then I finally told him he could only see the baby at my house until he gets a little older. He said that he would be over Saturday afternoon.

Chapter Thirty-Two

Shonda

I hate the fact that Malik's with me but all that bitch Kim got to do is call and say the baby needs something and he's gone. The baby needs Pampers, the baby needs milk, blah, blah. I knew I wasn't going through this bullshit with him for the next eighteen years. That bitch Kim knew Malik loved his son and was taking advantage. She was a stupid hoe. And to tell you the truth, little Malik didn't even really look like him. Well, I'm lying—yes, he did. Malik showed me a picture and he looked like a spitting image of him. Malik still was broke all the time and once again, I found out why. He was still paying for that bitch's ring, even after I told him not to. I confronted him about it and he explained to me that she was trying to buy a house and he couldn't mess up her credit. The way I feel about it is she charged it on her credit card, so let her pay for it. Anyway, I told him to put his foot down. She would only let Malik see the baby at her house. She said the baby is too young to be traveling. I know she just didn't want me to be around her child. But I got news for her, I don't want to be around her child. I don't like babies because they cry, you have to change their Pampers and hold them all day. Malik was starting to spend a lot of time with little Malik and neglecting me. Ever since Kim has started letting him see the baby, he has not taken me anywhere. I didn't feel I should have to compete with a little baby. I understand that little Malik is a part of his life but he has to find a balance. I'm not jealous, but right now I don't feel secure.

Kim

Every time Malik cries, Malik jumps up. He's been here every day visiting his son. He stayed all day today playing with Kevin and little Malik. I hated to admit, but I got to get some rest and wash some clothes while he was here. I was happy him and little Malik were bonding. I showed him the pictures from his last visit, and he asked me if he could have one.

"I got doubles. You can have it."

"Kim, what are you doing tomorrow?"

"Nothing. Why?"

"I was wondering if I can take the baby to see my mother."

"And where else do you plan on taking him?"

"I don't know, he's my son."

"Well, I'll tell you one thing. I don't want my son around that bitch."

"She's not a bitch."

"Now you're defending that bitch. You are not taking my child over to that whore's house."

"I didn't say I was taking him over her house, but if I was I don't see what the problem would be.

"You know, Kim, don't tell me where I can take my son. He's my son too, because I have rights. And secondly, I'm not paying for that ring anymore. I'm not going to let you take advantage of me. When you're ready to let me have my son like a father should be able to, call me."

We were at his doctor's office earlier, and they said that Malik had a little cold. But now it was three in the morning and he was wheezing really badly. I debated about calling Malik. I hadn't heard from him since his last visit, but I didn't know what to do. I wanted to take him to the hospital. I dialed his number and he answered.

"Malik," I said.

"What's wrong with the baby?" he asked.

"He's wheezing. I'm going to the hospital."

Malik said he would meet me there.

I got both the boys dressed. Kevin was whining, saying he was sleepy. I told him the baby was sick and he had to be a big brother and get dressed. He got himself dressed. I threw on jeans and a sweatshirt and we drove to the emergency room at Children's Hospital. Children's Hospital, even at 3:30 in the morning, was busy. It was so crowded. I looked around and grabbed the only two chairs that were empty. They were next to a fish tank. I sat down and took off Malik's snowsuit. Kevin fell asleep as soon as he sat down. Malik then had to see a nurse to get an arm bracelet and I had to fill out my insurance paperwork. I sat there holding little Malik. Malik walked into the waiting room.

"Is he okay?"

"They didn't see him yet."

"He's hot. Why didn't you bring him to the hospital earlier?"

"I was waiting to see if his fever and wheezing were going to get better."

"He's wheezing and a newborn, why didn't they see him first?" Malik said as he went to the nurses' station.

"Malik, I don't know why they haven't called him yet."

We didn't leave the hospital until about six in the morning. It took us two hours to be seen during that time. Me and Malik talked about the future of our child and how we were going to deal with little Malik growing up. I apologized to Malik and said that he could come and get him.

Chapter Thirty-Three

Shonda

Last night Kim calls Malik at three in the morning and says that the baby needs to go to the hospital. You know what he does? He gets up and leaves me. When I left for work, he still wasn't home. I didn't like him having intimate close conversations with Kim. I don't really think it could happen, but what if she starts trying to come on him, or tell him he can't see the baby unless she is with him? I wanted to go to the movies. I didn't know if Malik would be able to get away. I hated coming in second place in Malik's life. I called his phone, left him a message and I told him to call me at work. I got to work and still didn't hear from Malik. I called his office.

"Malik how is the baby?"

"He's okay. He might have asthma though."

"Really?" Damn I didn't want to ask him about going to the movies now.

"We didn't get out of the hospital until six. I just went back to Jarrod's place and changed my clothes. I'm so tired. I might leave early."

"Well baby, I just wanted to make sure the baby was okay."

"All right I'll call you when I get out of here." I guess I could rest easy about Malik.

I had planned for a day with me and Bree. It was Saturday and I just wanted us to do some shopping and spend some time alone. On our way out, Malik pulled up with his son in the car. We went back in the house.

"Aw, the baby's so cute. Can I hold him?" Bree asked.

"You can hold him, let me take his coat off," Malik said.

"No, Bree, he's too little. She can't hold him, Malik, he's too little," I said as I helped him take off the baby's coat. Other than pictures it was the first time I had seen him, and he looked just like Malik. I couldn't deny it. I held him, he was precious. I was falling in love with him.

Kim

I left Malik alone with Malik in the house, I had to go to the market and get groceries for my dinner. I was making a fresh salad, steak, and potatoes. When I came back, he was gone. I called his cell phone, he didn't answer. Then he answered.

"Where are y'all at?" I asked.

"My mother's house. I'll be there shortly to drop him off."

"Well Malik, I need my son home. I have to go to get ready for tomorrow."

"We'll be there."

I had a lot to do. I had to interview Stephanie for Lisa's position. Get on top of housework , pack lunches, wash clothes. I had to start work the next day and I didn't need this. I was going to put Malik in day care, but my mother said that she would watch him. I felt comfortable with my mother watching him more so than a stranger. Malik liked to cry and a stranger might get frustrated with him. I knew my mom would only spoil him more. Plus, I paid my mother seventy-five dollars a week and the day care he was going to go to would charge me $145.00 a week. Malik knocked on the door with Malik fifteen minutes later. Kevin ran to the door to greet them. Malik walked through the door.

"Next time Malik, can I go with you?" Kevin asked.

"Of course. All the guys will hang out together," Malik said.

"Next time, get my permission before you take my child out. It is too cold outside and I don't want him getting sick," I said as I took little Malik from him.

I spoke to Malik's mom, Ms. Gloria, today. I asked her about Malik's visit the other night. She told me she hadn't seen the baby since the hospital.

"I was calling to see when we can come to get little Malik this weekend," she said.

"I thought Malik brought him past over the weekend."

"No, I wasn't even home this weekend, I went to the race park in Delaware."

"Ms. Gloria, he is too little, but I'll bring him over this weekend."

After we got off the phone, I called Malik to ask him why he lied. I didn't let him get a word out before I said, "Why'd you say you went to see your mother? I know you took my son to see your little bitch—you didn't have to lie. Malik's too young to be going to strange people's houses. Now you fucked up, you can't take him at all." After I said what I had to say, I hung up on him. I felt like I was acting like a bitch, but so what? His girlfriend might be crazy. I don't know her. She might try to pinch or torture my baby when Malik is not looking. And if she did, he is so little he can't tell. I just don't trust that situation yet.

Chapter Thirty-Four

Shonda

Malik told me Kim found out today that he had the baby over here. I told him so what. He said she said something about the baby is too young to be around strange people. I knew that bitch just didn't want her baby to be around me. I told him that it's only two reasons why she won't let the baby come over. It's either because she doesn't know me and thinks I might be crazy or because she still wants Malik. She probably does still want Malik, because if she didn't, what real woman wouldn't want a father to be around his child? All these children growing up without a father and her silly ass wants to act stupid. Now if he didn't call and ask for the baby, she would be crying and try to drag him to court for child support. The good men always get the lousy woman to have children with. I told Malik she was using her son as leverage and that he was too dumb to see through it.

He said, "Shonda, she probably doesn't feel comfortable with her child around someone who said they were going to kick her ass on the phone."

"She threatened me first, Malik, and what does that matter now?

What are you, making excuses for her? That is old news. She needs to grow up. Y'all are not together."

"Listen, she'll eventually come around and let him come over on a regular basis. I can't force her to be ready."

"Well, I never seen a man not able to get his own son. That's some bullshit. You must be scared of her," I said.

"I'm not scared of her."

"Whatever. Malik, she's going to rule you as long as you allow it."

"It's not simple, you don't understand."

"I'm not trying to understand, Malik. You figure it out."

Kim

So far, so good. Malik's been a good father. All I have to do is call and he's here. He's been so helpful, he's good with little Malik, and he changes his Pampers and washes him up. He has been giving me money for him and buying him sneakers and clothes every time he gets a chance. His mom called me every day, asking about little Malik, and Nadia wants him to come over and spend the night, but I'm not ready for my baby to spend the night out yet. He is too little.

Last night, Malik was playing with the baby in the living room. I looked up at the clock and decided to let them play and I went to lie down for a moment. When I woke up, it was four in the morning. I went into the living room and Malik was 'sleep and little Malik was resting on his chest. I grabbed a blanket from out of the closet and placed it over Malik and the baby. They looked so peaceful, I didn't bother waking them up. I went back to sleep. I took a shower before little Malik and Malik woke up and I made Kevin some breakfast. I then woke Malik up and asked him if he wanted something to eat.

"No, I'm okay. What time is it?"

"It's seven."

"Really?" he said as he stood up and stretched. Little Malik woke up and he gave him a kiss.

He said, "I'll see you later, little man." He patted Kevin on his head, got his coat, and told me he would call me.

Chapter Thirty-Five

Shonda

Malik actually stayed the whole night out. I mean, it was time for me to go to work and I still hadn't seen or heard from him. All I know is, if he spent the night out with Kim or over there, I'm going to fuck him up. The only excuse he could have for not returning my calls was that he was dead, and if he wasn't dead, then I would kill him. My stomach was aching; I couldn't even think at work.

It was 12:00 P.M. and I still didn't speak to Malik yet. I had no other choice but to call—my last resort. I got Kim's number out of Malik's telephone book and I dialed her house; I had to know if he was there.

I let the phone ring and ring and I finally got her answering machine. I listened. It was pathetic. She had her son and the baby crying on the machine and she said "You have reach Kim, Kevin and Malik. We are not home. Leave a message and we will call you when we get home." If Malik was not there, I didn't know where he was.

* * *

Malik called me around three. I was about to go berserk on him, but instead I just calmly said, "Where did you stay last night?"

"I went to see the baby and I was putting him to sleep and I fell 'sleep." Was that the only excuse Malik could offer, one that was lame? So very lame. He fell 'sleep putting his son to bed? Yeah, right.

"Malik, you think I believe that?"

"It's the truth."

"Where was Kim?"

"She was in her room. I swear to God. It was just me and him on the sofa. Kim and Kevin were in their rooms. I'm telling you the truth." Malik must have thought he was talking to a fool. In no way did I believe that he fell 'sleep putting his son to bed. He could save that bullshit for somebody else.

"Remember, Malik, you cheated with me. You think I can't tell when you using the same line on me that you used on her? You must have bumped your head."

"Shonda, you know I love you. I just miss my kids. I would never cheat on you."

"You only have one kid. Her son is not your son. You're stupid. You're letting her manipulate you. You don't have to worry about me no more, it's over. It's over Malik," I repeated. "Yup, go fall 'sleep with your son again," I said as I slammed down the phone. Malik's story had holes in it, I couldn't believe he could hurt me like this. He stayed the night out on me and when I asked him for the truth, he continued to lie. If Malik wanted to be with his baby's mom/fiancée, I'd let him. I'm not going through no dumb shit with him. Please, I don't think so. I had too many other things to concentrate on, like selling a car before I left work.

It was payday and after taxes my paycheck was eighteen hundred. I was making in two weeks what I made in a month at any of my other jobs. After work, I went home, picked up Bree, and did some light shopping. I was also able to pay my bills, buy food, and still have money left over. My next pay I was going to start looking for a new place.

Malik was still on my mind, but there was nothing I could do if he wanted to be with his son. I had to let him choose his own path. He left me messages all night saying it was an emergency and to call him back. He left his number like I didn't know it already. I did not answer the phone. It's amazing what a man will say or do when he's in the doghouse.

Kim

It was a little late when Malik stopped over—he said he wanted to say good night to his son. I let him in. I was just about to get in the shower. We talked briefly and he went and talked to little Malik and Kevin for about an hour. I took my shower, dried off, and put my robe on. I walked past Malik reading to the boys. He looked up and said that he was getting ready to go. He gave them both a kiss and said that he was going home. Kevin went to his room and got in his bed and Malik placed little Malik in his crib. I walked Malik to the door and told him I was happy he was coming around and seeing the boys. He told me he was only doing his job and he missed me and Kevin when he wasn't here.

"We miss you too, Malik." It was an odd moment between us and then Malik hugged me. I hugged him back. I held him tighter.

"I'm sorry that I left."

"It's okay," I said as we separated from our hug and I pushed my hair back and looked down.

"Do you still love me, Kim?" he asked as he raised my chin and tried to kiss me.

"Yes, I still love you Malik, but I think you should go," I said as I turned away. I walked toward the door. Malik came behind me and pinned me up against the door. He kissed my neck and then removed my robe. I turned around and he kissed me. He suckled my breast in his mouth. Then he kissed my navel. I massaged his shoulders as he moved his tongue and head between my legs. He came up and he unclothed himself.

Malik then gave me what I missed and what I needed for the last couple of months. He made love to me like he loved me. Like he wanted me. We kissed and cuddled each other for three hours straight.

I never thought I would be creeping with my own man. It didn't feel right, he didn't feel like he was mine. I mean, I loved the way Malik was making me feel, but I hated that he had to get up and go when it was all over. I didn't know how to react. I was almost Malik's wife but I was playing the role of the other woman.

I wished that me and Malik could get back together. I missed our family, but it's less of a hassle now that we are not. I don't have to worry about where he is or what he is doing. With every visit, now, he comes to visit me and the boys.

I wanted to go get little Malik and Kevin's picture taken. I bought them matching blue and white outfits. They looked so cute. We were heading out the door when Stephanie called. I told her I was heading out the door to the mall. She asked could she go with us. I told her I didn't mind. She gave me her address and I picked her up from her new apartment.

Stephanie asked me about my labor and everything that was going on. I filled her in about the labor. Then she asked, "How has Malik been acting?"

"He's been over almost every day."

"Really? That's good."

I was about to tell her about the other night, but then I decided not to. It was none of her business. The rest of the ride to the mall we talked about old times and the boys.

Chapter Thirty-Six

Shonda

Now I believed Malik was telling the truth about falling asleep with son. He called a dozen more times before I forgave him. He said he wanted me to go with him to his mother's house on Christmas. I was so happy that he was finally going to bring me around his family. I couldn't wait to go. I even went to buy something to wear and bought his mother a gift. I was trying to get in good with her. I know that once she meets me she will like me.

Christmas morning, me and Bree made our rounds. We stopped past my dad and dropped off his gift and went to see Gram. We bought Gram a fuchsia pink silk pantsuit and hat to match that she could wear to church. After I dropped Bree at her dad's house, I expected to spend the rest of the day with Malik. He came over and gave me a red velvet box. Inside was a white gold and gold bracelet. It was solid and very pretty. I got Malik a few sweaters and a Roca-A-Wear sweat suit. After we exchanged gifts, Malik put his coat back on and said that he would see me later.

"Where are you going?"

"To my mother's."

"I'm not dressed yet, I thought we were going together."

"Uhm, Shonda, Kim is going to be at my mom's house and I don't want any drama."

"I'm not going to say anything to her."

"I know you won't, but she might say something to you."

"So, I can't go to your mother's house?

"Malik, I just don't believe you. How can you spend Christmas without me? How come I have to be excluded from certain aspects of your life? It's Christmas. You make me the fuck sick."

"Shonda, it's the baby's first Christmas. I have to spend it with the baby and my mom. I always do. I can't take you to my mom's house, having both of y'all there will only bring more confusion into our lives."

"That's not right, Malik. You still haven't even let me meet your mother."

"I will, eventually."

"When? Just get out of my face, just get the hell out of my face."

"Stop overreacting. I am spending Christmas with you. Just, half the day. You don't really celebrate anyway."

"So what."

"I have to be there for Malik."

"Well, it's not fair, Malik, and I don't like it. Whatever she says you run and go do."

"I do not run when she tells me and you're not going to tell me when and how I should see him."

"Nobody's trying to tell you what to do, but this is not right." Malik continued to try to explain why I couldn't go and I sulked on the sofa.

Kim

The baby's first Christmas was great. I went to my mother's house and helped her cook. Malik met us over there. Kianna was with her record producer boyfriend, Greg. Karen, Ryan, and Lonnie were there too. We made a feast: turkey, stuffing, salmon, macaroni and cheese, gravy and rice, string bean casserole, corn. My mother baked two apple pies. I dressed the boys alike and everyone loved taking the boys' pictures. Malik was treated like he was still a part of the family. We ate, played games and opened presents. Malik got me a white gold and gold bracelet. It was in a red velvet box. He bought Kevin a Playstation II, a bike, and a skateboard. He bought Malik more clothes and toys he couldn't even play with yet. After we left my mother's house, we went to Malik's mother's house. They were so happy to see little Malik. Nadia's daughter was all over him, kissing and hugging him. Malik's mom bought my baby some cheap clothes and Kevin a basketball and book.

Chapter Thirty-Seven

Shonda

New Year's Eve was a time for celebration—a lot of things had happened to me in the last year. I had a lot to be grateful for. I had Bree, I was working, making good money, I was about to move into my new apartment, and Malik and me were still going strong. His son was no longer putting a wedge in our relationship. I guess Kim came to grips that I was here to stay. I even accepted that Malik needed space and time to be with his son. I could respect that. The time he spends with his son, I use to spend with my daughter instead of pouting.

We spent New Year's Eve on the waterfront at Club Escape with Tae and her new friend, "the boah from New York."

At the stroke of midnight, I said, "I love you Malik."

"I love you, Shonda."

"I'm so glad to be going into a New Year with you. I felt like we have been with each other forever."

"Baby, there is nobody else for me," he said as he raised my chin up so our eyes would meet. "I love you and don't you forget it."

Kim

The previous New Years, I always spent with Malik. We would go to a party, or get a room at a hotel and celebrate. This New Year's was so very different. I was home in the bed with my boys, watching the ball drop in Times Square on television. They both were 'sleep when 2003 began. I gave them kisses, and said happy new year and went to sleep. I pondered what the new year had in store for me. My job was okay. But I think I want to go back to school and get my MBA. I had accomplished one of my goals this year and that was buying my house. My resolution was to acknowledge God more, because he got me through all of 2002. I want to get my finances together, save money, pay my credit cards down, and start making double payments on my student loans. I also want to go the gym and get rid of the little baby fat from little Malik. I decided I'm only twenty-five and my life is not over, with or without Malik. I even wrote by this summer, I want to start going out and meeting people.

Malik continued to come around. He spent so much time with us. I wondered how his little girlfriend felt about Malik spending so much time over here. She's probably mad, but that's on her.

Chapter Thirty-Eight

Shonda

I asked Malik nicely if he was in for the night or was he going back to Jarrod's. He asked me why. I told him I didn't feel like staying in the house and we needed to go somewhere. Malik said that I was spoiled and that we didn't have to always go out.

"Malik, I'm sorry, I like to go out."

"Well, go out by yourself, because I'm tired." I felt like Malik was trying to start an argument, like he was looking for a reason to be mean to me. His car was broke again, but he didn't have to take his anger out on me.

"Malik, why are you acting like that?"

"I'm not acting like anything. It's a new year and I'm trying to get my life together."

"What is that supposed to mean, exactly?"

"Leave me alone. Shonda, you brought nothing but chaos into my life from the beginning."

"I brought chaos into your life. What about my life? You didn't turn my life upside down?"

"No, I didn't. I didn't make you lose your family."

"Oh, so now I made you lose your family. You know what, Malik, your dick made you lose your family. If you want your family so bad, go back to them, I don't care. I don't have time for this, I'm out." I walked out my own apartment, got in my car and drove a few blocks, and I decided that I was wrong. I couldn't get mad at Malik for not wanting to go out. He was under a lot of stress. I drove back home to apologize to him, and you know what he told me? He said he loved me, but that we couldn't be together, that he had been thinking this over for weeks and it was for the best. I knew Malik had felt guilty from the beginning about little Malik, but the fact that he wanted to end our relationship was news to me. He didn't show any signs that there was a problem. He said that he was leaving and that he would talk to me later. I watched him walk out. I had no indication that a storm was brewing. Once, when I thought everything was going so right for me, it was still so wrong. Malik was gone and I was devastated. I never saw this coming. One week we are lovey-dovey, having a great time on New Year's and the next week he is telling me he has to leave and be with his family.

I thought it couldn't get any worse but it did. The next day Malik brought his bitch to my home to pick up his broke car. He needs his ass kicked so bad. I wanted to kill him. How could he play me like this? Just because she has his baby, he is going to be with her.

Kim

Malik called me from Jarrod's house and said he wanted to talk to me and can he come over. I asked him what was wrong; he said nothing and that he would be over shortly.

When Malik arrived, I asked him what was so important that he had to talk to me about.

He sat down on the sofa and asked me to join him. I did and then he said, "Kim, can I come home? I'm sorry. I miss you, I miss my boys. I don't need anybody else but you."

Malik wanted to come back home, that sounded so good, but why now, when I was getting over him? I had already started over with my life. Our relationship had been through too many changes. So I told Malik exactly how I felt.

"Malik, our relationship is okay the way it is."

"No, it's not. I realized I was wrong. I want to do right by you now," he said as he grabbed my hand and looked deep into my eyes. His lips were quivering, I knew he was serious. I told him that I would think about it.

The next day, he told me his car had broke down and asked me could I take him to get it. I didn't know his car was broke in front of his girlfriend's house, until she stuck her ghetto head out the door and screamed "Fuck you, Malik, and your stupid bitch." I ignored her. Then she said, "Dumb bitch, paid for her own ring."

I tried not to respond. But she kept saying it. So I said, "No, bitch, I didn't pay for my ring. Malik paid for my ring." I flashed it at her. "I got him and you don't."

Malik told me to get in the car.

Now that Malik was home, I wondered if I had made the right decision. I wondered if I gave in too soon. I know having him home made me feel vindicated, like I won, but what did I really win? Malik had left in the end of October and here it was January and he just decided to come home. I hope I'm not being desperate, but I want Malik in his son's life, my life. My feelings are secondary. I want a family.

Malik asked me did I think over what he said, I told him I did and said, "Malik, I can't."

Then Malik got on his knees and said, "Kim, we can get married tomorrow. I mean it. I am sorry. I want to be your husband and a father to my child."

"Malik, get up," I said. I was baffled. He was throwing my emotions in too many directions. Malik then got on his knees and asked me again to marry him.

"Kim, I'll do whatever it takes. Just say yes."

"Malik, I can't say yes."

"Say yes," Malik said. "Pick any day on the calendar, I don't care, any day. I want you to be my wife."

"No, I can't. Malik, I think it's best that you leave."

"I don't want to leave."

"You left before."

"That was a mistake."

"It was a mistake," I said as I broke down. All the buildup of Malik leaving me, being on my own, and everything else I went through when he wasn't here, came out. I shouted at him, "Why did you leave us? Why did you make me go through everything by myself? I was hurting, I needed you, Malik, and you weren't anywhere around."

"I'm sorry, Kim, I will never leave you again. I promise you, baby, listen to me. I'll be there for you. I'll be there for my son."

"I can't believe you. I can't trust you, Malik," I yelled at him.

Malik tried to calm me down, he told me to get myself together. He turned the shower on and I stood in there for almost twenty minutes. When I got out, he had made me some coffee and was waiting for me with a towel. We talked and I told him I would really think it over.

I thought long and hard about Malik and our family. I even prayed to God that he would help me to make the right decision. I confided in Stephanie and Karen. Both had mixed opinions as to what I should do, but ultimately, it was my decision whether or not to take Malik back and marry him. I couldn't let anybody talk me out of being with my man.

People say things like, I would leave him. He wouldn't have done that to me, I would have left him. But all that is just talk. People who usually try to convince you to be miserable are usually miserable and unhappy themselves. I'm tired of sacrificing. I'm staying with him; he's a good man who made a mistake. I'm not going to sacrifice love and family for everyone else. I'm scared to start over with anyone else, so I might as well try to make it work with Malik.

He was a good man that needed a little direction. He's my son's father and I love him. It would be stupid to let someone else have him. I'm tired of sacrificing for other people. Malik is a good man who made a mistake.

"Mom, me and Malik are getting married. I need your help to plan it. We're getting married on Valentine's Day."

"Valentine's Day, that's less than six weeks."

"I know, but we want to hurry up and do this."

"I am so happy for you. Okay, let me start preparing the guest list and find a hall. It's too late to hire a planner."

In less than five weeks my mom was able to hire a caterer, book a banquet hall, photographer, and a florist.

It was Malik's idea to get married on Valentine's Day. We planned for an afternoon ceremony so that we could take an evening flight to Puerto Rico for our honeymoon. I wanted to go to Miami or Orlando with the kids; Malik said that we could take the kids on vacation over the summer, when little Malik gets a little older.

Valentine's Day was the day of love and lovers, so it was easy to pick our colors for the wedding. Of course, I chose red and white everything. My mother continued to do most of the planning. She ordered my limo, and even persuaded her church to let us have the ceremony for free even though we weren't members. My mom was on her job, plus she was helping to pay for everything.

At home all the pieces were coming together ideally. Having Malik home was like he never left. He was so helpful with the boys, he washed little Malik before bed, read to them, he took out the trash and even cooked dinner, rubbed me down and let me relax. Malik had even applied for an accelerated business program. Since Malik was trying so hard, it was only right for me to give one hundred percent as well. I wanted everything to be right. I didn't want to give Malik a reason to ever leave me again. I went so far as to have Jarrod, who I hated, over for a football party for Malik. I invited Lonnie and Ryan also. I dressed the boys up in football jerseys and ordered hot wings and a lunch meat tray. The Eagles were playing the Miami Dolphins.

My invitations read:

> *The parents of*
> *Kimberly Brown*
> *and parent of*
> *Malik Moore*
> *would like for you to join them on*
> *February 14, 2003*
> *as they come together as one.*

I could not believe me and my baby was getting married. I had ordered the invitations and mailed them off. Malik had changed. I think he was just going through a phase, but I know right now that he's ready to be a good man and give me his all. I made myself forget about Malik and his fling; it was over and time to move on.

Stephanie called me and said she couldn't believe that Malik and me were getting married so soon, she had just received the invitation in the mail. I couldn't believe it myself; everything was happening so suddenly. It was surreal, that after all we had been through, we were together again.

Chapter Thirty-Nine

Shonda

I was hurt Malik had left; I felt like he owed me an explanation. I decided to write him a letter. I didn't feel like I could talk to him and I didn't want to risk forgetting what I wanted to say to him. I wanted to get my every thought on paper. Just the thought of him holding and being with her again put a sour taste in my mouth. I wanted to call Malik so bad. I missed him. I needed him.

Dear Malik,

Everybody wants security, and wants to feel like they belong. Even the hoe that does tricks longs to be somebody's significant other. I was someone's significant other. I was with my daughter Brianna's father for seven years, almost married. I always need somebody. I'm tired of needing somebody. You know what, I realized being apart from you, Malik, I don't need you—I love you and want you, it's a difference. Brian was security and Mike was a facade. With you it's real. I mean, you mean more to me than anybody I know other than my family. Remember you said I had your back, I do have it. Malik, you said it was me and you against the world. I miss you, Malik. I miss us. I miss you so much. I miss your jokes. I miss you lying next to me until I fall asleep. I miss us not getting any sleep. I miss our talks. I miss our walks. I miss our lunches. I miss your inspiration. I miss your patience. I miss us. I miss us. I miss you.

Love always,
Shonda

I mailed the letter to the office in a plain white business envelope he would have to get.

My letter had worked. Malik was standing at my door. *Thank you Thank you.* I fixed my hair, walked to the door with a smile and said, "Did you get my letter?"

"Yes, Shonda, that's what I came to talk to you about."

"Come in, don't act like a stranger." I welcomed him in. It felt strange at first, like we weren't together anymore.

"So what's up Malik?"

He looked at me with this serious look and said, "Shonda, you got to get over us. It's over. The invitations have been sent, I'm marrying Kim to be with my family."

"What, you could have said that on the phone. Are you crazy, Malik? Get out of my house, now! Fuck you."

"Shonda, calm down."

"No, you calm down. Please, Malik, you don't have to worry about me. You are a sorry ass. You're going to marry her just because she has your son. You're stupid. You'll be divorced in a year. It's not going to last, your child will grow up resenting you." I was uttering anything I could to make Malik reconsider his decision. I didn't want him to leave me, but it wasn't working.

"Shonda, you're making excuses, you just have to let us go. Get over me."

"Please, don't leave me, Malik, I can't take it. Please, Malik, I can't take it, don't leave me," I said as I held onto the bottom of his foot.

"Let me go."

He left. I cried. The door slammed. I cried. I closed my eyes and I cried.

I called Tae and told her what happened. At first she told me to try to call Malik again and talk to him. Then she changed her tune and said he wasn't good for me. "I would tell you the truth Shonda, but I think it's time to let him go and move on," she said.

"I can't let go, Tae."

"You have to, he's getting married. You had your fun, just let it go." I thought about what Tae was saying. Maybe she was right, maybe it was just time to let Malik go and be with his family. I loved him, but I had to do what was right.

Kim

I was getting ready for my big day. I had to pick out my bridesmaid dresses. I didn't really have any close friends, so I picked Karen and Kianna. My sisters were all I had. Stephanie begged me to be in the wedding, but we weren't that close, so I told her no. She was upset, but I told her she could help my mom coordinate everything and she was happy just to be involved.

We went to David's Bridal on Roosevelt Boulevard, not far from my house. The dresses were iridescent red, nice, classy, conservative, two-piece dresses. They were form-fitting taffeta on top with a long, sheer, layered skirt. Kianna wanted to wear the hoochie version of the dress I picked out. Leave it to Kianna to try to trick it out. She came to the back of the store and told me we needed to take it to a tailor and show some cleavage and show some back. I told Kianna she could have all that in her wedding dress, but at my wedding she was going to wear what I said.

"Fine, I'll wear this dress but this shit is wack," she told me. I had bigger fish to fry. I had picked out their dresses, but still hadn't picked out my own dress. I definitely wanted to wear white, but I was not sure if I was going to wear off-white or pure white. Then I saw my dress. It was off-white with diamond studs on the straps and had a corset top. Then the bottom of the dress was lined with the diamond studs and was satin. It was gorgeous. It was a size six. I was hoping that I could fit it. I still had a few leftover pounds from baby Malik.

My dress fit perfectly; my mother cried when she saw me in it.

"What's wrong, Mom?"

"You look so pretty."

"Stop crying, Mom," I said as I wiped my Mom's tears with my hand. Karen and Kianna applauded.

"You can't even tell you just had a baby," Kianna said.

"Yeah, it's holding everything in."

"Thank you. Should I wear my hair up or down?"

"You should get a weave and wear it down."

"Like what?"

"Like Shirley Temple curls or maybe straight," Kianna said. For once I agreed with her. I wanted something totally different for my wedding. I still had a few things to take care of. I had to get Malik's ring, my nails done, eyebrows arched, confirm my flower and limo.

Chapter Forty

Shonda

My cell phone rang. I answered it and heard someone yell, "What's up, girl!"

"Who is this?"

"Monique, girl, it ain't been that long."

"What's up? How you doing?" I asked Monique. I hadn't heard from her in months. I wondered what she wanted.

"I'm good. So I guess you heard."

"Heard what?"

"That your boy is getting married."

"Yeah, I heard."

"Well, how that happen, y'all was just together?"

"It just happened," I said, annoyed. Monique was starting to get on my nerves. I asked her what was up and what did she want.

"When did y'all break up?"

"About a month ago. Why?"

"Well, honey, girlfriend must have made those plans fast, cause you got exactly one week before Malik says 'I do.' Listen, Shonda, I just wanted to let you know the wedding is Friday."

"Why would they get married on a Friday?"

"It's Valentine's Day."

"Really?"

"Yup, I didn't think you knew."

"I didn't, thanks for the heads-up. I'll talk to you later."

"Shonda, just to let you know, I didn't call you to gossip. I called you because I never saw two people more happy together. When you worked here, y'all were so into each other it was sickening. I just thought you needed to know."

I thanked Monique, then pressed the red END button on my cell phone. I didn't even believe Malik, the other night when he said he was getting married. I thought he was lying. How the hell was he playing? What's wrong with him? What kind of person gets married on a Friday? It is definitely something wrong with that chick. Malik knows deep down that he didn't want to marry her, but I guess guilt will make you do anything. Deep down Malik knows he didn't want to marry her.

It's like, I had to do something. I couldn't let Malik get married. I wanted to call him or go up to the office, but I didn't want to get arrested. I thought of killing Malik. Just running him over with a car. Maybe hit him upside the head—anything to keep him from walking down the aisle.

Kim

When I put on my dress I felt like a princess. My day was turning out perfect. Even the weather was cooperating. It was a spring-like, beautiful, breezy day, as if it was April. I thought when we planned this it might snow or be cold, but it didn't, it wasn't, it was perfect. My dad was home for the wedding and doing well. Kianna's friend Heather did everyone's makeup so nice. My mom looked beautiful—Karen even looked nice. My mom made calls to the banquet hall to make sure the cake had arrived and that the caterers was there setting up. The flowers had arrived. The photographer came and took pre-wedding photos of me getting dressed and them doing my hair and applying my veil.

I waited for this day my whole life. My boys looked so handsome. I had a baby tux made for little Malik. Stephanie took the boys and drove in her car and we all got in the limo and headed for the ceremony.

I arrived at the church and saw all the cars parked outside. I was so nervous. I checked my hair in the mirror before I got out of the limo. The sun was shining so brightly. Red, pink, and white roses and azaleas were tied in stunning arrangements outside of the church. I peeked in and saw Malik in his black tuxedo; he had a white shirt under it and a black vest with a red tie. Little Malik was being held by Stephanie and Kevin stood in the front with Jarrod. They all looked so nice.

The music began to play. Everyone stood up. First my mother was ushered to her seat. Then Malik's mother Ms. Gloria was escorted to her seat. Kianna walked down the aisle, then Karen. I was so nervous when my father grabbed my hand and walked me down the aisle. I heard everyone say how beautiful I looked and cameras were flashing everywhere. My dad told me he loved me and that he was proud of me. He walked me down the aisle where Malik was standing. Malik smiled; the minister said everyone could have a seat. Malik and I recited our vows and Lonnie began to sing a song he wrote for us.

Chapter Forty-One

Shonda

I couldn't believe I was at Malik's wedding. I kept telling myself to breathe easy. I took long and deep breaths. I was nervous as hell. I was ready to smoke a cigarette before going in. I wished Tae would have came with me but she refused.

All I remember is, I was walking up the church steps and I sat on the last row so I would go unnoticed, then the Rev asked did anyone see why this man or woman should not be joined in holy matrimony, yadda, yadda, so I stood up and said "Malik, you can't do this, you know this is wrong."

First everyone turned around and stared at me like, *bitch are you crazy?* Then everyone stared at each other, shook their heads, and started mumbling amongst each other. Kim ran into the pew crying. Malik just stood there with his mouth open. One of Kim's girlfriends or cousins tried to act like they wanted to say something, but I didn't give them a chance. I said what I had to say and I was out. The wedding was over and I ran to my getaway car that I had left running outside. I called my god sister Tae as soon as I got in the car. I shouldn't have called her at all, since she refused to come with me. She could have been my backup. If things got ugly, ya mean. But she said I was wrong and she would not be my accomplice.

I frantically dialed her number on the phone. It began to ring, then she answered and I said, "I did it."

"You did what?"she asked.

"I went in the wedding and told Malik how I felt."

"No, you didn't, cause if you did I'm not speaking to you anymore. Come on, Shonda, I thought you were joking."

"Well, don't speak to me anymore. I told you I was serious."

"You are serious? Girl, you are crazy!" Tae screamed.

"I'm not crazy!"

"Really! You know how much heart it takes to go and stop a wedding."

"Uh, I don't know, a lot," I said as if I had to think about it.

"No, it takes a sick, crazy individual. CON-GRAT-U-LA-TIONS, it should have been me." Tae finally laughed between trying to sing like Vesta, this singer from back in the day who sung about going to her ex-boyfriend's wedding. They used to play the video all the time on BET. Now I can't believe I'm acting this shit out.

I was still hysterically laughing and answering all Tae's questions about the wedding as I drove into the Amoco gas station.

"I can't believe you did that shit."

"I don't know why, I told you I was for real,"I said as I got out of the car and walked into the convenience store.

"I know, Shonda, but damn, how did Malik react?"

"Do you think I waited around to see? See, if you would've come then you could have seen his face for yourself. Well, I'll be right there and I'll give you a second-by-second playback."

"Okay, how long before you get here?"

"Twenty minutes."After I pressed the red SEND button on my phone, I walked to the back of the convenience store. I opened the refrigerator door and reached for a Pepsi. I don't know what it was but something told me to turn around. I turned to my left and saw a tall light-complexed woman in a red iridescent dress, holding flowers, staring me down.

"Excuse me," I said as I tried to walk past the woman. She didn't budge. She just stayed there. It took a moment to click that this wasn't just any one woman. It was one of Kim's bridesmaids.

"You think you real funny? How could you do that? You know how much money my parents spent on that wedding?"

"Huh?"

"You heard me. You think you're real funny, but you're not, you are trifling."

"Listen, I think you want to get out of my way."

"No, I'm not going anywhere. You're going to hear me out."

"I'm not going to do anything," I said as I turned around and walked away.

The woman followed me and said, "My mother spent twenty-five thousand dollars on that wedding. You are a selfish, fucked-up person, you have no heart. My sister has a child, Malik, and another son, but guess what, there is something called karma. You and Malik deserve each other, he ain't nothing but a trifling dog, and you are a flea, and my sister is better than both of you." The next thing I knew I was falling into a rack of potato chips. The woman had hit me in the back of my head. I got right back up off the ground and tried to catch her but it was too late, she had already ran out of the door and into a white truck and sped off.

I didn't feel like going to Tae's; my head was ringing and I knew that woman was right. I was selfish, I was wrong. I knew Malik had someone and I still pursued him. I went home, I took off my shoes and fell on the floor and cried like a baby. I was acting tough, but deep down, I knew I had lost Malik. Even if Malik was making a mistake, he will think I was an idiot. A stupid idiot. What would make me do something so stupid? The scene of walking in the church and running out and seeing Kim's sister at the wedding just kept replaying in my head, over and over again. I felt like a complete fool.

Kim

After Lonnie finished singing, the minister said, did anyone see why this man and woman should not be joined in holy matrimony. I heard a voice from the back of the church. It was Malik's little girlfriend standing up at my wedding. She said, "Malik you know this is wrong. You can't marry her. You know you can't marry her, you love me." Then she ran out of the church. For a moment, everyone stood in silence or at least it seemed like that, then I heard gasps, and mumbling. I almost fainted. That bitch was ruining my wedding. The next thing I knew, Karen ran after her. My mother and Kianna tried to calm me down, but it was too late, I was out of it. I passed out. When I awoke, I was in a wedding dress in the hospital. Malik was nowhere to be found and I was heartbroken.

Shonda

Six months later

"So, aren't you scared one day he'll cheat again?" Tae asked with sarcasm.

"No. I mean, he knows I'm not playing with him. He's complete now he got his son and me. He's happy," I said with confidence. The day after the wedding, Malik was at my door thanking me. He said I saved him from a life of regret, that he didn't want to marry Kim, and how she wasn't his best friend and that he loved her but wasn't *in love* with her. He told me I was his best friend and he loved me.

"What about Kim?" Tae said.

"What about her? I mean, of course she'll never like me. Do you blame her? Malik says she's happy and even got a boyfriend. I guess she realized she had to go on with her life, because I wasn't going anywhere and I had won the fight. I mean, you know how the saying goes, I got a man, the boy is mine, don't mess with my man, ex girl to the next girl I'll take your man. You know how the story goes."

"You know you're crazy, right real crazy."

"I know, but Malik is with me and no one else. I have his heart and a ring that he bought me with his own money. He loves me."

GOT A MAN

DAAIMAH S. POOLE

ABOUT THIS GUIDE

The suggested questions are intended to enhance
your group's reading of Daaimah S. Poole's
GOT A MAN.

DISCUSSION QUESTIONS

1. Did Kim make Malik cheat by pressuring him to marry her?

2. Was Shonda wrong for continuing to deal with Malik even though she knew he had a family?

3. Would you charge your own engagement ring if the man you were going to marry couldn't afford to pay for the ring in cash and was going to make payments? Or would you settle for something less your man could afford?

4. Do you think Malik played on both Kim and Shonda's weaknesses, or did they both play a part in his behavior?

5. Do think Malik was confused about who he really wanted?

6. Did Kim worry too much about how her family viewed her?

7. What do you think contributed to both Kim and Shonda's need to have a man like Malik?

8. Would you have showed up at Malik's wedding? Did Shonda get what she deserved, when she did?

9. Will Shonda and Malik's relationship last?

10. How do you think Kim is going to move on with her life, since she didn't marry Malik? Would you move on with your life, or still try to fight for Malik?

You can visit the author's website at www.daaimahspoole.com